Silo Pilgrimage

A Novel by
Rob Jackson

Novak&Hall

Chicago, IL

Copyright © 2015 Rob Jackson

Silo Pilgrimage

Cover Photo by Cassandra Jackson

Novak & Hall Publishers
ISBN: 978-0-9905435-1-0

10 9 8 7 6 5 4 3 2 1

Printed in the United States of America.

Acknowledgements

Gratitude for support and inspiration: Dave Megenhardt, Jacob Snodgrass, Stephanie Carter, Don De Grazia, Dave Smith, Jon Erickson, Bill Reyer, Len Weinberger, Barry Marquard, Kathryn Koehler, Jeff Booth, Barbara Hilston Covert, editors of Great Lakes Review, my siblings Tammy and Myron and my parents Curt and Faye Jackson.

To: Carri, Samantha and Cassandra

CHAPTER 1

Dear Dr. Helmut Schmidt,

You can't imagine my surprise upon the receipt of your letter. When I published the article, I never imagined the circulation to include Europe. After the initial amazement, however, I was stricken with a pang of anxiety. Did I have my facts straight? God, I hope so! If one can imagine what it would have been like for a young man to take batting practice and all the time be unaware that Babe Ruth was in attendance, which is the closest I can come to sum up the feelings that I had at the time. As I declared in the article, I am by no means an expert on any type of religious phenomenon, though my work in psychotherapy, has on many occasions introduced me to theories in that arena. Rarely do I come across such material without your name being mentioned, so you see why I am so humbled by your lengthy correspondence. I assure you, dear sir, that I will do my best to answer your questions with as much clarity and detail that I can muster without boring you with too much detail. Forgive me too, Doctor, if my sentences seem to be abrupt and direct. My mind is racing faster than my fingers can go.

I completed my undergraduate degree in Sociology in the early '70s at Bowling Green State University, coincidentally a university that is only about a half hour away from the small liberal arts college where I am now an associate Professor. I learned of my acceptance into Stanford my senior year. Why Stanford? Only one reason.

1

The cultural anthropologist, Ernest Becker, taught there. Ironically, though, months before I enrolled Becker died at the age of fifty. The department also went through a de-Beckerization before I arrived. Therefore, the reason I came is to study with, in my mind, the greatest mind since Freud, and I came upon a complete regression of Becker's ideas. Becker's ideas were branded as fanciful (religious, god forbid) and inadequate to test any hypothesis. I was stubborn and steadfastly adhered to Becker's ideas. I was Paul. Becker took the Freudian view of sex and saw it as a by-product of death as you well know. Becker introduced me to Otto Rank, a thinker whose ideas still elude me when I approach him through primary texts. What I really understand of Rank comes through secondary texts, especially Becker's, but others too, including Zillmore and Welms.

To me, my curiosity about religion has always been more to do with it being a coping mechanism for the human animal. The truth of any dogma, or faith system, has always been secondary to its ability to provide a system for meaning or meanings. So, in a nutshell, my approach to the silo and the image on the silo was not that of a metaphysician trying to decipher a bridge between platonic realities, but rather the pragmatic potential of the human mind in relation to the image. So I approached the article with the giant shadows of you and Becker standing behind me. You no doubt noticed my lengthy quotations of both William James' *Variety of Religious Experience* and Otto's *Idea of the Holy.* I mention that because I had my first real exposure to those minds through your writing.

I must admit, and perhaps I should have been more forthcoming in the article, I have yet to visit the silo. I know you may find this incredible since it happens to be only about 20 minutes from where I live and you have traveled to Yugoslavia, Portugal and South America, just to name a few, to view similar phenomena. My excuses are two- fold: For one, I keep waiting for the crowds to die down. While I still do not by any means anticipate this event becoming another Fatima or Guatemala, I am amazed every day at its growth, exponentially on some days. Fatima, I understand draws 5 million a year, a town of only 8,000 people! When I decided to wait, I had to park over two miles away, and since I am engaged in a daily battle with gout, I could not relish the idea of such a tedious walk. I should have, though, because now the traffic to the main road leading to the silo is closed and the walk is extended to almost four miles. I can promise you this though: when you do arrive, I shall accompany you to the silo, even if I have to be pushed in a wheelchair. Secondly, I have been coping with quite a disruption in my family. I know that you have raised three daughters who have all lived through the age of my own daughter by a decade more and beyond. Perhaps you will be able to offer me more than scholarly advice on your trip here. If I sound desperate, I must ask for your pardon, but I am. As exciting as this is, bringing the world to our small county, the whole affair has been quite overshadowed by my personal distractions.

On a brighter note, I have had the opportunity to interview not only several people including secular curiosity seekers to modern day pilgrims, but I also had the opportunity to bring one Rachael Rasson to the college for a lengthy interview, which included psychological testing and a polygraph test. I have not only enclosed those materials but also the complete recorded interview with Rachael (I am not one of those scholars who is reticent about sharing his or her intellectual property with others in the field). Rachael was the lady who first noticed the image on the silo. She was on her way home from work shortly before midnight, and while rounding a curve in the road, she hit her high beams and there it was, so she claims. Some, however, do not appear to see anything! This has broadened the controversy, with some saying that it is not an image at all but an apparition, only revealed to selected members-shades of Gnosticism. I also enclosed copies of all newspaper articles that

3

I have, some, no doubt, you may find quite humorous, notice especially the two men peddling the t-shirts and coffee mugs that say "I saw the image." American capitalism at its best, or worst, I'm not quite sure which. I assume that that is an American trait but perhaps there are Fatima pens, hats, and bumper stickers. Also notice the quote from the young girl who proclaims in tears that she knows that this is the beginning of the end. I don't mean to sound facetious but such a reaction comes not from a sick or dying person but a nineteen-year-old girl who is apparently the picture of health, and as I have noted, though I find the remark ludicrous, I also find it fascinating.

Through your book on Mary apparitions, I understand that most of the people who first see the images of this kind or various apparitions happen to be Catholic. The woman who was the spark for this particular phenomenon also happened to be Catholic. More and more, it seems to me though, in America it is people who identify themselves as Protestants, especially people who identify themselves with the more conservative movements of Protestantism, fundamentalists and so on, who are not only the founders of these phenomenon but also the majority of pilgrims that come to the source itself. Of course I'm talking about images and apparitions of Christ not Mary. I would hope if a Protestant were fortunate to receive a revelation from a Mary apparition then they would soon after convert to Catholicism!

Most scholars in the field (and please feel free to correct me when I'm wrong in any future correspondence [and I do hope this is the start of many] on any misinformation) also tend to have a Catholic bias. You may now be the foremost expert in the field, yet you are a Lutheran. I wonder perhaps if this is a trend or an anomaly. By the way, I applaud your study on Tillich's existentialism. I would be remiss not to mention this book as another central influence on me. Not only did it clarify some confusing questions that I had on Tillich's theology but it also gave me a greater understanding of the Lutheran faith. Excepting the work I did for the article, I have without a doubt referred to your Tillich book even more than to your excellent study on religious apparitions.

Regarding your last question, a question that I deduce fills you with the most curiosity, what is my bias? If you couldn't ascertain my bias from the article itself then I am pleased. I have no religious affiliation. Your guess that I possibly may be a member of the United Church of Christ is an astute educated guess, being that I teach at a college that has a United Church of Christ affiliation. I'm assuming your guess came from this deduction and not from anything in the article.

I grew up an atheist with parents who championed atheism. I have read your comment that proclaiming one to be an atheist takes as big a leap as the leap of the believer, just in the other direction, and I can't disagree with that statement, especially after reading not only your work but that of Huxley's as a young man, and later Hume, though I still think the latter is excessive in his skepticism. So philosophically I am an agnostic, but if I was forced to abandon the safe harbors of agnosticism (that religious Switzerland!) and was forced to choose sides, I would have chosen the side of the atheists over the believers-- if I were to keep a conscience with any integrity. I must tell you, though, honorable sir, that knowing that you were standing on the other side would give me grave doubts if I should follow my own intellect and emotions, or if I should acquiesce my own will to yours, and cross the field and stand under the banner alongside you. Though my sentiments are indeed made with the utmost seriousness, any hyperbole is added only to show my respect for your work and your person. The fact that you are a believer at least makes me acknowledge with an open mind that I may be wrong, and I find a strange comfort in that.

Mine unbelief is based almost exclusively on my inability to rec-

5

oncile myself to evil, and the terror that the history of the world has endured under its brutality. I am no Job; I am far too weak. I need explanations of my suffering, and now, though only a small fraction of the affliction endured by Job, my daughter has my wife and me in an almost inconsolable state. (I must tell you, professor that my daughter is in no serious trouble, and as far as we know, she is in good health. She is just in a phase of inexplicable rebellion). If I could accept or create piecemeal an acceptable theodicy, then I may be well on the road to accepting a meaningful purpose to this life, but as of yet, all theories of evil have fallen hideously short. I do not use my own criteria but implement the litmus test of Dostoevsky: "No theory of evil is valid if you can't tell it to a dying child." And as I have written, I have found none valid or sufficient, and seeing an image of Christ on a silo beside a rural road will not do as a replacement for that elusive theory, but obviously I find the image fascinating all the same. I will await your arrival in late August, and at that time, I anticipate that we shall delve further into these issues. Of course, my wife and I want to extend an invitation to stay at our house as long as you would like while you tour the image and conduct any interviews or research that you may want or need to do. We insist and we will consider it an honor.

Best,

Thomas O. Granger
Associate Professor
Heidelberg College
July 27th, 1987

CHAPTER 2

Dear Sir,

I regret that many of the notes that I took pertaining to the events of which you have requested details have been destroyed when an unseasonable late winter rain flooded my home. I will, however, do my best in describing what I can. I will be the first to confess that I would be hesitant to trust my memory when describing events that took place nearly fifteen years ago.

The image of Christ was on a soybean oil tank and was discovered by a woman in her 50s (she also happened to be an ardent Catholic). As far as I know she still lives, but I do know that her family is very protective of her and have denied others interviews with her. Whether or not they have changed their stance is unknown to me.

I do remember that there was an electric feeling that summer and "the image" (as it became known) dominated the interests and discussions throughout the summer. At first, visitors to the image were nothing more than a slow trickle of locals who, with a few exceptions, were not convinced. Much to the surprise of the residents of the tri-county area (and to the dismay of the local law enforcement) that trickle transformed into a flood of humanity, including pilgrims. Pilgrims came from not only across the U.S., but also as far away as Europe and South America. Some of these groups are nomadic, and I for one, didn't realize that groups like these still existed. The generic term that one may associate with them would be "gypsies", however I did learn later that only one group were actually gypsies or more precisely, Roma.

The group that I remember most was a cult who had made the journey south from Canada. This group went by the name of Dukhorbors. (The image probably looked more like their leader, not Christ, or at least the historical Jesus). This group had a charismatic leader, and I can't remember his name, although I do remember that it was Russian: Ivan or something like that. Whenever I have infrequently thought about the strange events that transpired in our county that summer, it is this group that most often comes to mind. This group expressed its spirituality not through prayer or meditation, but through an esoteric ritual that combined the practice of becoming arsonists and nudists. I know what you must be thinking right now but what I write is the truth. They would simply set something on fire and dance around it completely nude in a fashion that I can only describe as bacchanal with qualifications. I shouldn't want to mislead you by using the word *bacchanal* into thinking that this particular cult was sexually free or involved with excessive alcohol or drugs. One of the things that I heard about them was they were-with the exception of their propensity to strip nude and set various structures on fire-very nice, clean people.

Another interesting fact about this group, and I hesitate to use the word *fact*, because I never investigated any of the rumors, is that Ivan was a descendent of the real group who lived in Russia and sought refuge in Canada after sustaining unbearable persecution from the Orthodox church. Tolstoy, as one rumor goes, may have funded this flight from persecution. Ivan, the leader, resurrected the group with the strange ritual, after studying the life of his great grandfather, one of the original exiled members. Again how much of this is true I cannot vouch for. I will say, though, that while I didn't know exactly what the nature of the disturbance was,

I did see a great fire roaring through the night across a field on my way back from the image.

Oh yes, and as far as the image was concerned, the Dukhobors were not, like most other pilgrims, seeking an image of Christ, but, instead, they believed these images were representations of their own leader (and images of Mary were investigated to confirm they were actually representations of the matriarch of the group). There was much talk about how much the image resembled Ivan if one stared at it long enough, but I, unfortunately, never got to see Ivan. This was not surprising considering that the Dukhorors rejected the New Testament in favor of what they called The Living Book, which wasn't really a book but just sayings passed on from various Dukhobor leaders. Even though the Dukhobors considered themselves Christian they had absolutely no interest in the historical Jesus. Instead, they were into the prophetic utterances of their leader. Ivan was said to speak to crowds and proclaim various prophecies. One prophecy pertained to the idea that the chosen ones would have to renounce property and military service; however, they were not true pacifists like the Quakers. I confess that I do not understand these paradoxes. Christians who reject the historical Jesus in favor of their human leader? Rejection of military service but not pacifists? Perhaps a closer examination of their theology could make one come to terms with these heterodoxies and paradoxes.

As I was told later, by a reliable source, I was actually witnessing the work of this group in the midst of one of their spiritual exercises. As I stated earlier, these were not Ignatius of Loyola type spiritual exercises but spiritual exercises that were centered around nudity and arson. Now, this group could become quite a nuisance to any community where one of these images appeared. I am not sure that if the fire I saw that night was the work of the Dukhobors but I do know that they were arrested for arson and indecent public exposure and that Ivan was deported. I do not know what happened to any of the supporters, which included disenfranchised kids, some who were run aways, who were recruited along the way, even a few who were local.

Beyond the mystics (none as colorful as the Dukhobors I assure you), the soul of America was hard at work. The capitalists were soon upon the scene. T-shirts, coffee mugs, and pins with a picture of the image were being sold faster than they could be made. I still have a coffee mug with a picture and a caption that reads: "I saw the image". Women pedaling coffee and doughnuts at dawn-ingenuity and entrepreneurship flourished everywhere. Mexicans who worked a nearby radish field sold burritos for lunch. They made more on their lunch hour than they did for a whole day of breaking their backs in the muck fields.

Though most of my notes were ruined, I still have a few newspaper clippings that I saved in a scrapbook. I have enclosed copies for your perusal. Notice, especially, the mother and daughter who held a vigil at the tank for over thirty days. The daughter has the priceless quote, "I know this is a sign of the second coming." She must be in her mid 30s to early 40s now. Good thing she was wrong! I have to wonder what she would think about her quote being scrutinized by scholars like me and writers like you. When you are done with your book perhaps she will get a copy. I imagine your book will rouse some interest among the locals. Though some seventeen years have past, those here are old enough to remember. I don't think before or since, the mostly rural tri-county area has had the eyes of the nation, the world for that matter, upon them. The image gave them their fifteen minutes of fame…which leads me to your final question.

As I have stated, the woman who discovered the image late one night on her way home from work, has been shielded from scholars, journalists, and religious seekers alike. Her story was covered well by the papers of the day, so you will find some of what you may be looking for. That's the best that I can do on that matter.

The man that brought it all to the end is not available either; he died a few years after the incident. I was able to talk at length with his widow however, and she disputes most accounts of the incident. She is easily in her mid 80s now but still very sharp. As you may well know, the argument that the man gave at his hearing was that he desecrated the image with paint because he was upset at the crowds, which hindered him from going to his favorite fishing spot. The widow had heard of the wailing and gnashing of teeth upon the discovery of the desecration. She knew that people in wheelchairs and people who were terminally ill had made the trip in hopes of being cured--some of them had traveled thousands of miles, only to see a soybean tank splattered with paint.

She maintains that he gave that excuse because he was an obstinate man. He actually was angered because he saw people grasping for help from an image and not through appealing to Christ through the word of God. She told me stories about how around that time many farmers were struggling, some losing their farms, and her husband spearheaded a relief campaign for the families throughout the tri-county area, doing everything from raising money to making mortgage payments to delivering dinners and gifts to farmers on Christmas Eve. Even so, she knows that if he is remembered it will be as the desecrater of the image, not as a charitable benefactor, although she is sure that the light sentence of 100 dollars and a weekend in jail was because of his known good works. Her pride of his light sentence is not something that I will soon forget. It seems like an odd solace for her after his death. It is sad that she could not separate his transgression from his reversal of fortune. I left there thinking that he was not, like Job, unjustly punished, unfairly maybe, but in her mind the two were linked. Forgive the ungainly prior sentence, I realize just and fair are nearly synonymous but it

11

is the small difference between the words that best conveys what I mean. What else can I tell you? As soon as the image was ruined the crowds left as quickly as they had come and life for most returned to normal. For the first couple of years I received inquiries like yours frequently, but after that only one every few months, then maybe one or two a year at the most. Your letter may be the first that I have received of its kind for three or so years, and it wouldn't surprise me if it were the last. Most people have forgotten about it and some have of course died or moved on. I suspect in another twenty years it may be completely forgotten. Of course your book may make it live on. I don't know when the last time I have thought about it before I received your letter. That is really all I have but feel free to submit any other questions to me and I will be more than happy to answer them to the best of my knowledge.

Sincerely,

Joseph Nash
Associate Professor
Bowling Green State University

CHAPTER 3

Dear Jason,

Yes, I am still surprised that you remember so well. You were so young when I worked with your father and after so much time I just assumed that I have been forgotten. None of my books that your father edited are still in print. I am very gratified that you have taken on this project. I wouldn't write the first word at my age and condition if I somehow thought that it was all done in vain. I have no doubt that this will be my last.

I have enclosed two letters that have been the genesis of the proposed book. One was given to me by your father and the other I wrote based on that letter. Your father was intrigued by the whole affair and wanted me to write about it. He had in mind more of a journalistic article but as I researched the affair I had the urge to fictionalize the account. After your father's untimely death, I put the project aside with no intention of working on it without him. Only recently, some fifteen years later, has the idea willed itself back into my consciousness. As much as I deem the idea as fanciful or improbable, it asserts itself even more.

So, I have a rough outline but I have much work to do. I need to reacquaint myself with the era and people who are like the characters that I have in mind. I may require your assistance with meeting such people because for the most part, I don't socialize much anymore.

One other obstacle that I face is the deterioration of memory. I can't for the life of me remember which letter was real and which was my own fabrication. Somehow your father became the owner of one letter, sent me a copy, and I fictionalized that letter, so, unless you and/or your saint of a mother have any insight, then I am not sure if I will be basing the idea on an actual historical letter or a fictional letter based on that historical letter. Perhaps with the technology at your disposal you will be able to assist me with this mystery.

I will be starting a journal, not for the sake of posterity, but only to assist me with my own memory. I don't trust it anymore. I have never kept a journal before so that too will be unchartered territory. I will be documenting the process that I hope will assist me to a completion of this project. My desk drawers are a graveyard of a decade of started and aborted projects. With your welcome commitment, however, I have a steadfast resolve to finish this one in honor of your dear father, to whom I owe all, including the letter that spawned this idea.

Yours,
E. Palamountain

CHAPTER 4

Mona had her teeth cut out in the morning. By noon, she sat, jaws swelled, spitting blood into a golden-colored spittoon. There was not enough room in her mouth for her wisdom teeth that began to invade the back of her gums near the end of her nineteenth year. James observed her from his chair with an expression that was half wince and half concern, and he noticed that he was feeling guilty, as if somehow he was responsible for this bloodletting to which he was a witness. Then he realized that this anxiety did not come so much from a source that he was directly responsible for her pain, but more that he was responsible for fixing her pain, and at this he was clearly failing.

It was not uncommon for Mona to go through drastic mood changes, and James became frustrated because he did not understand them. In fact, he had gone beyond the point of trying to understand the mood swings, and instead now went to work on trying to alter the mood, much as a painter may add yellows and greens to a landscape, with a canvas that was dominated by turbulent reds and defeated blues.

The reds of Mona's landscape would consist of unexplained outbursts. The outbursts were sometimes light reds, almost pink, going through a spoon drawer forcefully, where every move seemed to be intentional, every clink and clank meant to reach the ears of James, awake or asleep, no matter where in the trailer he may be at the time. Some of her outbursts were dark red, heading toward purple, and Mona's dark red phase resulted in damage. A broken chair, bruises, names and accusations of James's inadequacies that were meant to cut him off at the knees, or scratches that would make James wince as he looked into the mirror and applied hydrogen-peroxide with a cotton ball, watching the dark red lines on his cheek start to bubble and hiss in protest. Mona not only changed the color of her hair frequently but also the color of her moods.

Mona's blues were as dynamic as her reds. Her light blue, almost washed out to a gray, consisted of her insufferable silence. Not complete silence, but one to three word replies: Is there anything wrong: no. Are you sure? Yes. Do you want to go somewhere tonight? If you do. Do you mind if we stay home? I guess not. Are you sure? Yes, I'm sure. Are you sure there is nothing wrong? Yes, I'm sure. O.K., but I'm having trouble believing you by the way you're acting. No reply.

Mona's dark blues consisted of anything from sleeping all day to crying with her head down on the table, a crying that would last for hours, stopping sometimes for minutes only to resume again. James put a glass of water to her lips fearing dehydration. Sometimes James would emerge into the living area after he awoke in the morning, to find that some time during the night Mona's despondency had evaporated, and with the process of evaporation, the blues had altered to a neutral color.

Once James would disinfect his wounds and collect his thoughts, he would emerge from the bathroom with his palette covered with various shades of yellow and green. One of many challenges for James was that he was not a temper artist. He had no formal or informal training, no tools, no interest in the art. He learned out of necessity. In fact, he was nearly color blind, so he would end up blotting his yellows and greens blotch after blotch in trial and error, and with such inexact science, he would usually end by complicating the landscape more, destroying any harmony, even if the harmony was violent or despairing. Sometimes his sense of color was not the problem, it was instead his texture, occasionally not adding enough yellow and green, but more often than not, he added too much of a particular color, disrupting the balance, second guessing himself until he added layer after layer. Whenever Mona had a problem, life threatening or not, a general anxiety would spread across James's being, and he would bring forth his palette, desperately attending to the business of trying to fix Mona's problem.

This annoyed Mona.

"Can you eat anything?" James asked, with a voice full of concern.

"Nu-uh," grunted Mona, trying to formulate words around the cotton gauze at the back of her mouth.

"How about I go to the store and pick up some ice cream or pudding in case you're hungry later."

"Uh-huh," Mona gasped.

James patted Mona lightly on the hand and opened the trailer door and left. He stood on the 12 X 12 cement patio under the blue awning that was connected to the trailer and surveyed the surroundings. The trailer park was inordinately quiet, perhaps because of the intense humidity he thought. There were already small beads of sweat gathering on his forehead and he hadn't even started pedaling his bike yet. He rode his bike out of the lot up to a road that led to the main part of town. The town was small, consisting of fewer than a thousand people. The town had three bars, not including the American Legion, three small stores, two beauty salons, one barbershop, a library and a post office. The most striking part of the town was the large grain elevators, especially one in the middle of town that became known as "the tower." This particular grain elevator was built in the '40s, and it was constructed with such height that people would travel, mostly on Sunday afternoons, from as far as 100 miles away to view it. The tower could be seen for miles outside of the town. People would shield their eyes from the sun with their hand and tilt their head back as far as they could trying to view the top. When children viewed the tower standing right next to it, they must have thought it reached to the heavens.

James parked his bike in front of the store and turned around to look at the tower before he passed through the door. He had lived in the town all of his twenty-one years and his amazement never ceased while staring at the tower. Almost fifty years old, the tower was no longer functional, and now was surrounded by a fence, not only making it seem dangerous and abandoned but also forgotten by most who went by it frequently. James would sit on a bench staring up at the tower at times, watching as people walked by either conversing or just walking by thoughtlessly with downcast eyes.

The girl who waited on James, Diana, was the daughter of the owner of the drive-through. She had graduated two years before James and though she had been out of high school for five years she hadn't changed. She was short but appeared taller because of her big hair. Blonde hair that fell half way down her back and had big curls, and she had a mass of it piled on top of her head with a banana clip, and this in addition to stiletto heels increased her height.

"The ice cream for highty flighty girl?" asked Diana, while continuing to chew her gum.

"I wish you wouldn't call her that," replied James. "What band is that?" James asked pointing to Diane's T-shirt.

"Solution, they're a local band but they plan on moving to L.A. soon. They're really good. They play around almost every weekend. You should go see them, by yourself of course. I know Mona Nash would be above it."

By the time James returned, the ice cream he bought had already started to melt into a creamy soup. He poured it into a bowl and handed it to Mona along with a large spoon. Mona filled the spoon and let a little flow into her mouth, and, as if she had no energy left, put the spoon back in the bowl and stared at it. James went over and filled the spoon and brought it toward Mona's darkened and swelled lips. She again drank a small portion of the melted ice cream, but when James attempted to feed her another spoonful, she turned away. Though James did not have fresh incisions in his mouth, he too had a queasy feeling in his stomach, not helped by the pressured humidity that was bearing down on them.

"Come in," James said over his shoulder when he heard the light tap on the screen door. A burly man of sixty-five came through the door and looked Mona over empathetically, an empathy that was different from James's. Unlike James, this man with receding gray was calm. Mona instantly responded to his presence, her eyes opening fully, sitting up in her chair, silently requesting that he come closer, pat her head, anything at all to make her forget her pain.

"She's having a rough go of it Gus," James said.

"*Guten Tag*, Gus," Mona forced out.

"There there, no need to say a word," Gus replied as he continued to survey the damage. "Here, darling, put these right on the side," he said as he handed her two ice packs. "It won't only help you with the swelling and the pain, it will cool you off. This heat is suffocating." The ice packs appeared to give Mona some instant relief.

"*Danke*," She said conveying a smile, mostly with her eyes.

"You're welcome, sweetheart."

Mona had spent a good deal of her childhood in Germany and had become somewhat fluent during that time. Gus who had emigrated from Germany decades before was already fluent in English when he arrived, but after encountering lingering anti-German sentiment, he also mastered the dialect to a degree that he had no discernable accent left in his speech. In fact, it was only after Mona was walking by his trailer one morning and heard him speaking with his elderly sister in German that anyone became aware that he spoke German. Later in the day when Gus was planting flowers Mona came up to him and explained, *"Ich spreche Deutch ein bis-chen…"* and since then Mona spoke to him in German, though Gus would only answer her back in English. He explained to Mona all that this country had given to him: he had put two children through college, a teacher and an engineer; he had raised them in a well-kept split level home, a home that he sold only after he retired. His wife had died of ovarian cancer, and a trailer was all he needed for himself and his ailing sister, who he had been taking care of since she moved over from Europe nearly a decade before.

Though retired, Gus was constantly busy. He was involved in many charity programs, especially programs that helped feed and clothe children of farmers, farmers who had done well since the end of World War II but who were now barely hanging onto their farms and in some cases losing them all together. Gus especially took care of the elderly in the neighborhood. He would shop for them, run to the drugstore, or any other errand that was requested of him. In the winter he would spend his days, even at his advanced age, shoveling their driveways and their walks, and in the summer he would cut lawns and trim bushes, stoutly refusing any type of compensation except for perhaps a glass of water or lemonade. Gus was still a volunteer firefighter, a position that has earned him respect throughout the community and also enhanced his reputation as a selfless person.

The storm that all were anticipating was introduced by a boom that startled Mona and James. They went to the window and noticed that flashes of lightning were already crisscrossing the ominous dark gray clouds that marched toward their town. People who live in trailer parks often are psychologically different than people who live in homes when it comes to storms. There is a strange kinship with nature when nature is in its most violent state. The relationship is adversarial but it is a welcomed adversary, met with a defiance that produces a catharsis. One reason for this may be the fact that the first question asked when someone finds out that another person is a parky is something like "well, what about storms?" Or the most respected and feared adversary that nature had to offer, "what about tornadoes?"

Tornadoes! The very word to a parky excites an array of conflicted emotions. Just watch the news, for example. It's as if a tornado, like a bloodhound, sniffs out the section of a town where a trailer park exists, and proceeds to hammer through it--bent on total destruction. All anyone has to do is to ask a parky about tornadoes to see the person's eyes and lungs fill up with defiant courage. If you ever see people wearing T-shirts with "I survived the Xenia tornado..." then more often than not, they are a parky.

James could see several windows from other trailers and each one of them had at least two people staring out at the developing storm. The wind was blowing leaves and other debris in different shapes through the air at first, until one big gust sent everything in its path eastward including items such as lawn chairs and nearly empty charcoal bags. The rain that had started like a sporadic drum beating against the side of the trailer now had transformed into a downpour that created a constant cadence. The sound of the relentless rain was only occasionally disrupted by an exclamation point provided by thunder that seemed to shake the trailer, but the exclamation point was not unexpected because it was announced by a flash of lightning that made all reflexively move back away from the window. "One, two, thr...," Mona said lightly between the lightning and the thunder. "That struck close," she said more to herself than to James, trying to calculate how far the lightning had struck by how long it took the sound to reach them.

The storm was moving through, Mona could feel it in her wounded mouth. The lighter the rain became the more sporadic the lightning and the more distant the thunder. James could see the relief in her eyes and his own sinus pressure was gone, too. As the sun broke through the clouds, Mona smiled. "Let's go out on the patio," she said to James.

The heat of the sun had returned but the thick stagnant air was now light and blowing gently from the west. The trailer park began to fill with people surveying damage done to trees, fallen limbs and scattered leaves. As with nearly every summer day, the air began to fill with charcoaled smoke and lighter fluid fumes, and various men and women emerged, some wearing aprons of various designs. Some plain, others more sophisticated with matching sets of spatulas, forks and tongs. Before long the smell of meat and sauce overtook the fumes as talk of the storm was overcome by plans for dinner and the evening that lay beyond.

"Think we should check on Hank," Mona said.

"Probably," James replied looking toward a small black trailer. "I'll do it. You just rest, you may feel better but you're still swelled up pretty good."

James walked across the lot and tapped at the trailer door, and he waited and then knocked louder but still no answer, and then he jiggled the door knob to see if it was locked or not and it was not. He opened the door slightly and tried to peak through but could see nothing so he opened it a bit further. There was still no sign of anyone so he stepped inside the trailer and glanced across the kitchen and the living room but there was still no sign of Hank. James looked at all of the different icons and artifacts across the room and at the POW flag that was draped across the main window. Hank had Buddha statues sitting on tables, ying/yang medallions and crosses hung on the wall. Books were piled against the hall wall opposite the couch on a coffee table that had an ashtray that smelled of tobacco and pot. James walked back through the hall past a bedroom and then a bathroom and another bedroom at the end of the hall. James cracked the door and looked inside. On the bed facing away from James sat a man not yet forty with long hair tied into a pony tail, he was holding his legs as they wobbled back and forth and his body was rocking to and fro. James laid a pack of Kools on a chest of drawers and then turned quietly around and walked back down the hall, and quietly went out of the trailer and shut the door behind him.

CHAPTER 5

I turned fifty-three a fortnight last and I have never kept a diary. Not only have I not kept a diary, I have never confided in another human being my true thoughts or feelings. It is not that I haven't yearned for a confidant; I've even tested a few individuals, only to be spurned or betrayed. I anticipate that this will not be so much a diary but a confession. It is too early now but perhaps my confession will turn into a manifesto, a filibuster to keep at bay outside influences that attempt to rattle my mission.

Max will soon be here, his introduction card is the storm that rages outside. Max is a bum; he is not homeless though, just poor. He visits my flat when he is hungry, sick or cold. I assist him with clothes, medicine, and a place to thaw his bones. Max thinks that I am his only friend--I am not his friend. I observe Max. I can experience Max's despair without experiencing despair myself, observe his loneliness without being lonely, and can observe the suicide of Max without having to kill myself. I aid Max because I feel that I owe him. I got rid of him once, sent him packing, told him I had no time for his stories, his self-pity, his addictive habits. He left with a look that this was the end to our friendship that he had expected. He had obviously been in similar situations many times before and we were merely going through the movements of a life long ritual. As I saw him stumble across the street against sheets of cold rain, I felt no remorse--I expected that he would be found dead.

I finished my cup of tea and the crossword puzzle from the day's paper and crawled into my warm bed beneath a thick down comforter, and had no more thoughts of the situation--I would sleep with a clear conscious. When I heard the pounding at the door, I fumbled with the lamp switch until the light appeared and I could see the clock read 3:30 A.M. Another series of loud raps at the door accelerated my movements. When I opened the door I saw Max between two police officers. For a moment I felt the confusion that K must have endured.

"Erwin Palamountin?" one of the officers asked, looking suspiciously through me.

"Yes."

"This man says he belongs here." The police officer brought Max beneath the hall light so that I could see him better. "Do you know this man or not?"

"I do."

"Is this where he belongs?"

"It is."

"Who are you to him?"

"I am his caretaker." I have no idea now why I claimed to be the person who was responsible for Max's well-being.

"Well, you better start taking better care of him. We found him on his back in the middle of the street. He could have been killed."

"I see," I said, opening the door so Max could walk through.

"Well, next time there will be a problem. We'll contact Human Services and they will investigate."

"Good night, officers." With no direct comment on their threats, I nodded and closed the door. Max shook with fear or cold or both. The parka that I had given him hung from him like loose skin. The pockets that had already begun to rip when I gave him the coat were either now gone or hung by a thread. His gray beard had specks of ice that started to turn into water and glisten beneath the light.

I pulled out the convertible couch, brought Max a pair of sweats and a blanket and went back into my room. He said nothing nor did I.

There was such a strong chilled draft blowing across the hardwood floor I wondered if Max would be warm enough. The thought quickly died as I told myself I had done as much as I could, more than most people would. I considered turning up the heat but as I listened to the radiator hiss like a lizard, I was conscious of the cost of such a decision and buried that idea beside the previous one.

I turned out the lamp next to my bed and closed my eyes and although my body was tired, and my feet ached from gout, my mind raced on ignoring both. I thought about the German professor. What is to become of him? I don't create characters, they either come to me whole, completely formed, like Athena from the head of Zeus, or they tease me with fragments, hiding major parts of their personalities along with their history, their stories. Perhaps Herr Schmidt will be shy, reclusive and elusive and I will have to keep him where he is, an expert on religious apparitions who never makes the trip across the ocean. He will be a nebulous figure who we know only from the letters he receives from Tom Granger-I hope not, I am patiently waiting to see if he reveals more of himself. I also would like him to meet the native German, Gus, and unless I change my mind and change it, Mona speaks German very well. Why so many Germans? I'm not sure. I haven't finished the self-analytical process that I so often endure. I am from German descent so I'm sure that has something to do with it. That may also have something to do with my affinity for Max. He is German, second generation he tells me. I tend to believe him because I think he exhibits a great deal of the Germanic will--he realizes he is at odds with the world-spirit but instead of acquiescing to the great force he hunches his shoulders, grits his teeth, clinches his fist and marches against the turbulence.

But I have digressed...I would like for the German professor to occupy more of the story, if not make the trip to see the image, at least answer Tom's letters, but to this point he has remained invisible and mute, and it is his choice if he wants to come forth, not mine. Maybe it wasn't even his letter that came to me, perhaps it was Joseph Nash's letter, I'm confident that it was Tom who was my creation and that professor Nash is or was a living breathing historic person. Who knows, I may change my mind too. The best I can do is to stay alert, in case he decides to become more involved. I continue to lay awake, thinking about various characters who have lived with me, invited or not.

Occasionally a character won't come to me until I have sought out their inspiration. None of my characters are based on real people but sometimes they stay in some Platonic form, refusing to become material until they have some vessel of this world which gives them shape. A vessel that will ignite their structure, a spark that will bring them into this world through my writing. James, the bewildered young man whose first adult relationship has him outmatched, was born from a young blonde boy, twenty-one perhaps. I was sitting beside him or the subway and we did not speak. In fact, we barely made eye contact. James came to me through him, almost like the dead through a medium. For twenty minutes James told me his story, most of which I will never use--a biography of James wouldn't be very interesting. Most of his childhood was too average to integrate into any type of work. The meeting of Mona, this is where I started to pay attention and make mental notes. We were rudely interrupted when at a stop the blonde boy got up and left, exiting without any thought of what the repercussions might be, how by one action he may be changing what my life may become-- but thankfully James stayed. For reasons I'll never know, he did not exit with his spark.

I try not to put anything of myself into the characters. I some-

27

how think that I am betraying them when I do. When our interests overlap, I often wonder if I have interfered with them too much or if it is just a coincidence. Tom Granger quotes Dostoevsky and Dostoevsky is certainly one of my favorite writers. At times I have considered myself somewhat of an updated Dostoevsky-type character: a molish being that is prone to feverish hallucinations, bewitched by ideas that are not shared *en masse*. I have lived on the fringe of society for nearly twenty-five years.

While all of these thoughts continued to ruminate through my head I was conscious of the ticking of the clock, and also conscious that I was jeopardizing my strength for the next day and beyond. Though no doctor has ever been able to identify any abnormality with me, I suffer from a weak immune system and am often indisposed. It seems as if I just get over a case of inflamed bowels when I am struck by an ear infection or some other nameless, ominous infliction that stops any real progress.

I was more than conscious of the ticking of the clock but I was also conscious that Max was in the other room, and that I was spending most of this restless night with one eye open, waiting for the bedroom door to creak open. So that I could rest, I tilted a chair against the doorknob to secure the area, and while I finally fell asleep, I would often wake to make sure the chair was still there. The room was totally dark but every time a car would turn into the alley beside my flat the lights from the car would sweep across the room in a broad stroke and briefly make parts of the room visible, one part after the other. Once during the night toward morning a car light revealed Max who was standing over me grinning. I quickly rose up in my bed but could not see him anywhere. The dreary gray of morning was starting to seep through into the room and I could tell the chair remained unmoved-it must have been part of the dream. Still, I felt much better as dawn approached and the night had moved on. I went back to sleep for what seemed to be only a few minutes but in actuality was several hours. At 11:35 I finally removed the chair and entered the main living area. Max was gone and everything was in place as if he had never been there. Had the police brought him there the night before? I started to doubt myself and thought that that was also dreamt or part of a hallucination. A lukewarm pot of coffee that was half full convinced me otherwise.

Chapter 6

Two long black cars rumbled up the road and could be spotted by farmers who were busy in the fields. The cars drew attention because there were two of them; people gave pause, even if they did not give much thought. When they turned into the Hoffstetter lane two clouds of dust appeared, and grew larger until the cars looked like two small twisters heading up toward the house. Henry Sr. was standing outside the screen door, waiting. He stoically looked at the men. The four men stood in conference with Henry Sr. for close to five minutes. The men were dressed in black suits and all appeared to have matching sun glasses and even though there was no mystery about their identity, they still showed Henry their credentials. Henry pretended to view them, squinting his eyes against an afternoon sun.

The men spread out across the lawn and canvassed the yard that sloped down to the barn. The two men on the outside quickened their pace and walked close to the side of the barn peering through the many cracks that were formed by nearly over 100 winters and summers. Not until they were beyond the sight of Henry Sr. did the two men who were making their way to the back of the barn draw their guns. Henry Sr. centered his expressionless glance on the two agents waiting at the front of the barn. When the agents in the front heard the back doors being slid open they grabbed hold of the handles on the front doors and pulled them open flooding the inside of the barn with light. Not until the two agents in the front were inside and had walked to the sidewall did they bring out their guns. With a nod the four men each starting from a different corner began searching the space cautiously as they took steps while looking into pens and cages, never forgetting that the person they sought may be to the side, above, or even covered in the straw below them. The agent who had started at the right back of the barn was trying to shove pigs apart as quietly as he could so he could better view the space between them. The men eventually met back at the center of the barn and once again acted as a single mechanism, eight eyes turned upward. In a subjective unspoken language the agents communicated and two by two they ascended ladders that led to the loft. The tall one peered over the top of the floor scanning left to right. There were fewer cracks in the walls at the top of the barn that made it more difficult to focus on the objects.

The four men started to move the piles of straw when a cackle followed by an explosion filled the barn. The two agents on the opposite side of the explosion stood at the edge of the top floor trying to make out what exactly had happened when the tall agent, pale and nervous, held a headless, gun shot blood-stained rooster.

"Christ," gasped the tall agent, "this son of a bitch about gave me a heart attack. Flew right up in my face."

The other three began grinning and the agent standing next to the tall one started to chuckle, "Stan's been attacked by a chicken." The two standing opposite smiled at each other and relaxed their position.

"Screw you," said the tall one under his breath, visibly embarrassed.

The form moved from beneath the straw with such surprise that all four of the agents stood motionless, not trusting their vision. One, two, three long strides and then leapt high into the air coming down on the barn floor like a cat and darting out the back door as quick as one also. Before the agents registered the escape and descended the loft ladders looking out the back of the barn, the fugitive had a substantial head start. The barn door framed the scene like a movie shot-- the form becoming smaller as it made its way through a vast bean field toward the woods.

The woods that stood between a series of fields were not large but thick. As the officers canvassed the area they had to fight their way through weeds and briars and the more times they were poked and stabbed, the angrier they became. The first two through waited at the edge of the wood until the other two appeared at the other end, then the four converged at the middle.

"Where could he be? These woods are not that big."

"Yeah but it's thick. He could be lying on the floor of the woods like he was lying on the floor of the barn under that straw. We could a walked right by 'em and not have known it."

"Well, let's go through it again. This time we'll go east ta west."

"He may have already high tailed out the other side. He may be back through that bean field in that barn again. He may be in another patch of woods by now."

"One more time through."

"Hey," whispered the tall one. "Look." The eyes of the others followed his arm to the tip of his finger and onto the invisible line that connected his out-stretched index finger to a form that held tightly to a tree on the edge of the woods that stood 80 feet. The form was close to two-thirds to the top.

"Well well," said the leader, more to himself than to anyone else. "You c'mon down here now boy," he yelled cupping his mouth with his hands. "C'mon down here boy it's time for you to be a man and go serve your country." The gray-haired man paused and looked at his crew as if to say your guess is as good as mine. "Who can climb a tree?" he asked looking at his crew for volunteers. "Bill, how about you?"

"I can't climb that tree. Look how far up he is. He must be half bear."

"Well you're the youngest with the least seniority. It's time to prove yourself."

The other two nodded in agreement.

"Let's shoot him. That will bring him down."

"We can't shoot 'em."

"I don't need to climb that tree. I'll get the draft dodger down." Bill walked to the edge of the field and picked up a solid dirt clod and threw it at the young man. His first few missed but the other two joined in while the leader looked on, his silence being his approval. Every fourth or fifth clod hit the man in the tree and even though the man changed positions to shield himself, he could not hide himself from the barrage of stone and dirt and finally the man began to descend, and then took his second big jump of the day. This time, however, the agents were on top of him before he could make it to his feet. He fought wildly hissing and spitting. Once the agents had him handcuffed they brought him to his feet and started to drag him back across the bean field.

"You sons a bitches better never let me go. You better never give me leave 'cause I'll be gone. I'll never stay there. I'll never fight. You better never look the other way. I'll flee again and again and again." They took him for his word because he was never given leave during his entire tour of duty in Southeast Asia.

CHAPTER 7

A friend once told me that historians gravitated toward a specific time period because they had once lived during that time and had not finished what they came to do. Oddly enough, my acquaintance believed he was one example of this strange phenomenon. His area of expertise was medieval art, and, of course, he felt that he was a reincarnated king. For the sake of mental therapy, he went through a series of past life regressions, this therapy followed many other types of therapy including psychoanalysis, behavioral therapy, and even shock therapy when he was only sixteen years old. How odd, when he was made aware of his past lives through therapy, that he hadn't been a poor servant, slave, petty thief, or town drunk.

If I had had a past life what would I have been? A murderer I hope. Why? Because so often walking through the subway I have had the urge well up in me to grab by the neck some condescending or disrespectful stranger and choke the life out of him. In my first novel when I wrote the part about when Eugene first poisons and then mutilates the corpse of his mother's killer (who, unbeknownst to him at the time, happens to be his twin sister who was given up to adoption at birth (GOD, how I love a suspenseful plot!) and buries her beneath his cabin floor I came away from my writing desk a new man-temporarily anyway. I underwent some sort of massive short-term catharsis. The urge to murder placated by a creative act.

Even now, the thought that I had relinquished life in a past life, a committed crime for which I had not been caught, gave me a hint of satisfaction. Don't get me wrong. I have no desire to inflict any sort of pain upon the innocent. I am a pious man, and I mean well for most people but not all. One day a migraine without permission invited a writer's block and I wrote a list of vermin that I would like extinguished-child abusers and so forth were high on the list, a priority you might say, with white collar criminals rounding it out save one. I continued writing because that is the agreement that I had made with myself. If I wasn't going to focus and work then I was going to sit there and write--a self-inflicted punishment on most days, but not on the day of my kill list. It was a pleasure. Number one on the list was Jason. Why not? What could I receive, life in prison? The death penalty? Huh, I already have that. It would be a free ride.

I wouldn't though, but I want to. I would never want to see his mother suffer. Perhaps if she should go before the short time I have left, I'll revisit the matter, but, until then, he is safe.

I have solved the challenge with my little problem with Jason. He doesn't want to answer my letters in a timely fashion? I no longer have to worry about this damn book anymore. I'll finish but not in the way that I once planned. I don't have to worry about the 1,000 pages plus mammoth project that I envisioned three years ago, three years ago when I thought I had twenty ahead of me. No, last night I burned pages of notes. Graham's obsession with certain actresses that kept him from forming serious relationships. Hank's story overseas with his unwanted participation in Vietnam. That one I don't feel so bad about. There have been enough books and movies that any reader (phantom at this point) should be able to imagine what he must have went through, and how that experience must have shaped his personality. I do need to know more about him, and if Jason won't send me someone, I'll either have

Max go out and find one for me to interview, or I will go down to one of the centers myself where the vets hang out. This journal, this diary, or whatever the hell I should call it shall no longer stand in my way either. I am spending too much time writing my thoughts instead of my book. It is easier. A convenient excuse. Writing the book is too taxing so I avoid it. I may have to give this journal up or I may never finish. Now, Graham, look at my notes, they're a mess. Hmmm, a chapter in search of quotation marks. I wonder….? Just start writing. Not tonight though.

CHAPTER 8

Perry meets Parker. Perry opens his mail and answers the stranger. Perry goes to a party. A blonde man with blood shot eyes lectures Perry. Perry takes an oath. Perry attends his first historian show which concerns Lorenzo Da Ponte. Perry declines the opportunity to mingle. Perry reads a book at the party.

Perry walked down the street against the tide of strangers. He tried to keep his mind on past events to ease his immense apprehension. It is not that he necessarily thought that anyone from the crowd had singled him out for harm. He just could not stabilize the feeling of cold and unintentional indifference. He used to frequently and aimlessly wander the streets, spending the afternoon looking through shops of used books and records, stopping by one of the many bars, drinking imported beers, Long Island iced-teas, or, if he was short on money, which happened quite frequently, he would just drink coffee with free refills. He found companionship amongst other social outcasts who were daytime regulars. Daytime regulars differed from nighttime regulars. They consisted of hardcore drunks, the almost homeless, Vietnam vets, whores, and ex-art history majors who should have graduated ten or twenty years ago, but for one reason or another, more often than not, acquired a drug addiction, left school but never left campus.

He would be eager for the chance to talk with anybody, because he usually found everybody interesting, unless he was in one of his introspective moods. He spent so much of his time thinking alone, conversation gave him an innate peace, no matter how short lived this tranquility of mind existed; it was peace all the same. Perry's state of mind would be determined by how his efforts of conversation were received. If the person at the other end of the bar was willing to tell their story, he was usually willing to listen.

One such gentleman, who often told his story, each time with an embellishment which made it more dramatic, was a man in his late 30s who called himself Graham Parker. One story that circulated was that he changed his name from Leo (last name unknown) after attending a Graham Parker concert in the early '80s. This story, however, proved to be erroneous if one is to believe Graham Parker (the barfly, not the musician).

Parker approached Perry one day when he was drinking a Fiesta Liebermich beer, an import he had yet to try.

Do you like that book? Asked Parker, looking past Perry at the mirror on the back wall behind the bar.

Yeah, I do. Great idea. The book Parker asked Perry about was *Frank's World* by George Mangels. *Frank's World* is a book inspired by Frank Booth, a character in David Lynch's movie *Blue Velvet*. The idea of taking a character from a movie, especially one as creepy as Booth, and writing about his life and childhood, struck Graham as genius.

Yes, but I don't know if it is really about the Booth from Lynch's movie. It may be about the Booth in Wangel's mind, which was only inspired from the movie.

So, you've read it? Inquired Perry.

I've read everything, answered Graham Parker.

Really everything?

Everything.

Baptisms from the Dead by Don De Grazia?

Everything.

Have you read all the self-help books and all the Harlequin romances? Asked Perry, the pitch of his voice ascending with every word.

Let me clarify. I've read everything of consequence.

O.K. Have you read *Remembrance of Things Past*? asked Perry, slowly shaking his head, spreading his hands and fingers apart.

Like I said, I've read everything of consequence, and there is an argument to be made if anything French is consequential. But just the same, I have read the work that you are referring to, but, let me educate you on one small fact. People in the know, know that calling that book *Remembrance of Things Past* is a mistranslation. *In Search Of Time Lost* would be the incorrect misnomer. At this point Graham Parker dug his hand into a bowl of peanuts and scratched the bottom of the bowl several times to scoop up as many as possible and shoved them into his mouth. Several crumbs fell into his prematurely graying beard. *Ulysses, Man Without Qualities, The Recognitions*, said Parker, trying to chew a wad of mashed peanuts and talk at the same time, those are true *überwerks*.

Let's leave our heroes (term loosely used) and let them discuss books, their favorite art, what they think is overrated (Whatever you do, don't get Graham Parker started on Hemingway, said the bartender to Perry, he is on a one man crusade to have him removed from the canon) what they think is underrated. (How much longer can The Moronic Critic not take its place beside *Gatsby* when teaching, nay thinking, about the great American novel, how many more years must expire before *Insatiability* takes its place beside *Tristram Shandy* and *Don Quixote* as one of the great eccentric world classics, with each passing moment such thoughts sank Graham deeper into despair.) Let us continue to stay out of ear shot as the bond between these two men develops, strengthened by not only the novel, but music, the visual arts, cinema (the films of Viking Eggling on

39

acid did more for me, Graham had said to many people, and now Perry was a part of that list, than ten years of Buddhist meditation). Cinema would be the curse that kept Parker a bachelor approaching his fifth decade of life--but more on that later...

***

Parker (though not known as Parker at that time) had come to campus in the late '70s and for one reason or another he had never left. He had started many different projects, including a Ph.D. in cultural anthropology, a political party, whose main platform plank concerned smoker's rights (he equated the trendy political smoking bans in bars to the persecution of the Christians by Tiberius-scapegoats one and all). A plethora of abandoned art projects littered his psyche: novels, plays, short films, rock bands, Christmas CDs, mimetic contortionism, spoken word festivals, and Spanish-American War re-enactments (this gave Graham an excuse to wear his monocle, a family heirloom bequeathed to him by a great uncle who claimed to have done battle with the greatest rough rider of them all) and this was only a fraction of his aborted endeavors that were begun with passion and optimism, and ended in despair and confusion.

He lived in a small flat surrounded by students twenty years his junior. All the students assumed he was a professor so in return they always treated him with a certain amount of reverence. When he started to be called "Professor Parker", he never took the time or effort to correct the address. The fact that "Professor Parker" sounded very closely to "Colonel Parker" endeared him even more to the name. In a campus in excess of 50,000 students it was easy enough for Parker to protect his illusion. After all, he never said I am a professor; he just never corrected the assumption. Even that is not exactly true. He would certainly explain to someone who asked him about his professorship-waxing philosophically he would explain how he is a professor of life or a professor of existence.

It was only after the third or fourth "hi professor" that Perry finally changed the subject from art and asked him what he was a professor of exactly.

We'll get into that later boss, whispered Graham Parker.

***

The leaves were squash yellow and rust red and fell sporadically from the trees in slow motion like floating feathers. Perry went home and shaved and put on a clean shirt. He had been invited by Graham Parker to go to a party. He was to meet Graham in front of the Beacon and they would walk up to Summit Avenue. The party was being hosted by a friend of Graham's who had been a teacher's assistant in a wine tasting class presented by the horticulture department that Graham had flunked his freshman year. Perry opened his door and retrieved the mail from the box. He separated the junk mail and the bills and then stopped at an envelope with a familiar address. The envelope:

Box 908
Reinbeck, Iowa
50669

11211 East Indianola
Columbus, Ohio
442112

Perry opened the envelope and read the brief letter: **Dear Resident, to answer your last letter is easily done. YES. That is all**

41

that needs to be said on that horrific subject. Now, I have often thought about the limits of human knowledge. Not what we can know but if we can indeed know anything at all. We must be able to know if 2 + 2 is 4 for example. I don't personally know how to prove that but I assume there is a way. I am quite fascinated right now that I happen to use the word *assume*, very telling. What was the Alexander Pope quote? Ah, why, ye Gods, why should two and two make four? Or something like that. Metaphysics is a tricky thing. I'm preoccupied by my using the word *tricky* as in trick as in to trick. Are we being fooled? Are we in some kind of cosmic game? My question to you is thus: Do you believe that we can be absolutely sure about anything?

Perry put down the letter and opened his notebook. He took an envelope from his bill drawer and addressed it back to Reinbeck, Iowa. He tore a clean page from his notebook and began writing:

No. But I think there are degrees that fall short of absolutes. I'm not completely sure that I am sitting in an apartment in Columbus, Ohio right now but I'm more sure of that than I am for example if something happened the same way that it is relayed to me, and I'm more sure of that than if there is a God or a supreme entity and so forth and so on.

My question to you is as follows: Would you rather see the Hawkeyes win a national championship in football or basketball?

Perry stuffed and sealed the envelope. He stuck a new U.S. commemorative stamp of Millard Fillmore on the envelope and put the letter in the box.

***

The two men climbed a hill that led to a house that overlooked a small ravine. As they walked, Graham found it necessary to say *"crunch crunch crunch crunch"* imitating the sounds of the leaves as he stepped upon them. When they knocked, a grizzled and burly man in his mid-fifties greeted them. He had a tweed jacket, oversized red bow tie, and dark-rimmed glasses. He stared at them for a moment as if he weren't quite sure who they were.

Jack, it's Graham.

Graham who?

C'mon boss, its Graham Parker.

I don't know any Graham Parker. Who's boss?

You're boss and we're coming in.

Graham and Perry made their way past the man whom Graham referred to as boss (one of the many) and proceeded to go down a hall with hardwood floors. Graham walked on at a brisk pace but Perry couldn't help looking at the people who were disbursed through the different rooms. The house was big but the rooms were numerous and the ones that he could see were small except the room at the end of the hall, which was massive. The rooms that Perry passed gave him an inexact feeling that he couldn't verbalize. He thought that it must be the oddity of the rooms because each room was a different color, a color that one usually didn't find in wall paint--a blood red or lime green. The big room at the end of the hall was painted a conventional light brown, the hardwood floors continued throughout the room. In the middle of the room there was a massive rococo chandelier that had light bulbs alternating with real candles. At the far end of the room there was a wall that was entirely surfaced with bookshelves. All the books had the appearance of being very old. Most of the books had worn, cloth covers that covered many different shades of blue, brown and green.

Perry thought about his own 4 x 6 bookshelf filled with trade paperbacks.

Graham reappeared with two open bottles of Fiesta Liebermich. He took a look around the room as if he were memorizing every

43

detail.

Are you sure you know these people?

Of course I do.

Why is everyone looking at us like we don't belong?

Probably because we don't belong. But the fact that we don't belong doesn't necessarily negate the fact that I don't know them or that I wasn't invited. See the difference?

I guess.

You want to stick with me; you can if you're uncomfortable.

No, go ahead. I'll be fine.

Perry watched as Graham disappeared into a crowd. He looked around the room and decided to look at the books so he didn't look so out of place. He noticed that the books were alphabetized by author but they started with Z and ended with A. He picked up *Germinal* and started reading the first page.

Find something interesting? Perry looked around and saw that a man with extremely blood- shot-eyes and blond curly hair was looking at him with a smirk on his face waiting for a reply.

Excuse me, Perry said politely.

I was just wondering if you found anything interesting?

Perry showed him the book.

I'm Ness.

I'm Perry. Perry extended his hand to shake but the man did not move. Perry was thinking to himself that he had never seen a man whose eyes were blood-shot to the extent that there was more red to the eye than white. The curly blond hair accented the veiny redness of the eyes. Perry realized that the man had no intention of shaking his hand so he slowly brought it back to his body and used it to help his other hand support Germinal.

I'm here with Graham Parker. Perry offered this information mistaking the red-eyed man's reluctance to shake his hand as rude-ness, born of the fact that Graham had tricked him into crashing the party. He now assessed the situation and had come to the preliminary conclusion that Ness was the owner of the house; he had no idea who Graham was, and that he was about ready to ask the two of them to leave.

No offense, I just don't shake hands.

Oh, I see, said Perry still trying to make sense of the whole scene.

Do you?

Ness had now integrated an incredulous tone.

No, I'm not quite sure you do see. The fact is, my young Zola-ite, is that the common cold is crippling our economy. We know how it is mainly spread. Is it airborne? No, it is spread through the skin: you have it, I shake your hand, I rub my eye. Bingo! I am now a host to a virus that is going to perhaps put me out of work for a time or at least make me less efficient. Now, you tell me why we live in a century that put a man on the moon but has yet to figure out that a bow is a much more economical way of salutation than shaking hands. Think of not only the dollars saved but human lives, and yes people still do expire from complications of the common cold. So my refusal to shake hands in no way signals ill will toward you. I would not shake the hand of the President himself!

The two men stopped briefly interrupted by the sound of a bell. As the crowd turned toward a man in a white suit and tie expecting an announcement, Perry placed the book back at the beginning of the bookshelf and stood at partial attention with the rest of the people in the grand room.

Ladies and Gentlemen, said the man in the white suite. I have been sent to inform you that Uriah the historian will be speaking in the gray room in ten minutes at exactly one quarter after the hour. Thank you.

A quiet, respectful applause rippled throughout the room.

What exactly do you expect to learn from this? Said Ness, pointing his fingers at different parts of the bookshelf.

I don't know. Perry was obviously caught unprepared for the question. I guess I'll expand my humanity? No reply from Ness. Perhaps I'll learn something about myself and the world I live in or the way the world used to be or learn about history so I am not a part of the same mistakes that were made in the past.

Ness took a big gulp of air and exhaled through his nose, which expanded his flat nostrils and accentuated the red in his eyes.

Did you come up with that? Ness asked before continuing without giving time for Perry to answer. Or is that some hodge-podge of sayings that you have assimilated from professors at the university. Ness could tell, just as he expected that Perry had no answer, and if he did have one he was too unsure of himself to bring it forth. Well, said Ness, let me do you the favor of letting you in on a little secret and that secret is simply this: it is through people not books that we learn about humanity, otherwise, Ness continued with his eyes becoming mere red slits, we should refer to it as bookanity. Am I right or am I right? Everyone has stories, and it is through those stories that we learn about people. Let me tell you my story, and then compare it if you like to *Germinal*, although it is my hope that after you hear my tale, and although it is historical, I'm sure you will integrate the allegorical, if not now then somehow the lesson will manifest later.

Though my story goes further back I will be starting my story approximately where your story is at present. I came from a city but decided to go to a small liberal arts college in a small town. My parents helped move me into my dorm room at the end of August. The air was hot and moist and I remember how the room felt like an oven. My parents and I walked over to the cafeteria and ate lunch and afterwards I said goodbye to my mother and my teary-eyed father. When I got back to my room my roommate had arrived and was unpacking his things. I had talked to my roommate by phone

46

a few times and I had imagined that he looked like a jock or some-thing--athletic and clean cut. I was wrong. Before me stood a man about 5'2" and although he had the skin of an eighteen-year-old he was balding with long hair on the sides that fell to his shoulders. He had a thick black beard that grew to his chest but was so sparse on the front of his chin that it somehow complemented his prematurely receding hairline. The thing I remember most about him is his eyes. They were obscured by the thickest glasses that I have ever seen before or since. His glasses were so thick and they had such a dark tint to them that to this day I could not tell you the color of his eyes. If I had to guess, I would guess brown, but I don't know why I say that now.

We shook hands and then he got out a nylon stringed classical guitar. The two of us sat on the edge of the bed singing folk songs in harmony. He stopped playing and the two of us continued a cappella and he put his hand beneath the F hole in his guitar and produced two drops of acid. Without missing a beat we both dropped. We went from singing folk songs to performing songs by Love and The Chocolate Watch Band. He wanted to cover a Vanilla Fudge tune but I refused, staunchly refused. This angered him and he took his guitar and walked out of the room. I looked out of the window and could see him walking across the lawn until he rested under a tree. He started playing his guitar again and I opened the window to listen. I could hear that he was playing a slowed down version of "some velvet morning". Three young students in retro tie-dye shirts came up by him and started playing hacky sack kicking the sack on the beat, adding percussion to his dirge.

The walls were beginning to melt around me so in a panic I exited the room then the building. When I got out in front of the dorms I looked down the road and noticed the sidewalks were moving. They were expanding and at the same time they were rolling in an up and down motion. I was laughing to myself. I'm not sure why, if it was because of the funny sidewalks or something else I can't be certain. When I finally was able to stop watching the moving sidewalks I saw that there was a group of students dressed up and they were waiting to get on the bus. I asked them where they were going and this girl said that it was meet the president night for first year students. This struck me as funny also so I was trying to talk through my laughter. President Reagan! I said. You're going to meet President Reagan! And she said nowa, yeah she said no just like that with a *wa* on the end. Nowa, not President Reagan, President McCutheon, you know the president of the college. Didn't you read the itinerary? We all go to his house and walk through and shake his hand and have refreshments. Well, by this time I was laughing so hard, I could hardly stand and I could tell that they were all staying clear of me so I walked off trying to hold myself up.

And as you may imagine, I never fit in from there on out. It was a small college and I got the reputation as a druggie and a misfit. And up to that day I had never been either. I spent a good part of my time after that not going to class but trying unsuccessfully to try and learn the drums so I could play in Evan's band.

Who's Evan?

The roommate who gave me the acid. Evan left at the end of the semester and I left at the end of the year. After I left I never picked up another book. I committed myself to learning all I could about human nature through humans, real humans. Now, I want you to join me in my crusade. Put down your books. Look around you. All these interesting people who have stories, stories full of drama, tragedy, comedy. It's all there--men and women--with stories filled with expansive humanity. I want you to take an oath, an oath that you will seek knowledge through the flesh and the blood, not through artifice.

Perry looked around in confusion and if all these people had interesting stories to convey about their lives...he would be surprised. Put your right hand on my shoulder and repeat after me.

Do you promise? asked Ness with his blood-shot-eyes wide open. Perry thought that his very soul was being observed. Without realizing it Perry found himself nodding in the affirmative. Good, good said Ness. I want you to put one hand on my shoulder and repeat after me. I will not seek. I will not seek, repeated Perry. Knowledge and experience through paper and celluloid. Film too! Cried Perry. O.K. I can see that is more than you are willing to sacrifice. Just paper, just books.

The lights started blinking indicating the historian was about ready to start. This filled Ness with anxiety and made him rush the rest of the oath. Ah, he said, you promise to uphold the seeking of knowledge through the stories of humans told first hand instead of books in which the truth may be to shifted to ascertain. What does that mean said Perry? Do you promise! Yes, I swear said Perry. O.K then, said the blonde man, let's hurry so we can get a good seat, and with this exclamation he took off at a brisk pace and disappeared through the crowd.

***

Perry came into the room that at some point had been converted into a chamber theater. The room was very large and contained by four black walls. The room was built up with stands that were highest in the back and gradually descended until at the last row of seats, which was closest to the stage area, one could plant one's feet firmly on the floor. The room was dimly lit and all the seats appeared to be full and there wasn't much room left to stand against the walls. Perry spotted Ness on the opposite side of the room toward the back packed in the middle of the crowd. Ness was on his tiptoes anticipating the start of the historian. Down near the front Perry saw a man frantically waving to him and it didn't take him long to notice that it was Graham Parker. Perry made his way through the crowd amongst an array of diverse people, none too happy that he was moving ahead of them. He sat down beside Graham. Thanks a lot, he said, leaning his head over near Graham's ear. Good thing you were looking out for me, you can barely see from back there.

In the words of Emerson, Graham said, Oh, what a lucky man you are.

The house lights were dimmed and then repeatedly flashed signaling for the crowd to quiet. The room was still when the person who had answered the door earlier in the night walked onto stage and stood in front of the microphone. His presence created a small stir with light applause, and he was wearing the exact same thing but had at some point changed his bowtie and now wore a black one. Ladies and gentlemen, he said, esteemed colleagues, honorable guests, please allow me to introduce to you Uriah Theeeeee HISTORIAN!!!!!

The crowd erupted into applause and various shouts of bravo and the like could be heard across the room. An old man emerged from stage left and began to make his way toward the microphone. The man had to be at least ninety, probably older, Perry thought. The man crept along hunched over with a timid glance and a feeble wave of appreciation to the crowd. His white hair was thin on top but grew long down to his shoulders on the side. He wore bottleneck glasses and had Chester Arthur sideburns that only left about an inch of skin showing on his chin. He, also, was dressed in a bowtie and he held a pipe cupped in his arthritic left hand. The old man continued to wave, smile, and nod to the crowd in appreciation of his enthusiastic reception.

He converted his waves to motions with his hands that were meant to quiet the crowd. When the crowd was quiet the historian put his mouth near the microphone and said thank you. This mere two-word utterance was enough to make the crowd once again erupt in excitement-the applause grew louder. After several repeats of the same episode Uriah the historian began to speak, mostly about how touched he was by the reception. Perry was struck how his voice did not match his physical presence. Where his body was weak and wasted by osteoporosis his voice was a strong bass and fluidly smooth. He had not only the voice of a young, strong man but age had not damaged his talents as a skillful and effective orator. His voice easily resonated to all corners of the room and it took Perry some time to get used to this anomaly.

There was an Italian Jewish wordsmith, gentlemen and ladies, who lived in the later part of the 18th and into the 19th century, who would raise the libretto in opera to a whole new plane, started the historian. His life was at once transcendent and tragic, magic and miserable, prolific and putrid. His name! Lorenzo Da Ponte. And tonight I tell his story. He raised the bar, someone shouted out of the audience. Yes, he raised the bar, repeated the historian. Lorenzo's father, Antonio, was a pressman, a diligent worker and a religious fanatic. He was an outspoken Zionist over a century before the birth of Theodore Herzl, and it is this, even more than the invention of the idea of the integrated motion wine press that has made historians since refer to Antonio as a man before his time.

Antonio was a great fan of poetry, especially the Italian sonnet, and had not only read the entire collected works of Petrarch but he had also submitted and had published, though with limited success, his own Italian sonnets in poetry journals throughout the area. No one suspected of course that the Da Ponte's were Jewish, which would have not only further limited his opportunities in the poetry business but also in the vineyard game.

So you can imagine Antonio's surprise one day when he had the four-year-old Lorenzo with him during a daily inspection of the grapes, when the young lad seemed to be babbling to himself, but upon closer examination of the young boy Antonio realized that he was actually reciting Italian sonnets, and not just any Italian sonnet, but a beautiful, lush sonnet ripe with meaning. Well, as you may imagine, after Antonio recovered from his disbelief he demanded of the boy an explanation, since he knew the lad was not yet old enough to read, so he figured he must have somehow memorized the text from an oral presentation of the sonnet. But the boy had no idea how he knew it--he just did. Antonio made the boy repeat all of the sonnets as he transcribed them. He spent the next few weeks scouring through every possible source that may contain the Italian sonnets, but try as he may he came up empty. Antonio interrogated every single person from his wife to the farm hands to see if they had ever read anyone's or recited their own poetry in earshot of the boy when he was either awake or asleep. He couldn't even find anyone who read poems or knew a poem by heart. In fact, most of the people were confused by the word *sonnet*; so inevitably, Antonio faced the fact that the sonnets were the boy's own creations. But how? What did a four-year-old boy understand about love, desire, sex, and death? The answer was that he knew nothing more than any other four-year-old. The boy did not understand the meanings behind his sonnets but week after week he created more. Antonio came to the conclusion that his prodigy had a gift from God, and he was not an ultra-smart poet musing on the meanings of life but merely a vessel--a pencil to the hand of God.

Antonio soon realized that the vineyard was small change compared to what the talents of his young son could bring him. He no doubt would be a wealthy man very soon. He took young Lorenzo throughout Italy first and then he made several tours throughout the whole of Europe, often performing in the royal courts of Prague, Budapest, Paris, and Vienna. Once while in London he astounded the crowd and delightfully surprised his father when after he finished an Italian sonnet he would then take the same subject matter and form it into an Elizabethan sonnet. One court master claimed that he had not seen such skill in a wordsmith since Shakespeare. His first book of sonnets was published at the age of five, his first epic poem by the age of eight, and his first full length play, which was reminiscent of the restoration comedies of Wycherley, debuted in Paris, April 1765 when Lorenzo was the ripe old age of twelve. We have multiple attestations of the young boy being brought back out onto the stage for numerous encores by publications of the day.

Lorenzo remained productive throughout his teenage years but tensions with his father began to grow. Lorenzo wanted more and more to make his own decisions and to have more control, especially over his finances. Where Antonio had always been somewhat frugal, Lorenzo became a lavish spender, fancying more and more not only the expensive styles of the aristocrats but also superior wines. By the time he was eighteen he had fully developed the main character flaws that would eventually lead to his downfall. While wine and uncontrolled spending certainly did not help his cause, it was gambling and women that would bring him to the brink of ruination--his road of excess would not lead him to the palace of wisdom. But I'm getting ahead of myself.

It is the 1780s in Europe, in Vienna particularly, and the liberation of The Enlightenment has made a perfect marriage with the containments of classicism and a beautiful paradox is born. The reforms of Joseph II make it a grand time to be an artist and a liberal-- this is the emperor to whom Beethoven will dedicate his fifth piano concerto in 1818. Lorenzo is introduced to Herr Von Schinelmietz who happened to be, next to the Esterhazy family, the biggest patron in Vienna. Von Schinelmietz attends a reading by Lorenzo and is mesmerized. He is at the beginning of funding a new opera by Mozart based on the Don Juan legend that is slated to be called *Don Giovanni*, and the libretto has already been started by the librettist Karl Vegshorn. Von Schinelmietz promptly dispatches one of his assistants to relay the news to Vegshorn that he has been relieved of his duties and that the libretto will be written by Lorenzo Da Ponte. Von Schinelmietz arranges a meeting between Mozart and Lorenzo and it is a disaster. Von Schinelmietz understands that he has a clash between titan egos but will not relent on his demand for the collaboration. He works it out so the two do not have to work together but finished scores are instead delivered to Lorenzo. Lorenzo is secretly thrilled with the music as is Mozart with the libretto but neither lets on that this is the case. *Don Giovanni* is a brilliant success in Vienna and throughout Europe. Lorenzo is a star and is received by royalty as if they were the servant and he the master. Everyone in society publishes in the newspaper the nights in which Lorenzo calls.

Though both Mozart and Lorenzo secretly hoped that Lorenzo is asked to work on Mozart's next opera, *The Marriage of Figaro*, both artists claim that they do not want anything to do with the project. Both artist, however, are deep in debt because of lavish spending, especially Da Ponte, who has already started to pawn gifts from admirers to cover his ever increasing gambling debts. Rumors are also starting to circulate about various illegitimate children that Da Ponte has some financial arrangements with throughout Europe. To this day these rumors have never been confirmed but we do have one source that they were started by a vengeful Karl Vegshorn. Needless to say, Lorenzo Da Ponte is overjoyed when he hears word from Von Schinelmietz that he will indeed be the wordsmith for *Figaro*.

The premiere of *Figaro* is slated for October 9th, 1788, but in Prague, not Vienna. Von Schinelmietz presents the premiere to his beloved cousin, the Hungarian born Czech, Countess Gzukhewitz. This gift is to celebrate the 50th birthday of the countess. The premiere is not only the biggest success of Lorenzo's career but also of Mozart's. In fact, Mozart has a little over two years to live and he will never equal the success that he attains in Prague with *Figaro*. Lorenzo makes so much money that he is able to keep his creditors at bay and temporarily stay out of debtor's prison, and with the premier of *Figaro* in Vienna only six weeks away, Da Ponte plans to pay off all of his debts. Lorenzo is introduced at the Vienna premiere and received with vigorous applause. The overture is played magnificently by the orchestra, and the performers are some of the most talented in Europe. Lorenzo feels himself becoming quite uncomfortable as the performance progresses through the score. He is not certain why, but he isn't sure if he is paranoid or if he is being stared at by the audience. Throughout the opera, occasionally someone will leave their seat and hastily exit the building. When the opera ends, there is sporadic applause, but the applause is nearly drowned out by hisses. As Lorenzo exits the theater and walks through the street, other people who have in the past been quite friendly to him are now cool toward him, to say the least.

The next day all the major papers report Figaro to be immoral and a threat to human decency and call for the opera house to be shut down, but on the influence of Von Schinelmietz, *Figaro* manages to be run four more times with the last performance having fewer than twenty people attending. Needless to say Da Ponte is ruined and it doesn't take long for creditors to start calling his gambling debts due. There are talks about taking Figaro to smaller venues throughout the city but everyone knows, including Da Ponte that the charge of immorality is a red herring, and the true cause of *Figaro's* fortune is his political subservience. Yes, my friends, on the surface *Figaro* seems to be a harmless opera buffa but in reality it is an indictment of the aristocracy and a call for democracy.

It is well known that Lorenzo has had passionate conversations about the new country across the Atlantic and the political experiment based on The Enlightenment. In fact, a few years later in Paris, Franklin and Jefferson will go see *Figaro* four straight nights because they have no problem at all understanding the sub-text, and they both write about the genius of Mozart and Da Ponte. Furthermore, Jefferson and Franklin are avid Freemasons, so they also see clearly the presentation of that ideology. If the ideas of democracy by itself would not bring about reform the subversive beliefs of freemasonry surely would bring an atavistic Europe to its knees, and little did the American diplomats know that all they had to do is to hang around Paris for a few more months to see the implications of *Figaro*. My friends could it be possible that the pen and not the sword prompted the storming of The Bastille? A wordsmith was the match that lit the most important revolutionary keg in the history of the world? Well, Da Ponte liked to think so and he was so confident that Vienna, Munich, London, and Rome would follow the anarchy in Paris that he started to openly defy his critics and creditors, but it was an accusation of sexual misconduct that would wholly alienate Lorenzo from everyone around him. Word spread that one of the most important aristocrat's young teenage daughter had been impregnated by Lorenzo Da Ponte; there were even accusations that force was used. To make matters worse the young victim was no other than Fraulein Von Schinelmietz, not only Da Ponte's most fierce defender, but also the man who used his influence to keep Da Ponte out of debtor's prison. But no more. Von Schinelmietz withdrew all support from Lorenzo and instructed a moral court to be organized. The court was organized and chaired by no other than Karl Vegshorn. The court lasted just under two hours and a note was sent to Da Ponte stating that in the opinion of the court, the only way that Da Ponte could keep his honor and escape a public trial with a probable public hanging was to drink the poison that would be given to him at ten o'clock the same night.

Even with all of Da Ponte's transgressions he was still not without his admirers, the most ardent of whom lay locked up in her room pregnant with his child, and the young Fraulein Von Schinelmietz had a staunch ally of her own: her mother. Her mother would do anything to make her daughter happy and she could see that the death of Da Ponte would probably be the end of the young mistress too. She struck a deal with her daughter that if she could help Lorenzo escape that the daughter would never see the man again. Though the daughter was bereaved at the idea of never seeing Da Ponte again, she knew she had to swear to this to save his life.

The mother arranged through some of her relatives with connections to have Lorenzo disguised and transported to London. Lorenzo knew he would not stay in London but that he would find away to cross the Atlantic to have a new start in America. America: the grand political experiment. We have statements that the philosophy that gave birth to The United States was so close to his own that he felt that he could have written *The Declaration of Independence* and *The Constitution* if he would have only had the chance. In fact, when on occasion he would cite his favorite writers, Sterne and Fielding would only be mentioned after Jefferson and Madison, for their work represented The Enlightenment as well.

And now friends, one of the greatest minds of The Enlightenment was heading into exile, sailing across the Atlantic Ocean. Da Ponte's good friend and supporter Ricardo Casanova would control the damage by claiming that he was not only the one who had violated the youth but he took the blame, or as history would have it, the credit, for fathering all the rumored children, but this gesture would remain unknown to Lorenzo, and also the ironic fact that Casanova's well-intentioned deed would cost Da Ponte a piece of immortality that would have put him on equal footing with his own creation, *Don Giovanni*. Moreover, many would later claim that Lorenzo was inspired by Casanova when writing *Don Giovanni* when in reality Lorenzo relied almost exclusively on autobiographical memories for the libretto.

See friends it doesn't matter if you are one of the greatest minds of the age, the masses do not recognize such genius, whether you are a master of libretti or an associate professor who is on a fast tenure track and at the tender young age of 27, and you have already published one of the seminal works on the meaning of The Enlightenment, offering ground breaking analysis on figures from Voltaire to Danton, and just because you work at a conservative university in the South and have some communist sympathies and you are set up and photos are taken of you out of context with a male grad student and you are forced to step down and your career and everything you have worked so hard for is tarnished, oh, Lorenzo Da Ponte, others have carried your burden, but I digress. Excuse me gentlemen and ladies. I just need a moment. Very good. Where was I? HE SAILED ACROSS THE ATLANTIC OCEAN! Someone called from the audience. Oh, yes, said the aged historian, he sailed.

Lorenzo entered the harbor and stared across the New York landscape full of optimism; he felt as if he were being released from jail. He was going to live the great experiment, and he was now in a land that would fully appreciate his talents where people wouldn't become so perturbed about a character flaw or an indiscretion here or there. But, alas, though the new country was built with immigrants it had already at such a tender age developed a case of xenophobia that would leave Lorenzo bitter within months. Da Ponte spoke fluently not only his native Italian but also French and German, but he struggled with his English. He tried his best to break into opera but no one was interested. It would be another forty years before the cult of Mozart would reach the New World. Now if Da Ponte would have written the libretto for Papa Haydn's *Creation*, that would have gotten someone's attention.

One conductor felt sorry for the confused immigrant. He was impressed with Da Ponte's passion and amused by his delusions of grandeur, so he arranged for Lorenzo to become a stagehand. A stagehand, *mama mia*! Fumed Da Ponte, and with those words he turned and left, slamming the door behind him. Four days later he returned, walked up to the conductor, got down on one knee, took the conductor's hand and kissed it, thanking him for his generosity, all the while never making eye contact with him. Four days living on the streets, sleeping in abandoned buildings, and one bowl of chicken broth had made him reevaluate his dire situation. Lorenzo threw himself into his work, which included the rearrangement of sets and the raising and lowering of the curtain.

Every day he sank deeper into despair until after about six months he was numb. He lay in a small flat that he had rented and realized that the America of Thomas Jefferson and James Madison didn't exist; America was a land of the haves and have nots. This really only bothered Da Ponte because he was grouped with the latter, at least on this side of the Atlantic. Now that political consequences were expressed as realities instead of hypotheses over champagne in a Viennese drawing room, he no longer had much use for them. It was one thing debating capitalism with democracy, but it was proving to be quite another living it. He had tried everything, writing to people who had helped him in the past, including Von Schinelmietz, begging for forgiveness and for funding to get back across the Atlantic, back to proper civilization. But no replies ever came.

Da Ponte, dehumanized and in despair, decides that the time has come for the end. On a humid summer night he walks along a cobblestone alley for the harbor, intent on swimming back to Europe, which he knows will be futile, but all the same, he decides he will be better off either way. As he descends a hill he notices two lights, one at the end of a pier, and one in a shop on the water's edge. He walks with resolution toward the light at the end of the pier when he is stopped cold. He suddenly finds himself on his knees facing the other light on the water's edge, and hears...

59

he hears my friends, one of the finest tenor voices that he has ever heard, and mind you he had worked with some of the finest in Europe. He got himself up on his feet and walked wearily toward the storefront, which was the source of the light. He listened closely with tears streaming down his face and he heard the grand tenor voice emit: *alla pompa che' appresta, Meco, o shiava, assisteria*. Lorenzo wiped the tears from his eyes and came through the door with the most ardent bass harmony that he could muster and sang a perfect fifth harmony and joined the tenor and they continued, *Tu prostra nella povere, Io sul trono, accanto al Re*...and this pleased the tenor very well, and he put his cleaver aside and wiped his bloody hands on his butcher's apron and shook the man's hand as they continued *Vien, mi segui, apprenderai. Se lottar tu puoi con me*...and on and on through the night until Lorenzo's voice broke and he collapsed in the man's arms.

Lorenzo's fever broke three days later and he found himself in a comfortable bed being fed soup by the butcher's daughter Maria. We thought you died a few times, she told him while spooning broth into his mouth. Soon the butcher, Mario, came to him and also attended to him with much tenderness, and when Lorenzo recovered he started to earn his keep, and Lorenzo's newly discovered butchery talents endeared him to Mario even more, until there came a day within a few short months that Mario started to view Da Ponte as his own son. Lorenzo my boy, he would say, you are now my apprentice. Look, a foreigner here less than a year and already a butcher's apprentice, only in America! And Mario could not have been more pleased when on Christmas Eve, Lorenzo approached him and told him that he was in love with Maria, and she in love with him, and he was now requesting his blessing for a marriage. Mario broke into song and Da Ponte once again joined in: *Oh, come e' bello e morbido! Non pui le mani allividite, il tepore le abbellira...sei tu che me lo doni*...and the two men walked out onto the beach and sang until darkness covered the land.

With the help of Maria, Lorenzo Da Ponte rediscovered the Catholicism of his youth, and it was now clear to him that he must put away his pen forever. What he thought had been his blessing was actually his curse. It was his words that had made him a master seducer, and it was his seductions that made him take the wrong turns in life. Over the next few years Mario passed away but before he did, he received the greatest joy of his life, a grandson. The couple named their young son Mario Lorenzo. Mario grew up and reminded his parents very much of his namesake; he even had a beautiful tenor voice. Mario excelled in the art of butchery also.

Through the years there were grandchildren and Lorenzo grew the business until it was one of the most popular butcheries in the neighborhood, and everyone knew him by his name and when they would stop after work to buy their daily cuts they would look at the fine chops and at the impressive surroundings and say Lorenzo, you have really done a nice job and Lorenzo would say only in America! Only in America!

Lorenzo worked on until he was in his early eighties and one day he signed the deed over to his son and went home. Lorenzo thought that he only started to live once he found Maria and he had never disclosed his past. But it was nearly fifty years since the death of Mozart and his music had been rediscovered--the cult of Mozart was at its peak. Since all of this information was beyond the knowledge of anyone who knew Lorenzo over the last fifty years, you can imagine Mario's surprise when the old man approached him and showed him a Philadelphia newspaper with an announcement of the American debut of *Don Giovanni* and the old man requesting that he wants to see it before he dies. But why, inquired a confused Mario. I have my reasons, the old man said as he turned to leave, and if you won't take me, I'll travel there myself. In those days gentlemen and ladies you have to realize that traveling from New

York to Philadelphia by carriage was not easy for a young, healthy man, let alone an old man with severe arthritis and a heart ailment, an old man who was brought to the brink of death by pneumonia twice in the preceding year. Mario could tell that this was a part of the dementia of his recent days and that the old man was not to be deterred, so travel plans were made.

It rained most of the trip and the roads spread out in pools of mud and the horses labored through with little rest. The carriage had to be stopped twice to fix wheels that had been broken by exposed ruts in the road. They were behind and as the rain poured faster Lorenzo feared that they would not make it to Philadelphia in time, and he was disconcerted by his son's apparent lack of urgency, so he told him. He told his son that he must have the men hurry at all cost because it is I, Lorenzo Da Ponte, who is the librettist of *Don Giovanni*. His son looked at him speechless, full of pity. The old man who once had a sharp mind and a full sense of reality had slipped away from him for good now. I can see you don't believe me, but it was I, and not only *Don Giovanni*, but the *Marriage of Figaro*. O.K., papa, said Mario, whatever you say. He could see the man was upset to the point of stroke. To appease the old man, Mario went to the top of the carriage and spoke to the men and gave them money. At the next stop the men traded for new horses and drove the carriage as fast as they could, pushing the fresh horses to their limits.

They arrived in the city at dusk and there was no time to find a hotel, so Mario instructed the driver to go directly to the opera house. Mario helped the old man out of the carriage. Lorenzo looked shaky and pale more dead than alive, but they could hear the overture ring out so they climbed the concrete steps with all the energy they could muster toward the large, classical pillars. By the time they got to the entrance they were greeted by a man of perhaps twenty-five. Sorry, the show is full tonight, he said looking at the gray-haired old man who had mud caked up to his knees. No, cried Lorenzo, gasping for air, it can't be, you have to let me in. Sorry, I would if I could but we have a full house. Lorenzo grabbed the young man by his shoulders put his mouth to his ear and whispered, I am he, Lorenzo Da Ponte, librettist of *Don Giovanni*, long thought dead, but it is I. The young man realized that now he was probably in a situation best handled by someone other than himself; he wasn't going to take a chance of letting the antics of a senile old man get him fired. He slipped through the door and an older man emerged and asked what seemed to be the problem. Mario asked his father to step aside and let him handle it and he did, letting himself become lost in the overture. You see sir, said Mario, we have come all the way from New York and have endured many hardships to see this performance. Really, said the man. Why? Well, you see, said Mario, my father wants to see it before he dies. Really, said the man. And you see, continued Mario, lowering his voice so his father could not hear, my father thinks that he wrote the words to this opera, and you must understand that he has lost control of his faculties, and I haven't been able to bring him to his senses. I see, said the man with a look of sudden comprehension on his face. Wait here. The man returned with two programs and instructed the men to follow him. He led them around to a side door that was open. We are completely full, but this door is open and you can see part of the stage and hear the music clearly, it is the best I can do. Mario looked around to see the disappointment on the old man's face but Lorenzo was too absorbed in the opera to notice. He was mouthing the words verbatim: *Ma che ti ho fatto che vuoi lascriarmi.* This struck Mario as odd even though he had heard his father and grandfather sing large parts of operas in his childhood. He found himself involuntarily looking at the program just to make sure: *Don Giovanni* by Wolfgang Amadeus Mozart.

Mario watched the old man immersed as he continued through

the night, even as the sound of the rain competed with the opera, the old man continued *Di molte faci il lume*…Mario noticed that the old man was being transformed and instead of being bent over he was standing erect with his foot tapping time and energy seemed to flow through his limbs and the further into the performance, an hour and a half or so, he continued on *ah, ah, ah questa e' buona*…and as Mario stared at his father he noticed he was no longer old. He still had the physical appearance of an old man but his spirit and his movement and his clear, stern eyes matched that of any young man, and then the thought occurred to Mario, my god! He is not crazy. He did write this sometime before he came to America. Papa, he said in his ear, I believe you. I believe you. Lorenzo diverted his bright eyes in appreciation then quickly returned his gaze to the stage and continued to recite the libretto to himself. The son stood behind his father with his hands on his shoulders and became more proud of his father with every passing word. The rain fell harder and flashes of lightning filled the sky and illuminated the faces of the men.

As the finale approached every fiber in Lorenzo's body was moving as he was now singing the words as loud as he could but still his voice was being mostly drowned out by the rain and the crash of lightning. Lorenzo spread his arms out wide and bellowed: *Questo e' il fin di chi fa mal; E de' perfidi la morte alla e' sempre ugual*… and he held the last word of the opera as long as he could and when he finished the roar of the audience and the sound of the applause exceeded the volume of the weather and Lorenzo Da Ponte, a paradigm of The Enlightenment and the human spark of The French Revolution held his arms high above his head with his eyes closed and his fists clenched in triumph, and when the applause started to die down he collapsed and lay unconscious on the wet grass.

Lorenzo lasted four days in a sick house before fluid filled his lungs and he breathed his last. Gentlemen and ladies, tonight you have heard a story of a man who lived a miraculous, redemptive life. He was a great figure of the European Enlightenment but also a great American. He lived a life that it would have taken two men to live, and his two lives were vastly different from one another. He was certainly ultimately more fulfilled with his domesticated existence in America, but we are more benefited by his maverick days when he was producing and co- producing some of the most transcendent art known to humanity. And I would like to suggest that when he stood in front of his creation listening to his words ring out into the Philadelphian night that he somehow understood this, that his life was full of meaning, for him because of the life he built for himself in America and for us because of the work he completed before he got here and I thank you.

The crowd erupted to its feet in vigorous applause. C'mon, said Graham Parker, let's get out of here, they're going to bring this guy back for at least two more curtain calls and I'm thirsty. Parker and Perry made their way through a sea of enthusiastic fans. Perry looked toward the corner and didn't see the blonde man Ness anywhere, nor did he see him going down the hall or in the grand room with the bookshelves. Perry waited leaning against the window as he waited for Parker to return from fetching beers. Perry looked out the window and he noticed the wind was now tearing dead leaves off the trees at an accelerated pace. He watched the golden colors fly by the window lit by a street lamp. He followed the track of a leaf to the ground and standing underneath the lamp on the corner was Ness. He was doing nothing apparently but watching the leaves carried by the wind swirl past him and Perry envied him. Ordinarily Perry appreciated the chance to talk to people and make new friends, but tonight he wanted to leave the place and find a big pile of leaves and lay back on them and watch the flying leaves fall like shadows across a partly clouded October night. He was at once uncomfortable and anxiety filled, so he just wanted to be alone with the leaves.

Hey, boss, said Parker extending a beer to Perry, what ya thinking about over here by yourself.

I don't know, Da Ponte I guess, Perry responded.

Yeah, we have a lot to discuss over some beers sometime. Yep, I'm left with more questions than answers though I gotta tell you. Well, this place is filling up again let's join the soiree, what a ya say?

Actually, I'm a bit tired and I think I'm going to call it a night.

What! O.K., listen, I got one person I need to talk to then I'll go with you, we'll stop at a bar on the way home. I just need fifteen minutes.

All right.

Good deal, Lucille. I'll be back in a jiffy.

Perry watched Graham Parker disappear into the crowd. He was somewhat of a people watcher but after a quick surveillance of the room he didn't find anything that captured his attention. He found the falling leaves more interesting tonight. He placed his hands on the ledge and put his hand against the window so he could see out without the interference of the rococo chandelier. He looked down at the corner and the blonde man Ness was no longer there, so he turned around and perused the room and saw no sign of him there either. He looked again out the window and scoured the area that the street lamps would allow him to see. When he was reasonably assured that Ness had left the premise and probably would not be back this night, he casually walked over to the book shelf, picked out the book *Sock Full of Holes* by Jacob Snodgrass and began to read.

CHAPTER 9

I don't know. There are a lot of problems with this chapter I fear. I wonder if the part about Proust is too pretentious. I think not because I am obviously describing a pretentious character. Why do writers shy away from characters who talk about art or writing? Obviously there are a few but I think the intellectual as well as the pseudo-intellectual is vastly underrepresented in the contemporary novel. Even though I am certainly no expert on contemporary novels, I know there are still a few, like that delightful little novel on that amorous professor who although he senses his own mortality, he refuses to go gently into that good night. Delightful little book actually, read it in one sitting. As I am examining my feelings right now (after all, isn't that supposed to be one of the functions of a diary!), I am feeling a bit of the hypocrite.

Why don't I read more contemporary novels? And, how can I not read more but yet rail against the world for ignoring mine. Note to self: something to explore, a character who like me is a hypocrite. Change it somehow though to protect identity. Wouldn't want any snoopers thinking it is autobiographical. How about a composer, twelve-tone minimalist perhaps, Dr. Faustus type character, who is discouraged because the world buys very few of his compositions, barely enough to keep the label from dropping him, which infuriates him, but he buys only recordings from Bach, Mozart, Beethoven, Mahler, etc...and does little to explore and support the music of the day, therefore he is part of the ignorance which he rails against. No, still too obvious. I wouldn't want anyone to know it is I and that I simply changed the circumstance from literature to music. Too thinly veiled indeed. How about I make the composer an African female, that should do it. Ah, even better, I shall make the composer an Inuit hermaphrodite! Yes, some novel in the future will explore the life of Inuit hermaphroditic twelve-tone minimalist composer. Possible title: *The Eskimo Serialist*. How could anyone possibly become wise to my cover with a name like that? Not PC enough I'm afraid. I am uneasy being disrespectful toward a whole people, especially one where I have not met a single member. This may be my first real attempt at Realism. Or Naturalism. Note to self: look up the difference.

But where is the contemporary novel where two men have an intensely philosophical conversation, 2 bottles of vodka drank, one with a fever of 104, the other out of his mind with syphilis? Ah, the good ol' days.

I need to reread the chapter to Max. I'm unsure about the ebb and flow of diction in places. Do words like bequeathed and plethora work in the context in which they are placed? I'm uncertain. How about the line "The leaves fell like pillow feathers in a dream"? I like it but I don't think most people will. Maybe it's the way Max raised his left brow when I read it, I'm not sure. I don't think the image would work if I just stated that the leaves fell like pillow feathers, but a dream somehow slows the image down, makes it more meaningful, and perhaps taps into something mysterious. I'm uneasy. I'll probably go back and change it. The last two problems may prove to be the most crucial challenges. Do the speech patterns of Ness and Uriah the Historian sound too similar? At one point Ness was going to be Uriah's son but now I'm not sure, which makes their similar speech even more of a flaw. I'll go back and toy with Ness's speech and see if I can make it more distinct. Perhaps infuse it with some "you knows" like Dorothea Brooke's uncle. And lastly, and most importantly, is Perry too passive? I want him to be an observer, a prism through which events are filtered, but I must also make him a knowable character who breathes and bleeds and hurts and laughs. I must allow him to be passive but not to the point to where his flesh is dissipated, not to the point where he is merely a shadow. I need to run that by someone other than Max, perhaps I'll give the punk down the hall ten bucks again to listen, but I don't know if I can bear his apathetic disposition. It's all unbearable to me right now. I'll let it sit for a while and come back to it with fresh eyes--can't be too hasty.

How am I to start the next chapter? I have a vague idea. Two beings came upon the horizon at daybreak...

CHAPTER 10

Two beings came upon the horizon at daybreak. They cast short, wavering shadows against the concrete. The man, a giant, smoked a Marlboro and dressed like a cowboy. His face was battered with one eye swollen shut, and he still had a limp though over a week had passed since his vicious encounter. The girl, pale with large almond eyes and long black hair, which she brushed straight back over her head, ambled along at his side. The heat of the day was already baking the street; steam was swirling around their feet. The giant was an Indian who was born in Bombay and had been moved to Nashville as a child. The girl was a daughter of an Air Force Captain and had lived many places in her youth, including Alaska, Texas, and Germany.

The giant Indian went by the name of Conway Jones Jr. This was a stage name suggested to him by his mentor, Tennessee Bob Smith, back in Nashville. It was hard to say exactly how big Conway was but there was little doubt that with his boots on he surpassed seven feet and he was well over 375 pounds. Aliesha, his girlfriend was not taller than 5'7" and maybe topped out at 145 pounds.

No one here knew that this tough guy, Conway Jones Jr., was once the King of Karaoke. What is known about him, however, is that he came from India and began his life in humble origins. His father, Hari, had come to America in the late '60s after being transferred from a two-year stint in London. This travel and opportunity was made possible for Hari after he was accepted into university and scored extremely high on his exams. Hari was so brilliant in mathematics that the decision to study chemical engineering was impassionedly endorsed by his mother and father. After school Hari found work with a British company and neither his brilliance nor his work ethic escaped the notice of his superiors. Hari was offered a position that would mandate that he move to London for two years, after which he could apply for relocation back to his homeland. Hari accepted on one condition: only after his wedding which was slated to take place in 45 days. Hari was anxious to marry and he was also excited to meet his new wife who had been selected for him.

A week after the wedding Hari and his new bride Sarbojaha were attending a religious ceremony when news reached them that there had been an explosion that had caused several deaths and untold damage at one of the chemical plants owned by the British company. This explosion was of such magnitude that the company had to re-evaluate its business plan, and one of the changes made was to postpone the expansion of the main research lab in London. Though the original plan was to delay any new staffing for six months to a year, it would be over three-and-a-half years before Hari and his family would set foot on British soil.

During this time the couple had a child whom they named Satyajit. Hari, a man of the university who considered himself rational and above superstition, explained to his wife that the largeness of their son, especially his hands, feet, and head, was because of a genetic anomaly, not because anything they had done to offend the gods. Sarbojaha could not be consoled.

This son was sent to her as a curse. She had either inadvertently offended the gods, or she was paying the price for one of her ancestors' offensive actions. It seemed the more time she spent praying at the altar the larger their son grew. Hari, who had been introduced to Christianity at university without converting, had developed an affinity for the monotheistic Western religions. His own religion seemed more primitive to him, and as a scientist, and soon to be a Western scientist, he would just as soon leave non-Western customs behind. He realized soon enough, though, that his wife would have none of it. She would hold fast to the sacred texts and the customs of her people to her dying day, though she would eventually come to accept her giant child as a blessing not a curse.

When they boarded the plane in London to travel to New York, the six-year-old, Satyajit, was almost as tall as his mother, and would grow taller than her within two years. The taller he grew the less abnormal his appearance became. His torso and legs were catching up to his hands, feet, and head. On the first day of the sixth grade Satyajit was attending history class when a balding man with a light-gray handle bar mustache appeared in the doorway. Satyajit's teacher went to the man and exchanged a few whispers before she turned and asked Satyajit to step out into the hall.

Satyajit sat along the wall by himself on an oversized chair that was equipped with wheels and a desk that would extend when he extended a lever on the side. Hari had designed the chair for Satyajit a few years before when it became apparent that Satyajit would no longer fit in any of the desks at the elementary school. Satyajit would roll his seat from class to class, with the exception of Phys. Ed. and Industrial Arts.

Satyajit stepped out into the hall with great apprehension. He had rarely been in trouble and the few times that he had been had either been a misunderstanding or a rule broken in ignorance. The man gave him a confident smile while he sized him up with great pleasure. He reached into a duffle bag that hung around his shoulder and pulled out a basketball.

"Do you know what this is?" said the man.

"A ball," replied Satyajit cautiously.

72

"Good good, that's a start."

The man introduced himself as Coach Collins and proceeded to instruct Satyajit in the basic ideas of basketball. Satyajit listened intently. He had seen the game on T.V. and he was well aware that his parents had grown tired of the joke about the possibility of an early retirement because of his NBA salary.

The coach looked up at Satyajit and put a hand squarely on his shoulder. "Satyajit, we both know that you're tall enough, now the only question that remains is if you're man enough." The coach paused and continued to look up into the sixth grader's eyes, "Satyajit, are you man enough to make a commitment to play for the Brown County Red Devils?"

Coach Collins could tell that he was working with a young man who needed direction. Coach Collins embraced the challenge of turning a reticent young person into a fierce competitor. The coach told Satyajit that he would give him some time to think but he would stay in touch with him weekly, if not daily. Coach Collins wanted to leave him with one important fact, and that fact basically was that no less than three boys who went through his program had gone on to be a Volunteer with a full-ride athletic scholarship, and if the coach had anything to say about it, Satyajit may very well be the fourth.

Satyajit was an imposing presence on the basketball court, though soon enough it was evident that he had no body control. The other boys--though shorter--could easily dribble around him and shoot the ball before Satyajit could react, and no matter how many drills Coach Collins put Satyajit through, Satyajit saw no advancement in his skills.

To say that Satyajit's size had raised the hopes of the Red Devil community would be like saying that JFK had raised the hopes of the Catholics in the 1960 Presidential race. Though it was never confirmed, one of Coach Collins' cousins said that he heard he

73

was offered five collegiate athletic scholarships before Satyajit ever stepped on the floor. Coach Collins did not speak to the local paper about Satyajit's progress, so when the Red Devils made their debut in late autumn, the gymnasium was packed and there were crowds lined up outside who could not get in.

After the first quarter the gym was half empty, and there was no one in attendance, not even the most fervent of optimists could make the claim that it was half full. Satyajit was called for a 3 second violation every few minutes, and when he did not have his large frame parked right in front of the basket, the smaller, more athletic members of the opposing team would fake a move and fly around him for an easy layup. Coach Collins had seen the warning signs in practice. Satyajit would stick out his hand to defend a player a second and a half too late. He would raise his hands for the ball in the middle only to let a near perfect pass sail through his hands, and the ones he would catch he would toss toward the basket, tottering, arms flailing, only to watch the ball bounce off the rim or the glass back into an opposing player's hands. Coach Collins could not disappoint the excited community by not letting them see the giant play. He had held out hopes that the crowd would spark something in this man-child that would ignite something within his basketball abilities. Though it was rare, Coach Collins had seen such phenomena before.

The Red Devil fans who did stay for the second half witnessed a curious site. Satyajit would stand underneath the basket and jump out of the way. Sometimes he would jump out of the way right when an opponent was charging for the basket. A few "boos" started rippling through the crowd, and every time Satyajit would jump out of the way of an offender the chorus gained strength until any type of communication between players and coaches was rendered impossible. Finally, Coach Collins benched Satyajit, and the crowd erupted in a standing ovation.

Talk started that Satyajit was obviously throwing the game. How else could anyone explain the way he was jumping out of the way of the opponents, seemingly giving them an unhindered access to the basket? Was Hari a gambler? Had he had his son shave points for profit? Those who knew Satyajit's family knew that this was impossible. Hari and Sarbojaha had impeccable characters and possessed the highest degree of ethics to all who knew them. The real story was that Coach Collins in a last ditch effort to salvage the glory that Satyajit could bring him, instructed Satyajit to stand under the basket and count to three, and then jump out of the red zone, and then jump back in to avoid the continual violations. Satyajit was simply following his coach's disastrous advice. To his credit, Coach Collins would always look back at this as his worst coaching decision.

After the game Satyajit was surprised and deeply hurt that everyone had avoided him. After all, this was not his idea, and he had only agreed to do it because he thought it would make people happy--at least that is what he had been told. Not only were the kids avoiding him, they were mumbling things to each other as they passed. Knowing how boys can be, one can surmise, that they may have been so angry with Satyajit, that they may have been planning to do him physical harm: a beating in the shower for example. While this thought may have been discussed amongst the boys, the sheer girth of the boy giant was a more than decisive deterrent for any such nonsense. Satyajit was too young to understand exactly what was going on. Under the coach's iron hand, the boys encouraged Satyajit and were patient with his lack of coordination, but the fact remains that there was an undercurrent of suppressed anger and resentment that was only now beginning to surface. The boys garnered much local attention the year before on their own by not only going undefeated, but also by not letting any opponent finish within fifteen points of them.

Since Coach Collins had recruited Satyajit, all the attention and the hopes of the community had been put squarely on his giant shoulders. The community had gone beyond the reality of an undefeated junior high team to the projection of a future high school state championship. Now, though the boys had lost their first game in over a year, there was a feeling of gratitude, if not superiority, that the giant had been exposed. Satyajit was oblivious to this resentment up to that point. He had no doubt felt like an outsider all of his life, but now felt the near universal hatred leveled against him. His inclination was to dress and leave as quickly as he could, but something made him sit still, his oblong face buried in his gigantic hands.

Once the locker room was clear he put on his hat and gloves, both specially made by a local widow. Clothes would always remain a challenge for the boy Satyajit. He looked around and made sure he had everything. He had an inclination to clean out his locker but he would not quit. His father had instilled in him the importance of hard work and commitment, and the idea of working hard even with things that did not come easy to him, and for Satyajit that was just about everything--including tying his size twenty-one shoes. He walked over to a wooden ledge that extended over a hissing radiator and surveyed the equipment. Lying among various athletic equipment were the handgrips bought by Hari. Hari bought the grips for Satyajit to strengthen his hands when he was younger. They were odd looking: whereas most handgrips were made of shiny metal springs with black grips, Satyajit's handgrips were rusty, with orange grips and they would squeak and crunch when Satyajit would use them. It was obvious to Hari that Satyajit's strength did not match his size when he would continually drop anything that he held. The grips, though used continually, did not seem to help, so Hari thought maybe it wasn't just a question of strength but of coordination, or perhaps nerves. Anyone who had seen the game that night would have undoubtedly argued for the former. Satyajit stuck the handgrips in his duffle bag and went out the door and started for home.

The time change had occurred and it was dark already, which was fine with Satyajit. As long as he could walk in relative seclusion he could think more clearly. As he walked he kicked the newly fallen leaves off to the side of the walk. He walked slowly. He was in no hurry to go home and tell his parents what had transpired. Whenever he tried to explain an experience to them that wasn't positive, they would somehow try to make him understand that there was something cultural that was giving him a negative impression. That is how his parents came to first tolerate and then accept a whole host of behaviors, including racist actions. Satyajit came to a stop because he was trying to make out a faint thud and hum in the distance. He couldn't quite make out what the noise was so he walked toward it. It led him down a driveway to a garage in back of a house. Satyajit listened from a few feet away as he stood mesmerized. What was that beautiful music, a music that seem to be crying out to soothe Satyajit's soul. He stood there listening for several minutes as he inched up closer to the garage. Soon he was close enough to look inside of one of the small, square garage windows. He saw many men in a closed circle playing instruments. There was a man singing into a microphone, a big man by most standards, even though he was full-grown, he was still considerably smaller than Satyajit. The big man also played an acoustic guitar. Satyajit noticed that he was accompanied by a violinist, a drummer, a stand-up bassist, and a man sitting down playing a slide guitar. Satyajit continued to listen to the music and did not notice his uncoordinated toes tapping perfect time to the music. He had left the weight of the evening's experience behind him, and let himself join with the music.

With a disruptive clash Satyajit was jolted out of his hypnotic trance. The drummer had spotted his gigantic face in the window and had responded by jumping up in fright, bringing his equipment crashing down. Satyajit recognized the look of horror in the man's face. It was familiar to him. He ran down the drive and down the street and didn't look back. When his parents asked him why he was out of breath he said that he was more determined than ever to get into shape. He assured him that the night went fine but he had to keep working hard to meet his potential. When he lay in bed that night he was no longer worried about basketball, all he could think about was the music he'd heard. He wouldn't quit though. He would finish out the season but in his spare time he would concentrate on learning more about this music.

***

It's not as if Satyajit had never heard country music before. The family had been in Nashville for a few years now. But for some reason, maybe because of the vulnerability of his psyche considering his basketball experience, the music had not quite spoken to him like it did that night outside of the garage. He checked out a book from the library on the history of country music and was reading it in study hall when Coach Collins tapped him on the shoulder and motioned to him that he wanted Satyajit to follow.

"Satyajit," Coach Collins said looking up into his eyes, "I have to tell you--I am extremely disappointed."

"I know. I'm sorry. I will work hard to do better," replied Satyajit.

"I'm afraid it may be too late for that."

"Really coach, I can do better," Satyajit replied in a voice that was barely audible. "I will figure out basketball."

"Son," continued the coach, becoming angrier, "this is not about basketball, this is about being a thief." The coach waited for

78

a response but did not receive even the slightest change in Satyajit. "Well, aren't you going to say anything?"

"I don't know what you mean."

"The hand grips." The coach snapped back as his face flushed.

"My hand grips."

"No, Satyajit, my hand grips. This school's handgrips. The taxpayer's handgrips. The handgrips that two boys, yes, that's not one but two witnesses saw you put in your duffle bag. Do you deny taking the handgrips?"

"No," said Satyajit putting his head down, and then continued saying in a whisper so low that the coach could not make it out "They're mine. My dad bought them or made them for me." The last part of this sentence was mumbled because Satyajit started to choke up and even though he tried to hold it back, tears started to stream down his face.

"What did you say? I can't understand a damn word you're saying thief." The coach got up on his toes, his eyes only coming to the chin of the boy giant.

Satyajit forced out "My Dad" but that's all he could manage because he was afraid that if he tried to speak any more he might really start shaking and crying because he felt himself becoming more upset and he thought his knees were going to buckle.

"I wouldn't worry," the coach continued, "I'll get a hold of your Dad and the police. Would you like that?" Satyajit stood there pressing his thumb and index finger of his right hand against his eyelids. "So here are your choices. Give them back right now or I'll call the police. I am going to follow you to your locker and you are going to give the handgrips back." The coach took Satyajit by the arm and led him to the gym. Satyajit got the rusty, orange-handled grips from his bag and gave them to the coach. The coach looked at them and placed them in his back pocket. "O.K., this ends here. But you are no longer a part of the basketball team. We don't want thieves around us."

Satyajit sat on the bench in the locker room. He felt like he had been punched in the stomach and couldn't get his air. He truly was a gentle giant but he felt a rage and a hate boil up in him like he had never felt before or again. For the first time in his life he felt he had the desire to kill. He would never see Coach Collins again without feeling this hate well up to a point that made him dizzy. He composed himself well enough to get through the day, and after school he walked the streets and for the first time in his life he felt his difference not only physically but also emotionally. He realized that he was alone. He waited until dark and walked back toward the garage.

While listening to the country and western music, he was once again overcome with the same sensation until his trance was abruptly interrupted by a jab in his back.

"Don't make a move there partner," said a man holding a shot-gun, pressing the barrel into the small of Satyajit's gargantuan back. "Move nice and easy and put your hands up where I can see'm." The man led Satyajit around the side of the garage and into a side door. The band one by one within two seconds stopped playing their instruments and stared at the prisoner. "George, this what ya'll saw gazing at ya through the winder?"

"Yup, that's him alright. I'd never forget that mug," replied the drummer.

The large man who was now obviously still much smaller than Satyajit said. "Boy, you some kinda prevert or somethin?"

"No sir," exclaimed Satyajit, casting his eyes toward the ground.

"Crimeny sakes, you sure are a big fella. How old are ya?" The man continued his examination of Satyajit, trying to see what he was up to and to see if he was friend or foe. The man's real name was Bob Smith but he had gone by his stage name Tennessee Bob

Smith for over twenty-five years. Tennessee Bob is what most of the Nashville music community called him. Tennessee Bob had never cracked the big time but he was still well known on the circuit. He had put out a few 45s in the late '60s on a small label, but other than some local radio stations, his music never really caught on. There had been dozens' of incarnations of The Tennessee Bob Band and the newest one that Satyajit had stumbled across was going to be called Tennessee Bob and the Smokey Mountain Boys. Tennessee Bob had long ago quit trying to play only originals in hopes of getting signed by the major labels of Nashville, and now he had long since resigned himself to playing cover songs of all the classics and making a living playing clubs and festivals across the area.

Satyajit explained himself with such respect and humility that Tennessee Bob and the gang took an instant liking to him. Tennessee Bob invited Satyajit to sit down and listen to the band only after advising him to be more cautious in the future; otherwise he may end up with a bullet in his back: Satyajit thanked Tennessee Bob for this advice.

Satyajit continued to go to the garage instead of basketball practice through the winter. Tennessee Bob gradually started to view Satyajit as the son he never had. Tennessee Bob attempted to show Satyajit a few chords on the guitar but quickly gave up. Satyajit's hands were too big and his fingers were too thick. With much trepidation Satyajit asked Tennessee Bob if he could try singing a song with the band instead. Satyajit had memorized "They Saw it Comin" by Porter Wagoner. Tennessee Bob sat down while the band started the music. Satyajit began to sing the song and the band started to exchange glances. When the song was over nobody made a move and Satyajit feared the worst. Tennessee Bob finally said, "Boy if I could sing like that I would be singin at the Opry instead of the Hillside Lounge on Saturday." The bassist broke with a "YEHAWW!!!" as the rest of the band extended their congratulations to the new vocal prodigy.

Tennessee Bob loaned Satyajit several hundred records over this time--Johnny Cash, Kitty Wells, Hank Williams, Patsy Cline, Faron Young, just to name a few. Hari and Sarbojaha had a record player that they rarely used. Hari was indifferent for the most part about music and Sarbojaha would put sitar oriented indigenous Indian music on from time to time when she was homesick. So Hari and Sarbojaha were torn with the conflicted feelings of consternation and optimism when Satyajit would come home and spend most of his free time in his room listening to country and western records. The consternation came from the fact that they did not understand this music. In so much of their music God was praised, and from what they could make out this music talked about adultery and falling into burning rings of fire.

It wasn't just the music that concerned Satyajit's parents. Tennessee Bob had given Satyajit an oversized cowboy hat that was given to him as a gag. Tennessee Bob had gotten the oversized hat as a gift for a birthday and he assumed it would always be decoration. However, much to his surprise it actually fit Satyajit. He presented the hat to Satyajit with a pair of cowboy boots that he had specially made by his cousin who was a taxidermist by trade but made a few pairs of boots a month by hand. Tennessee Bob's cousin looked at him with disbelief when the order was put in. Tennessee Bob assured his cousin that there were no mistakes. Satyajit liked his gifts so much that he only took off the hat and boots when he absolutely had to. When Tennessee Bob gave Satyajit the boots the initials CJ II was branded into the outside of both boots.

"What does it stand for?" inquired Satyajit.

"Well, I've put a lot a thinking into that voice of yours. And ya know how sometimes you think ya should know somethin but ya can't think of it? An how it just needles at ya an almost drives ya distracted until ya think of it?"

"Uh-uh, I guess."

"Well, that's how I was with your voice. I set right cheer one night for hours on end tryin to think about your vocal style. And then it hit me. You have the absolute best qualities of Conway Twitty and George Jones, and I like Satyagit and all..."

"It's actually pronounced Satyajit sir."

"It's a fine name. But I don't think it works for a singin cowboy like yourself. Damn, if I had a voice like yours I would be singin at the Opry Friday night instead of a class reunion at the Brown County Fairgrounds. That's why ol' Tennessee Bob is goin call you from now on Conway Jones Jr. I thought about Tennessee Bob Smith Jr. but I don't want to give you my 30 years of Nashville baggage. Look what it did to ol' Hank. But I like the junior part, even if there really ain't no senior. No one'll have to know it but I really will be the senior. I always thought I liked to be known as Conway Jones, juss never worked out. Tennessee Bob stuck."

The consternation of Hari and Sarbojaha was softened by Satyajit's new attitude. They thought that even though the whole country and western philosophy and dress was so alien to them, it might well be for the best, because for once Satyajit felt that he fit in, and because of his size and ethnicity, he had gone through his whole life never feeling like he was a part of something (outside of his family). Now he had a second family, Tennessee Bob and The Smokey Mountain Boys. It was the excitement and the near elation of the usually moody boy that made his parents reluctantly agree not to call him by his birth name, but to henceforth address him as Conway Jones Jr. At first this was very awkward, but Conway pointed out to them that they didn't have to say Conway Jones Jr. every time, that, in fact, Conway by itself would suffice most of the time. Hari and Sarbojaha obliged. Hari was actually more comfortable about his son's westernized name; he had always been the activist in the family for assimilation. Sarbojaha, on the other hand, felt that she was being further removed from who she was. She still resisted wearing only western clothes and rarely spoke English. All she had left from everything, including the religious festivals to the daily rituals of her youth, were memories and impressions--memories and impressions that had been ravaged by the vicissitudes of time and chance.

Under Tennessee Bob's tutelage, over the next few years Conway learned hundreds of country and western standards. Tennessee Bob arranged to have Conway brought into a studio to record a song that Tennessee Bob had written years ago called "You're The Only Liar Lying in Front of Me." The song was pressed into a 45 and sent to a handful of local radio stations. The song was being played by most of the stations and began receiving very favorable reviews, but more importantly, it was creating a buzz that didn't go unnoticed by a few A & R people and record executives. Tennessee Bob made it official when he had an entertainment attorney draw up the papers--he was now Conway's manager, and he would see to it that Conway's career was handled the right way. Tennessee Bob had made mistakes with his own career, and he was determined to make things right now. Not only could he help out Conway, but now he realized that Conway might be his ticket too. He loved playing music but he could use a break from playing at lounges and festivals, and he wasn't about to rest until he saw Conway on the stage at the Opry.

"I wunt to tank you, Tennezzee Bob, for all you've done for our son." said Sarbojaha. "But we are so conzerned about his zchul. Right, you undaztund Tennezzee Bob, yezz?"

"Yes, ma'm, I sure do."

"Very gud den. We put country muzic on hold till afta zchul, yez."

"Ma'm, my mamma taught me to obey my elders. And if that's want you want that is what we will do. But I hope you have taken into consideration that Conway signing now might be a chance of a lifetime and we pert-n-near have ourselves a bonafide record deal," said Tennessee Bob wiping his brow with a handkerchief.

"Yez yezz, Tennezzee Bob, but I tink you agree wit me, that education in America, also chanz of lifetime? If diz don't work for Satyajit…"

"Please mom, call me Conway," Conway interrupted from across the room.

"If thiz doez naught work for Conway," Sarbojaha continued with her voice lowered, as if somehow this was not a conversation that Conway should be a part of, "den collage. No high zchul degree. No college. Yez, Tennezzee Bob?"

"Well, I reckon mam, if that sort a thing is important to ya. I just hope the oppritunity is still thar. Your boy has a gift. There may be one a decade come through this town if that."

"We are on agreement denn Tennezzee Bob?"

"I reckon. Well, what I mean is yes mam. If that is what his mamma wants that is how it will be. I always listened to my mamma, God rest her soul."

"Tank you, Tennezzee Bob."

Tennessee Bob explained to various interested parties that he was going to put the boy's career on hold until he graduated school. What would a few years matter? Tennessee Bob had a plan. He told Conway about different contests that he had recently become aware of himself. These contests were fun plus many of them had cash prizes. They called the contest Karaoke, and all you had to do was get up in front of some speakers and a monitor and sing along with a recording. Tennessee Bob was skeptical at first, but he had so much fun his first night out that he continued to go to the bar that had nightly contests. One night on the way home Tennessee Bob was thinking about how hard it was to keep all the bands going that he had started over the years, and how there were always various personality conflicts, and girlfriends in the way, and members who got too drunk to finish the second set. It got a bit tiresome after a while thought Tennessee Bob. With karaoke, there was no setting up or tearing down, just stress-free entertaining, and even though he was a traditionalist, he had to admit that he was very fond of these new contests.

And it was perfect for Conway. He could hone his skills and become comfortable in front of crowds a few times a week without a big commitment to band members and the circuit. If he fell behind with his homework, he could take some time away from the contests. The word started to spread. Before long, lines of people begin to appear outside of the restaurant about 7:30 in anticipation of Conway's performance. Tennessee Bob would stop by in the afternoon and sign up Conway, and the owner of the establishment began requesting that Conway go last, because she sold more beer and food throughout the evening then.

Conway would win the contest and collect the $100.00 prize a few times a week. Before too long, any serious competition wouldn't bother signing up for the contests that Conway was in, this would leave a line- up of bad drunks to perform before Conway. A few of the owners figured out that they did better business if they just featured Conway for a night's worth of karaoke. One chicken wing establishment even went as far as advertising the night in the paper, and displaying a sign outside to alert passersby of the upcoming show. One night much to Conway's surprise, he spotted Hari and Sarbojaha standing in the corner, stoically witnessing his performance. Conway did not disappoint, his crooning of songs like "Mama Tried," "Woodchopper's Ball", "Blue Side Of Lonesome", and "My Woman, My Woman, My Wife" brought the crowd into first a sing-a-long and then a standing ovation.

***

"Do I always see you at these things?" Conway asked the girl in front of him looking down into her eyes.

"I don't think I have missed you sing in this city in the last six months," replied the girl. "I absolutely love your voice. You are my favorite singer." Conway blushed, his oblong face burning crimson. He was not good with compliments so he just looked out over through the window across the street. "Conway," the girl continued, "I am Aleisha and I am your biggest fan."

Conway tipped up his hat and mopped his forehead with a bar rag and thought to himself, "you don't look that big to me." But he continued to stare in silence. Aleisha, in her early 20s, knew how to handle shy boys. "It's nice to meet you too," Aleisha said with an edge of sarcasm.

"Excuse me mam?" Conway said as if coming out of a slumber.

"I said it is nice to meet you too."

"I'm sorry, where are my manners," Conway said as he removed his hat and extended his hand, "it is a pleasure to make your acquaintance." Aleisha hesitated before she put her hand inside his palm, but any fear was soon put to rest when Conway enclosed her hand and with a gentle movement, he went through the greeting ritual. He gently released her hand and placed his hat back on top of his head.

"I sing a little," Aleisha informed Conway.

"Oh, yeah," Conway replied becoming more animated than he usually allowed himself to be. "Maybe we could do a duet sometime. Uh, I dunno, Johnny and June, Porter and Dolly, George and Tammy. I know 'em all by heart."

"Whoa, I don't know about that. Well, what I mean," Aleisha continued, sensing that she risked having Conway recede back into his shell if she handled the encounter wrong, "is that I'm not that good. I mean I can hold my own with most people but you have perfect pitch, and your phrasing and dynamics are flawless. I've never heard you make a mistake. I would hate to make you look like anything less." Again, Conway looked through the window across the street. "But if you wouldn't mind, I would like to sing with you but not in front of a crowd, not yet anyway. I think I could learn a lot and if I could learn to harmonize with you I would be learning to harmonize with the best." Conway continued to avoid eye contact with Aleisha. "But I know you are probably busy."

"I'd like that," Conway mumbled. "I'm not that busy. I could make time. How about Sunday afternoon? I could give you directions to the garage where I rehearse."

"O.K. O.K, I'll be there."

After writing down the address for Aleisha, Conway returned to the microphone and performed a set that was truly inspired. The bass of his voice resonated through the room and held everyone's attention. He tried his best not to look at Aleisha but when he did and saw her smiling and clapping he had to look away quickly so as to not break his concentration. After his last song he didn't walk by her again. He exited the room with most of the crowd congratulating him on his performance.

Conway layed in bed that night thinking of Aleisha. He had never had a date before. Most girls who he went through school with were either scared or freaked out by his enormous stature. Even if a girl had been drawn to his quiet demeanor, she would have never considered going to a school dance with him. The peer pressure and teasing would have been too much to withstand. Aleisha, however, had never been a girl to not do exactly what she wanted to do. And right now she wanted to get to know Conway better. She was fascinated by him and his size, and his freakish looks did not deter her at all, if anything, she like his uniqueness.

The two became inseparable. She drove him to school in the morning and picked him up in the afternoon, and the radio would always be tuned into a classic country station and the two would be full of passionate comments either about the song or the performer. On the weekends they would stay up late either on the phone or in person and talk about music or what they wanted to do in the future. Conway for the first time started to really want to be a part of the Nashville scene. Before, he observed himself passively, an object at the mercy of nature's chance, but now, he was starting to feel that he had a part in his destiny.

Conway and Aleisha lay in bed late at night at Aleisha's apartment. The two were having their usual conversations on music and the Nashville scene, and smoking, a new habit that Conway had acquired since his relationship with Aleisha began. This new habit did not bother Hari since he had indulged in smoking tobacco through a pipe given to him by his father when he was young too. Conway started smoking a cigarette or two a day, but now had developed such an appetite for Marlboro reds that he went through at least a pack a day. They would smoke flicking their ashes into a tray that lay on top of Conway's chest. Aleisha wanted Conway with her constantly, and when she went to work, and Conway was not in school, she wanted Conway to stay at her apartment and wait for her. She wanted to help Conway make it to the big time and she was suspicious that Tennessee Bob did not have Conway's best interests in mind, and that in fact Tennessee Bob actually viewed Conway as a means to an end--his last chance to become successful in Nashville. Monetary gain was only part, though the main reason, that Tennessee Bob had latched on to Conway, Aleisha had concluded. She thought Tennessee Bob was trying to live vicariously through Conway, trying to recapture his youth and to finally achieve all of the things that he had failed at so far. Aleisha also saw the annoyance that had begun to be shown when she continually attended Conway's gigs and rehearsal. The seeds of a dramatic confrontation were being sown. Two forces pulling for the entire being of Conway Jones Jr., and Tennessee Bob had seen this scenario played out so many times in the past, that even though he knew he was in the right, and would fight with everything he had, it was a battle that he was destined to lose. He had no tools effective enough to battle the allure of a first love.

"Conway, you're eighteen now, I think we should get married O.K." Sensing the upcoming battle, Aleisha knew that now was not the time to be passive.

"All right, then maybe after we will move into Graceland," Conway replied with smoke rolling out of his nostrils.

"You don't think I'm being serious, do you?"

"No, you're not, are you?"

"Yes, I'm being very serious O.K. I think that you must not either believe me or that you must not feel the same about me." Aleisha's eyes were starting to fill with moisture.

Conway took one last hit off of his cigarette that drew the red ash up to the edge of the butt. He put the cigarette out, put the tray on the nightstand and then rolled his massive being up on its side. He looked down at Aleisha and put his palm over the back of her head and drew her toward him. "There are things that I haven't told you."

"What sort of things?" Aliesha said suspiciously.

"Things that I used to think about almost every second. Until I found music and then I started thinking about it less, until then I would only think about it every hour, then every day, and then sometimes not for weeks. And when I would think about it I would think how I must have a talken to you. Bout how it was unfair not to let you know everthing about me before this came to this point."

"Go ahead. O.K."

"Alright then, I will. Do you know anything about mythology?"

"Huh-uh. Not really."

"Well, I was assigned an assignment at school on mythology.

Some of the Greek gods to be more specific. Well, even to be more specific than that the group of the gods they call the Olympians. Nasty gods really in so many ways. Anyhow, I was rollin along in this report and then I came across a part that said that these gods were immordel, unlike the Nordic gods. I don't know exactly why, but I re-read that line several times and then I just kep a starin at it. So right then and there I decided to check outta book on these Nordic gods, and reading bout them was a life alterin experience for me. One of the three actually.

"The other two bein music and you honey. An before I go any further explainin myself I want you to know that right off the bat."

"O.K., O.K." Aleisha said quickly, wanting the suspense to end.

"I did some reading on these gods. My ma's religion has many different gods too so it interested me from that way. Now, where most gods you see are immordel, meaning they would live forever, the Nordic gods are doomed and they know it but yet they are still gods. They lived everday with the knowledge that they are gone ta die and they know how it's going ta happen. Just like me."

"What are you talking about?" Aleisha looked at Conway with concern. She had never seen this side of him. First of all, he nev-er said much--she did most of the talking, and besides that when he did have something to say it was never depressing. Now not only was he talking about strange gods he was claiming he was doomed.

"Yes, that's right. I'm doomed. If I don't die unexpectently of something else-a freak accident or someth'n-then I know what will kill me and about when."

"I wish you would stop this now you are starting to really scare me." Aleisha set up and moved away from Conway as if he had just told her that he was a leper.

"Please, I'm not trying to scare you but I need to tell you this."

91

"O.K., O.K." Aleisha started to twirl her hair. A nervous habit that she would never be able to break.

"See, I'm so big because I have glands that don't work properly. It's not natural. It's a disease. I was diagnosed with it many years ago but I never really understood it until a few years ago. My glands have made me grow much bigger than I shoulda. And the reason that I know that I'm doomed is that my body is too big for my organs--my heart, and lungs, and kidneys--and my body is constantly putting too much stress on my organs, and one day they will collapse and cease ta function, and like 'ol Wodin, I will be no more. Please don't cry, don't cry, just let me explain. Not only do I know that I am doomed, I know that people with this disease live to be an average age of 36, which means I've lived half of my life probly. So ya see, I find great comfort in the Nordic gods, but, not nearly as much as I find in you or ma music. Especially," he said drawing her back over to him, "you."

Aleisha now had tears running down her face faster than Conway could dry them, and the more he tried to comfort her the louder she sobbed, until her face was red, her eyes were swollen, and her whole body convulsed. He stopped speaking for several minutes except for an occasional whisper: "there, there, it's all going at be just fine," he would mutter over and over. When she seemed to be settling down he continued, "but I'm fine with it. I have my music and I have you and before that other than my parents I had nothin. Well, I know you are not crazy about him but I have Tennessee Bob, and I gotta credit him for startin me down this road to self-discovery. You don't have to say nothin right now. I realize that this may be too much for you ta handle and I respect that. You may not be able ta go on with me, and while that will be sadder'n I can think about right now, I'd always understand and think properly of ya. I don't want you to be a thirty-nine year ol' widow. I want nuttin but the best for ya."

The wedding reception took place twenty-nine days after Conway's high school graduation, and the ceremony was conducted by a Southern Baptist minister from the church where Aleisha's parents were members. The reception was held at a local VFW where Aleisha's dad had been a member since he retired from the Air Force. The layout was simple and the entertainment was provided, much to the chagrin of Aleisha, by Tennessee Bob and The Westward Wranglers, a band, which contained only one original member, the bassist to be exact, from the Smokey Mountain Boys. The highlight of the night happened when Tennessee Bob announced that Conway was going to sing with the band and perform a song that he had written in honor of his wedding. As Tennessee Bob was coming off the stage he shook hands with Conway and offered him another congratulation. When Conway had proposed the idea to Tennessee Bob, Tennessee Bob had asked if he could see the song but Conway declined. Conway's reasoning for this was that he simply wanted everyone to hear it for the first time on his wedding night. Tennessee Bob, however, took this as one more sign of Aleisha's interference and the continuation of her badgering of Conway to assert his independence.

Conway stepped up to the microphone after handing the chord changes to the band. "I want to dedicate this song to all of you, especially my lovely wife," said Conway looking directly at Aleisha. She smiled broadly as the guests all turned their gazes toward her. The drums started a beat with the bassist playing a simple pattern and then the sound of the slide guitar flooded through the hall. Conway closed his eyes and brought the microphone up to his mouth. Before he began singing he said along with the music, "this song's called 'Woe Is Me.'"

I lived eighteen years inside this shell
Though I didn't realize until now, it was hell

You came along in time
To throw me a line
But I want you to know
I have a pickup full of trouble I'm a loadin
Woe is me, woe is Wodin

Though it's too late
To try and fight fate
I'll make every moment count with you
Until my time on earth is through
But I want you to know
I have fields full of trouble I'm a mowin
Woe is me, woe is Wodin

Aleisha was standing on the dance floor, face flooded with tears that were thought to be by the crowd tears of joy, but in fact were tears of anguish over her husband's fate. Tennessee Bob had a perplexed look on his face, trying to figure out the lyric, and Hari was standing next to him with a broad smile, his toes tapping and his fingers snapping off beat, like he was listening to a ragtime tune in his head. Conway continued after the steel guitar solo:

Today I have given you a ring
Few know what the future will bring
Lord knows I can't worry about the things I can't change
But I want you to know
That I'm head'n out to the open range with a cold one
 Woe is me, woe is Wodin.

Conway took a bow as the crowd gave him an enthusiastic applause, because even with the obscure lyric he still had that voice. He came down off the stage and picked up Aleisha and swung her around. Her shoes dangled almost two feet off the ground. The dancing continued, and during the Chicken Dance, it became obvious that Conway's coordination had not improved since his short time as a junior high basketball player. Conway then slow danced with his new bride and told her how the thought of having another fifteen to twenty years seemed like more than he deserved as long as it was spent with her. Now, he just had to somehow find the courage to tell Tennessee Bob that Aleisha had found new representation for him, and from here on out he was going in a different direction. This would not be easy because he felt that he wouldn't have either music or Aleisha if it weren't for Tennessee Bob. Aleisha wanted him to do it right away--no sense dragging him along, she told him. The sooner it was done the sooner he could get over it and pin his hopes on somebody else. Conway wanted a month even though a sick feeling stayed with him whenever he thought about facing the daunting task. For now he just wanted to forget about his responsibilities and enjoy himself. Nashville had waited this long. Another month wasn't going to hurt.

A few weeks later Aleisha came home from her job. She had been hired as cashier at a local drug store. She sat down next to Conway who was watching T.V. and using Conway's cigarette as a light she lit her own.

"Who is Ralph Emory interviewing tonight?" Aleisha asked as she exhaled her first cloud of smoke from her cigarette.

"I forget his name. Somebody new on the scene. Hopefully he will be interviewin me soon," Conway replied as he looked over at Aleisha.

"O.K., O.K., I know what your gettin at. I don't know why that guy didn't show up but I got some news. I ran into a boy I met singin at a club one night and there's a lot of buzz on him too. Not as much as you of course. Quite a bit though still the same. And he knows all about you and he said that he would talk to the guy that he is talking to and tell him about you what'd ya think about that. Good news, huh?"

"Seems a bit far-fetched in some ways I reckon."

"What a ya mean. That doesn't make any sense to me whatsoever."

"I mean who is this guy and who in the sam hell is the guy he knows? Maybe we should call Tennessee Bob and see if we can patch things up."

"O.K., O.K., I can see you are getting frustrated but it has only been a few weeks. I can get this thing going O.K. Just give me a few more weeks O.K.? I mean it's not exactly like I have failed. One guy didn't show up one time o.k. So let's not start overreacting O.K. Bob Smith is not the answer to this problem O.K?"

"I just hope we are not making a big mistake." Conway laid his massive head back against the wall.

"O.k., here is the deal. This guy wants to meet you. He invited us to a party and I have the address. We got to look at every chance that comes our way."

"If nothin comes of it we then we contact Tennessee Bob and make amends, deal?"

"O.k., o.k."

They walked down an uneven, cracked sidewalk through a neighborhood full of rundown century homes, homes with large windows, thick velvet curtains draped to one side. A full moon hovered partially obstructed behind thinned out dark clouds, clouds that were being propelled by a cool breeze that made Aleisha press herself against Conway as they walked. Aleisha occasionally would stop and take the directions from her leather jacket, scrutinizing them, trying to judge their accuracy. They finally walked into the side of a long rectangular gray building, and proceeded to climb a dimly lit stairway with a strong smell of mildew.

There was no doubt in their minds that they had reached the

correct place because country music was blaring, mixed in with the sounds of talk and laughter. Aleisha knocked. A young, chubby cowboy with blond hair and a red face answered the door. He had boots and a hat on, and a gut that was held in by a thick belt that had a gold plate and steer horns on for a buckle. Aleisha inquired if Gerald was there and the young cowboy motioned them into the house. The party was expansive and covered all four rooms of the 2nd floor apartment. As the boy lead Aleisha and Conway through the crowd, everyone stared, as people always stared at Conway. He was so used to it that he didn't even think about it anymore, he just ignored their stares and kept walking. They were led to a kitchen where a group of cowboys was sitting around playing cards. Most of them were smoking which gave Conway the urge so he lit up a Marlboro red.

"You fellas hold on there for a moment," said a young man with a black hat on. "Hello, Aleisha. Hello Conway," said the young man looking up at Conway. "I saw you maybe six months ago at a dive singing along with a karaoke machine. I enjoyed it."

"Thanks," replied Conway. "Do you mind?" asked Conway pointing toward a keg that set beside two rows of plastic cups piled on top one another.

"No, not at all. That's what it's there for." As he said this, he turned and winked at the other men who were playing cards. "I'm going to finish this game, you two mingle and make yourself comfortable."

"And then we'll talk business?" inquired Aleisha.

"Sure sure, no need to rush into all of that though, we are all here to enjoy ourselves."

Conway didn't say much, he just leaned against the wall and chain-smoked and drank beer. After about twenty minutes Gerald and a few of his gang approached the couple. Gerald asked if they were having a good time and added a few other friendly exchanges. One of the men with Gerald, named Matt, stepped forward and started a conversation with Conway about the music scene in Nashville. The couple loosened up and drank and generally started to feel very comfortable among the people present. Aleisha was surprised how much Conway was talking and laughing because he barely, except for a few isolated occasions, talked or showed any emotion, even to her. Maybe he was finally among his own, meaning other young, talented musicians who had hopes of making it in this town. Just perhaps he finally found people that he could relate to and just maybe this is what he needed to become the person that he was meant to be.

Conway looked across the room at Aleisha and noticed that she was smiling at him, so he smiled and nodded to her, and his nod was an acknowledgement of two things. One, that he was indeed enjoying himself and two that he was all right without her. When they went out in public Conway would usually not leave her side, somehow he felt like she protected him. Aleisha tested the boundaries of her freedom by roaming into other rooms and striking up various conversations on a variety of different subjects, but subjects that were, nonetheless, directly or indirectly related to music.

Aleisha let the better part of an hour go by before she checked on Conway again when she was once again assured that he was doing fine. She went back through the kitchen and refilled her cup, and by noticing that the keg was beginning to float, she assumed that the party would be over soon, which was fine by her since she knew that both she and Conway had drunk too much. When she turned around Gerald was standing there smiling at her.

"Hey, I want to show you something." Without asking, he took a hold of her arm and led her back through a hallway into a room. "I want you to hear what I've been working on." He started a reel-to-reel player and placed headphones over her head. She was impressed, especially with the quality; all she could think about was how she needed to get Conway into this studio with this producer. She was not dumb nor naïve and she had had her share of experiences with boys, so she was neither surprised nor offended when she felt his arm come around her hips and his lips come up against the back of her neck. She handled the situation by matter-of-factly removing his arm and stepping away but continued to listen to the demo. He was not deterred however, and tried again but this time he was more assertive.

"O.K, O.k., that's enough I'm going back out there," said Aleisha as she put the headphones down and tried to free herself from Gerald.

"C'mon, what's the problem?" Gerald started making his case "we're all just havin a good time here."

"This is not what I call a good time. It was until now but I call this a bad time."

"Don't you want to say you slept with a star in a few years, I've seen you hangin roun musicians for two years now," Gerald said, kissing her neck.

"O.k., o.k., that's enough I'm outta here," said Aleisha as she pushed him away.

"Goin back to that negra freak," Gerald replied with frustration in his voice.

"Excuse me?"

"That negra freak that you want me to help you with. If you want me to help you, you have a funny way of showin it."

"I don't need your help that bad. Not with the talent he has."

"You know what, darlin, I don't care how well that freak can sing. This music ain't for foreigners; it's for Americans, full red-blooded Americans like me. Nashville ain't all about talent, it's also about image, and there ain't nobody goin to sign that freak. Nobody in this town likes him and they're a little sick of all the talk about him and all these karaoke contests are a joke."

"You're the freak. You don't know nothing about him. The biggest thing about him is his heart and you'll realize that someday unless your small red-neck mind is too stupid," Aleisha said hotly as she walked out of the room.

She didn't want to concern Conway so she gathered her composure and took a deep breath before she entered the room.

"Hi hon," he said taking her hand.

"Conway, I think we should go."

"Why?" he said, feeling a bit disappointed.

"I think I drank too much."

"Alright, I'll just tell these fellers goodbye."

"O.k., o.k. Just hurry O.k."

Conway shook hands and zipped up his jacket and grabbed Aleisha's hand. Someone turned the music down and called to them.

"What's that bud?" Conway said politely looking back at Gerald.

"I said what's the hurry?" Gerald repeated.

"My lady here ain't feelin so good. But I want to thank you for your hospitality."

"You mind helping out real quick before you go? I have some light bulbs that need changed and I ain't got a ladder." Even though this sent a wave of laughter through the circle of men standing around Gerald, Conway was ready to oblige but Aleisha stopped him.

"Oh, c'mon honey, don't tell me you don't take advantage of the freak's largeness if you know what I mean. C'mon Goliath, I need my ceilings painted too, no hard feelings what a ya say?" Conway finally understood what was happening and the expression in his face changed as he surveyed the people laughing at him in the room, the very same people that gave him hope for the future only minutes before, and as he had done so many times in his life

100

he started to walk away.

And Conway fell hard. He couldn't recall who stuck out their foot and tripped him up he just remembered being on the floor, his nose bleeding, and his ears burning. Aleisha bent down and helped him up on his knees but a kick in the face with a boot heel sent him reeling back on the floor again. Though he was dazed, he didn't take long to react when he saw Aleisha jump on Gerald and start scratching his eyes, and when Gerald threw her off with a motion of violence, Conway reacted. He didn't think at all because he was being led by instincts that had not surfaced until now. By the time Conway swatted Gerald to the floor he had five or six guys on his back or around his legs, punching, kicking, and clawing. With a powerful yell Conway fought back with strength that matched his size, strength that was beyond anything that he had ever felt before, strength that he was unaware of until now. He picked up Matt by his collar with one hand and threw him against the wall mixing the sound of shattering mirror and breaking bones. With every punch, swat, or throw there were bones breaking and teeth flying. Conway added to the heap of bodies as he would turn with a growl inviting the next contender that dared approach him. Two men dove at his feet and locked their arms around his ankles and attempted to drive him back. Conway bent over and took their skulls and started to beat them together like two coconuts. Gerald re-emerged from the hallway and jumped on Conway's back and locked his arms around his neck attempting to cut off his air supply. With a raging yell Conway let go of the two men around his legs who were hanging on like two wolves who had attacked a deer. As he stood up to attend to Gerald, he grasped at the arms around his neck to free him, he was then able to loosen one arm and while he was grabbing the second arm he felt a shock sizzle through the entire length of his massive body. Aleisha was screaming at the top of her lungs and when she saw what happened she started running around the room screaming for help in hysteria. Conway calmly surveyed the room to try to make sense of anything. He looked at the half-shattered mirror on the wall and saw an image of himself with a large switchblade knife stuck through his throat as blood poured down his neck. He attempted to pull the knife out of his neck, but his adrenaline would carry him no further, and he collapsed, hitting the floor with a brutal thump.

The hose protruding from Conway's throat would make a sucking sound followed by a gurgle. Someone was by his bedside nearly all the time. Mostly Hari and Sarbojaha at the beginning but then Tennessee Bob would send them home to rest and sit next to Conway through the night. Tennessee Bob had sat in the waiting room for seventy-two hours when Conway was in critical condition. He had lost so much blood that it was touch and go for a while, but now he was on the mend, even opening his eyes and blinking to let people he saw know that he recognized them. Aleisha wasn't there at the beginning. Doctors had discussed hospitalizing her too because of symptoms of a complete nervous breakdown, but they decided to send her home and prescribed xanax for her. She prescribed vodka for herself, and by mixing the two remedies she lost more than ten days. When she finally broke out of the haze from xanax and alcohol she learned that Conway had pulled through, and that he had written her name on a piece of paper.

The first person she saw when she entered the waiting room was Tennessee Bob. He got up and went over to her and put his arms around her and she buried her face into his chest. Soon she was sobbing and trying her best to tell him how sorry she was. Water under the bridge he kept telling her and he also told her what was important now was that Conway was alive and that they all do what they can to make sure he has all the help he needs. The two sat down and talked and Tennessee Bob told her fighting back his own tears that Conway would never sing again, and that he would have trouble enough just getting any type of voice back, and that she might have to learn to sign or something just to communicate with him. Aleisha tried to identify Conway as something other than a country and western singer and she could come up with nothing else. Though Conway could not talk he had come out of a coma days ago and he could think clearly, and he knew that it was his voice that Aleisha had fallen in love with, and without the voice she would probably fall out of love with him so he might as well start preparing himself for being alone again.

She knew she had to be strong but when she entered his room and saw all the I.Vs and hoses coming from his body she had to turn away and catch her breath, and when she sat down beside him and put her hand on his and saw the pitiful look he gave her and the pain in his eyes, her eyes once again let go of the tears and they fell down her face in a stream. She stopped crying and didn't say a word. She just sat there beside him holding his hand as the room darkened from the descending sun. She knew what he must have been thinking. She knew what everyone must have been thinking. She was determined to prove them wrong. She was determined to spend the rest of his life with him. Though they were unaware of it at the time, Conway's voice would recover and while he would no longer sound as he did before, a mix of Conway Twitty and George Jones, he would heal with an unique voice with a rare gravitational pull and most would judge it far superior. This knowledge wouldn't come to light for a while and so he spent his days thinking all was lost.

Within a few months Conway was able to make hoarse sounds though not without pain. He never was much of a talker but now he limited himself to one-word conversations. "Thirsty", "light", "cigarette" were examples of complete conversations for him. He had no desire to leave the apartment and would smoke and watch television all day and into the night. When he would smoke he would hold up Aleisha's vanity mirror and watch the smoke roll out from beneath the gauze on his neck. Aleisha would come home from work and try to tell Conway how her day went but he paid little attention. She was not one to give up easily and she continued to try and support him emotionally for months, thinking that he may snap out of his depression, but the snow flew and then spring came and Conway receded further into himself, and now when Aleisha was in the apartment she simply ignored him. He could speak several sentences now but he still held his remarks to one or two words for the most part.

One evening Aleisha came home and looked with concern at Conway. She was holding a newspaper and she handed it to him. Conway read the front page and learned how Gerald, Matt, and the others were found not guilty on all charges. The jury had found that they had acted in self-defense. Conway put his hands on his head and Aleisha again, after months of not trying, tried to comfort him. He removed her hand and she broke and shouted, "It's not my fault." Conway picked up a lamp and threw it against the wall shattering ceramic and glass into pieces, and then he put his boot through the TV, grabbed his jacket, put a scarf around his neck and disappeared into the Nashville night.

He walked into a tavern and sat at the end of the bar. "Scotch," he whispered in a hoarse voice. He drank a steady stream of beer and scotch and kept to himself. Conway no longer had soft features. His age and his experience had hardened him and now he had an imposing presence, so he did not look like someone that anyone should have the nerve to approach. The bartender would just point at his glass and Conway would nod. The scotch began to warm his blood and he started to force a whisper to sing along with the jukebox, and when the music would stop he would fill the machine with change and pick his favorite selections. A man with a tan and premature gray hair entered the bar and walked up behind a woman in her late 30s who had been drinking and chain-smoking for most of the night too. The man grabbed her arm and demanded that she come with him but she told him to get lost. She was staying. The man grabbed her by the back of her hair and pulled her off the bar stool but the force of a blow to his head made him release his grip before he fell to his knees. Conway stood behind the man and opened up his fist and with his open hand slapped him hard to the ground. The woman slurred that she could take care of herself and that Conway should mind his own business. She helped the man who now had no idea where he was to his knees and wedging herself under his armpit she helped him up and the two of them stumbled out of the door.

"That's quite a punch you pack," said a man with a straw hat who was smoking a cigar. Conway looked at him and without replying sat back down in front of his drink and lit a cigarette. "One helluva punch."

"You looking fur trouble mister?" Conway whispered with his grainy voice.

"No, no, you misunderstand me. I ain't looking for no trouble. I'm a looking for opportunity. Dell, get this man a drink on me. Name's Tim James." Conway nodded but did not offer his hand. "I just thought you may be interested in a little money makin venture. I can see you're a man a few words so let's have Dell bring us the bottle while I explain."

Conway sat on the passenger's side of Tim James's '65 Ford pickup. The houses became scarcer and the light dimmer as the city street turned into highway, state route, county road, and finally dirt road. They had been on the road for an hour and Tim had done all the talking, Conway listened to the AM radio and hypnotically looked at the dark road just ahead of the headlights. James had given Conway a detailed explanation to why it would be in his best interest to disappear and not come back to Nashville for a long time. The man he had pummeled in the bar was a bad character from a family of bad characters. If Conway stayed in these parts, James explained, things would no doubt end badly for him. As they pulled into a lane and passed a farm house James reminded him that he would collect money, if there was any, and then give Conway half. They drove across a grass yard and parked behind a barn where there were several other automobiles parked. As they walked toward the barn they heard a chorus of encouragement that grew louder as they came closer. They stopped in front of a side door that a man stood beside holding a rifle.

"Bill," James said tipping his hat.

"Tim," Bill said back, looking at Conway. Bill grinned and shook his head. "Damn Tim, whereja find this one here."

"I can't give my secrets away."

"Damn hesa biggin. Should be some show."

Conway entered the barn lead by Tim James who glowed like a businessman with a trophy wife. He was known for his finds and this may be his best yet. Many in the crowd looked on in envy but not surprise, and some tried to conceal their envy, not wanting to let James enjoy his moment. Tim James sat Conway down along some benches as he went over to talk with some men who were gathered in the center of the barn floor. When the men separated, James came back and told Conway he was 2nd but he had to pay out $200.00 dollars because he hadn't had a reservation.

The barn was dimly lit except for two bright lights that hung above the center floor. The first man who came out was 6'2" and 245 pounds, his head was shaved and he wore a mustache, and as he took off his shirt, he gave the thumbs up to a group in the north corner that were obviously rooting for him. The second man who stepped out into the center was an inch or two taller but deceptively thin. If anyone in the crowd were to make a bet just on the looks of the two the odds would be against the thin man, but obviously the thin man had his share of supporters dispersed throughout the crowd. Though when the thin man took off his shirt and stepped into the light he transformed into an ominous image with scars covering his body and a look that betrayed no fear. When the bell rang the two converged into the center and began an innocuous shoving match not unlike one could witness on a grade school playground. The bald one struck first with a blow that hit the thin man's shoulder and knocked him to the ground. Before the bald man had a chance to jump on top of the thin man, the thin man had bounced back to his feet and was quickly going around the bald man, and every time the bald man would reach out to grab or hit, he came up with nothing but air, and then he would become frustrated with the thin man's reluctance to engage so he dove at his knees and though he missed he got a hold of the thin man's pant leg, but before he could grab for more, like a snake the thin man brought the heel of his boot crashing down in three consecutive strikes on his opponent's bald head.

Though dazed the bald man grunted and shook his head like a bull and rushed at the thin man, but the thin man continued to run around the bald man until the bald man's body heaved for air. The bald man continued to chase his opponent until his opponent threw himself to the ground, sticking out his leg tripping the bald man, and then jumped on top of him, taking his ears in his hands and smashing the man's face against the floor making blood ooze from his mouth and nose. The bald man tore a red flag from his belt and the fight was over, to the sound of both cheers and boos from the crowd. The winner was congratulated and the loser collected his shirt and stumbled out the back door, and after money was exchanged and much conversation a man appeared in the center. Above average in size with a battle-worn look, the man stretched his body in preparation, but nothing could prepare him enough to hide the fear in his eyes when he saw a giant coming toward the center to fight him.

***

The sun was coming up and Conway tried his best not to wake Aleisha. He slid his boots off by the front door and walked as gently as someone who is almost 400 pounds could. He walked into the kitchen and poured himself a glass of water so he could take four aspirin, hoping that he could calm his throbbing head. He walked into the bedroom and looked at Aleisha sleeping. He lay down on the bed and closed the one eye that wasn't swollen shut only for a few seconds before a violent gasp startled him.

"Oh my god, oh my god, what happened to you! Oh my god Conway."

"Settle down, settle down now," Conway said grabbing Aleisha's arms as he tried to calm her before she snowballed into hysterics. "I got into a fight. I'm fine."

"You're not fine," she squealed. "You're going to the hospital."

"No, I'm not going to the hospital. I'm staying right here. I'm hurt, I'm really hurt but I'm going to be O.K."

Aleisha got up and grabbed her hand held vanity mirror and placed it in front of Conway. Conway's face had swelled further and he looked worse than he had known. "That's not fine, that's not O.K. You are going to the hospital. My god, Conway, who did this to you? We have to call the police."

"No we ain't callin the police and I ain't goin ta the hospital and that's final." And Aleisha knew that it was final. She knew no matter what she said or did that he wasn't going to do any different than what he said he was going to do. She got some peroxide and cotton balls and cleaned him up the best that she could. As she was cleaning him up, directed by his winces, she decided to tell him what she had wanted to tell him last night when she waited up for him.

"O.K, O.K, This has really been depressing and now you're getting into fights and getting yourself beat up. I'm sorry for what happened to you that night. I blame myself. I don't know what else to do but to keep telling you how sorry I am. I can't even think about what you've lost without crying. I'll be at work and I'll just start crying. I love you but I have to get out of here for a while. I hope you understand."

"Where'll ya go?"

"My sister needs somebody to drive her car up north. I've volunteered to do it. It would get me out of this apartment for a couple of weeks."

"I got a better idea. Let's both go," said Conway looking at her with one eye. Conway wasn't against the idea of some time apart but he knew this was his chance to take Tim James' advice and get out of Nashville.

"That might be an idea," said Aleisha turning over all the positives and negatives in her head.

"In fact, I say we get out of here for a few months maybe longer."

"Leave Nashville?"

"Why not? Lot a bad memories an there ain't much here for me now."

"Where we going to get the money."

"Hold on," Conway said as he got up and crossed the room and picked up his pants. He took a wad of fifty twenty-dollar bills and tossed them unto her lap.

"My god, where did you get all this money Conway?" Aleisha asked with a look of astonishment.

"Honey, mind if I tell you about it tomorrow? I can't think straight my head is hurting so bad. I need ta sleep. Just tell me that we're going and we're going together."

"Of course...of course we'll go together...O.K, O.K....we have to leave in four days," she said kissing him on the head. Conway laid back and she covered him up and turned the lamp back off and left the room. He lay there watching the morning sun escape through the shades with one open eye. He wanted to sleep but couldn't, and not because of the pain but because of the thoughts--the same thoughts that had kept him awake for months. It is a rare thought that can become as obsessive as a thought filled with the desire to seek revenge. He had to somehow dissipate this thought, and he had come to the conclusion that only an act would drive away the thought and act he would, and only when he made this decision did he close his eyes and fall asleep.

***

Conway drove his sister-in-law's blue Chevelle through a dark alley between two brick buildings. He got out and walked about half way up the alley and then walked into the darkness under an awning beside a large green dumpster. He sat there in the dark. He wasn't sure how many minutes or hours had passed when he finally saw two people walk by him. The people didn't even suspect that there was a person lying in wait only feet from them. What if he wasn't alone? Conway had thought of that possibility and if that ended up being the case then he would have to do it another time, probably in another place. A few more people walked by and Conway would squint and try to see if anyone of them was the person he was looking for. Conway started to wonder if the man he was waiting for was not there. He had been in there every Friday night since Conway had started stalking him, dreaming of his revenge, filled with hate. Conway was thinking that he had somehow missed his target when a tall angular man walked by him with an unsteady gait. Conway knew. Conway stepped out of the shadows and called the man's name, and though surprised, the man with a sure calmness squinted up at Conway, and as if he had seen an old friend he smiled and stuck out his hand to Conway in a gesture of good will. Conway took the hand, grasped it, and pulled the man hard against him placing the other hand over his mouth to muffle a yelp that was traveling up the man's throat. Conway put his hands around the man's neck and lifted him eight inches off the ground. The man's face turned red and his eyes bulged as Conway squeezed tighter and with one quick motion the giant snapped the man's neck making his body go limp. Conway opened up the top left door of the dumpster and threw the man in it. He looked around for witnesses and saw none, and then he took off the gloves and stuffed them in his pocket. He walked to the car and when he started to put the key in the door his hands were shaking too much for him to finish the task. He got down on his knees and clasped his right wrist with his left hand and guided the key into the lock. He sat in the seat, wiped the pouring sweat from his forehead, started the car and drove away.

***

"How did you sleep?" Aleisha asked Conway as he came out of the bedroom.

"Great, ready to go."

"We're all packed, you just have to eat, shower, and carry the luggage down to the car." The morning was sunny and warm, and Conway woke up relaxed. In fact, other than a slight mental recognition of the murder, he gave it no further thought. Most of the arrangements had been made well in advance so little further preparation was needed, and the car was loaded and the couple was on their way, a stop at the gas station for a fill-up was the last unchecked item on Aleisha's list. They decided that Aleisha would drive first and that Conway would take the last leg of the trip. Conway felt strange, not because of what he had done the night before, but because of the way he was seeing things around him. It was like he had never noticed the terrain of Nashville. He had told himself the night before that he was never coming back, but instead of seeing the city for the last time, he felt like he was seeing it for the first time. He absorbed in his mind-- the buildings, the gardens, the lights, the people, the signs, his own neighborhood for the first time in his life it seemed.

They pulled into the gas station and Conway pumped the gas as he watched a group of people stand around drinking coffee, sharing a paper, talking rapidly. Aleisha looked at the people and then at Conway and with a look that communicated what she was thinking: obviously something newsworthy had happened that was causing somewhat of a stir.

Aleisha went into the mini mart to pick up cigarettes and pay for the gas. Conway looked toward the small crowd and noticed Aleisha had become one of them and was gathering information. He looked back and forth between the pump handle and the meter only with an occasional glance at Aleisha through the glass. When the car was full Conway pulled it around to pick up Aleisha.

"Someone was murdered," she said closing the door.

"Really, that's awful," Conway replied as he was pulling out onto the road.

"Yeah, a basketball coach from Brown Junior High. His name was Steve Collins. He was killed outside of an American Legion and put into the garbage. Wasn't that your basketball coach?"

"Yeah, I forgot his name but it must have been. Too bad, I hate to hear that."

"Well, I'm glad we're getting out of these parts if there is a murderer on the loose."

"Me too...me too," Conway Jones Jr. said as he watched the

crowd becoming smaller in his rearview mirror.

CHAPTER 11

Hath she her faults? I would have them too.
They are the fruity must of soundest wine.
Or say, they are regenerating fire
Such as hath turned the dense black element
Into a crystal pathway for the sun

The first thing that James would do when he got home in the morning from the factory would be to scan the want ads. The thought of working in the factory any longer than he had to filled him with angst. For the first two hours after he returned to the trailer his mind would still be mired in drudgery. Even when he closed his eyes the hot plastic parts would come at him down the conveyer belt as he would pick them up and, with a paring knife, shave the excess plastic from around the circular opening, making it smooth and workable. He would repeat this procedure: pick up, sheer, pack, tape, move, sometimes for twelve hours straight with a half hour lunch being the only thing to break the monotony. Even though sometimes he barely kept up, he was always able to sheer the pieces and stack them in the box six rows deep, three up and three down, then tape the top of the boxes and stack them on a fork-lift which would carry them onto a semi-truck.

He had hoped that if he got a new job that a re-occurring dream that he had would cease. In his dream he was not able to keep up with the plastic parts and they piled up on his end of the conveyer belt until they started to tumble one at a time and then more on the concrete aisle all around him. At first there was only a small bounce and the pieces would roll down and around the other machines, and his co-workers, some who had been there more than twenty years, took great delight at his inability, and when the parts hit the ground and started to pop into the air like they were being popped in a microwave popcorn bag, the co-workers started to become an audience, and they would howl in great delight.

He actually had no reason to fear his co-workers any longer. He was hired under a program meant for short-term employees. These employees worked the summer and then either started or returned to college. James was undecided about his future plans and this provided him with needed funds--especially now that he was supporting Mona. He was certain that he would not enroll in college this semester anyway, but he was equally certain that he did not want to continue working at the factory, especially third shift. He had gotten into a routine on Thursday mornings, when the weekend had officially started for the third shift. Many of the workers headed for the bar to drink beer and play pool. The first time James went along, the feeling of drinking beer first thing in the morning struck him as quite odd, but not nearly as odd as walking out of the bar certifiably drunk, and instead of experiencing the depth of night, a bright noonday sun made James squint and shield his eyes, which were made even more sensitive from the alcohol. And today, in particular, he had drunk even more alcohol than usual, celebrating his last day at the factory.

Mona was rarely amused by James but when he arrived home in this state, she was quite proud. James drunk at midday she said, shaking her head. She made him a sandwich, and put him to bed, figuring that he would probably sleep until about eight or so.

"Guten Tag, wie geht es Ihnen?" Mona said to Gus as she passed by his lawn chair in front of his trailer.

"Good day to you too, my young lady, I'm fine thank you, and you?"

"Es geht mir gut…bis bald."

"Very well, you have a good day."

Mona knocked on Henry's trailer. By a lack of response, proceeding to a second knock, most people would have turned away but she waited. Henry always took longer than most to answer his door and nobody really knew why. Some suspected because of his paranoia he peeked out of every window, making sure that "they" were not after him, others, including Mona, thought that it may have something to do with drugs, but whatever the reason, sure enough, Henry appeared at the door. He looked at Mona and then looked past as if he were expecting to see James too. She had never come over alone.

"Where's James?" Henry asked.

"Drunk, passed out and I'm bored." Henry nodded. "What are you up to?"

"Not too much, trying to relax, read a little."

"Want some company?"

"Where's James?" Henry asked uncomfortably.

"You've already asked that and I said he's passed out drunk. He usually gets up around three or four but he stayed at the bar until almost one in the afternoon which means he won't be up until eight probably and that trailer is so small that I can't watch T.V. or listen to music and I read all morning. How about chess?"

"You play chess," Henry said, thinking over the possibilities.

"Every time I come over here with James and see your board I tell you that."

"O.K., come in," Henry said as he opened the door before surveying the surroundings with a nervous glance.

"Do you have a beer?" Mona said, sitting on the couch making herself at home.

"I don't drink," Henry said, still standing just inside the door.

"Do I make you nervous?" Henry said nothing. Mona waited for a reply.

"You don't talk like you're nineteen," Henry said finally breaking the silence.

"That's because I feel like I'm thirty. I was more independent at fourteen than most people in their 30s, smarter too." Mona squared the chessboard. "Let's play and I'll show you."

Henry was a competent chess player. He played in a club in high school and continued to develop in Vietnam, and he never turned down a challenge at the local bar back when he still drank, but lately challengers had been few and far between, and while he would still occasionally study moves from a book, he rarely had the opportunity to play. His rust showed initially when much to his surprise Mona took an early advantage.

"You're not letting me win, are you?" Mona inquired.

"I wouldn't have let my mother win when it comes to chess," Henry replied.

After Henry got over the initial surprise of Mona's fast start, his concentration deepened. He was even able to block out the short cut off jeans and the skimpy blouse that she was wearing. He slowly outmaneuvered her, taking a rook, bishop, and both knights, and within fifteen minutes he had her queen and now it was only a matter of moves, and within a few minutes he began to put her into check and soon after check mate.

"Not bad. Not bad at all, actually I'm quite impressed. I was afraid early on that you may have me," Hank said rubbing his chin as if he was trying to mentally correct his early mistakes.

"Well, I was taught by master."

"Your dad?"

117

"Yeah."

"He must be a good teacher."

"To be honest with you, I've never really played that much. Early on, in sixth grade maybe he started teaching me and we would play a lot but I lost interest and after that I have only played sporadically."

"Wow, you should play more often. Want to play again?" Henry was appreciating the chance to play-- it had been awhile.

"Maybe." Mona was looking restless.

"Why maybe."

"Got any dope?"

Henry looked cautious. "Why do you ask that question?"

"You don't think I smell it. I smell it walking by here at night, or evening, or sometimes in the morning."

"I'll be right back," Henry said after quickly contemplating the situation. "Then you will continue playing, right?"

"Yeah," Mona said cheerfully.

Henry returned holding a rolled bag of marijuana and a small pipe. He packed the pipe--one of the souvenirs that he still had from Vietnam. He paused before he lit the pipe just to make sure Mona was still interested. If Henry had any doubts about her willingness to participate, he had them no more. He lit the edge of the pipe moving his lighter in a circular motion to inflame the whole circumference of the pipe. He inhaled deeply, his cheeks puffed out as he put his hand against his chest as if that would somehow keep the smoke in his lungs longer. He was so concentrated on the ritual that he momentarily forgot about Mona, and it was only after he exhaled that he realized that she was there, and waiting, once again. He passed her the pipe and it was hot against her lips and Henry made the same circular motion once again with his lighter, while she drew the smoke in, but unlike Henry she was unable to keep the smoke in and she expelled it from her body in one hoarse

118

convulsive cough. Though most young women would have been embarrassed, Mona simply waved toward her hand backward in a gesture meant to signal Henry to return the pipe to her mouth so she could try again. This time out of pure will she kept the smoke in her lungs longer and only released it in short spasms. Once the pot in the pipe was burnt, Henry tapped out the ash and asked her if she wanted more, and while Mona was determined, she was not one to do what she did not want to do for the sake of appearances. Henry decided that he had had enough for now too. Mona sat back as the room around her started to descend and she had the feeling that she was levitating because she could not feel the couch beneath her.

"What?" Mona asked.

"Are you ready to play?" said Henry, setting up the last few pieces.

"Ready as I'll ever be."

The two began to play and Henry had the advantage very early. Mona sat staring at the board and could not decide what her next move would be.

The pot had made her unable to concentrate and she now just wanted to get the game over without seeming to throw it. Henry finally gave her an out when he told her that it was obvious that she "wasn't really into it."

"Got any music?" Mona replied in a way that indirectly affirmed Henry's statement. Henry pointed at a record bin. Mona flipped through the albums and every record she came across made her emit some sound that showed her disapproval. She told him that she would be right back and headed out the door, and though she could see no one through the yard she somehow felt that everyone was watching her and that because of her blood-shot eyes, they knew exactly what she was up to. This only bothered her momentarily, and then she walked more easily because she realized that

119

she did not care who knew what and what they knew. She checked on James and as she expected he was still out cold. She grabbed a few cassettes and a cassette player and considered if she should grab a wine cooler. She had more of a buzz than she had bargained for from the pot but decided to grab the cooler anyway.

When she returned to Henry's trailer she walked through the door without knocking. She gave him his choice between REM, The Cure, and U2. He looked them over and chose the new Cure, songs from which were all over the radio that summer.

"Well, what do you think?" asked Mona after a few songs.

"It's alright. I've heard it around some."

"Alright, are you crazy? Beat's anything in your freedom rock collection. God, doesn't anybody listen to anything but classic rock in this hick town. I have James finally turning the corner. Looks like now I'll have to work on you next."

"Hey, I just like music. I guess most people have what was popular during their formative years."

"This wine cooler is good. Too bad you don't drink anymore."

"I have a feeling that you wouldn't say that if you knew me when I drank," Henry said as he repacked his pipe.

"I can't imagine you were that bad. What did you do that was so bad?"

"Fighting mostly. I'd fight anybody and everybody and I needed very little reason."

"Did you win?"

"You never heard any stories about me?" Henry said pausing for a reply.

"Not about fighting. Just that you keep to yourself a lot."

"Yeah, I won, mostly."

"Can I ask you a question?"

"Sure."

"Out of the Vietnam movies, which one is the most accurate?"

"I wouldn't know."

"Why not? You were there, weren't you?"

"Yeah, but I never watched any of the movies."

"What, *Apocalypse Now, Hamburger Hill, Platoon,* you've never seen any of them. Not even on T.V.?"

"Nope, why would I need to see them when I was there? I don't need to watch them. I know what happened and what it was about." Henry said as he exhaled and passed the pipe to Mona. Mona hit it and exhaled slowly, finally getting a hang of it. Mona got up from the floor and sat next to Henry.

"Why do you spend so much time alone?" she asked, looking directly into his eyes.

"Because I'm not a big fan of people. I like my own company the best."

"Do you like my company?"

"Yes, and I like James too," Henry said.

"Maybe you just haven't met the right people."

"No, I used to like people and they used to like me but all that changed."

"How so?"

"When I was in high school I was the high school quarterback. I was very good and I probably could have went to college to play. Not only would I have gotten a free education but I wouldn't have been put in the draft. I couldn't stand the thought of more classes and more homework. Not that I wouldn't have went. I just didn't want to start right back up right away. I remember Saturday mornings when I would walk up town many of the men in town would be having breakfast and reading the paper, usually about the game the night before. People would actually cross the street to shake my hand and tell me good game. They would hand me a copy of the paper and tell me to read about myself. I was a local hero be- cause when I led my team to victory the whole community somehow felt good about themselves. Fast forward a little over a year. I'm walking down the same street, now in my uniform, and those same people would not make eye contact with me, some would even cross the street so they wouldn't have to pass me. Now I had been involved in a conflict that made them feel really bad about themselves. I'm talking about some who were VFW guys who were at that time maybe ten years older than I am now. They had saved civilization but we had somehow added to its possible destruction, for doing the same thing. Doing what was asked of us, and in my case, doing what I was forced to do. I moved out to Arizona for a few years and when I came back, I had long hair and a beard and many of them didn't recognize me and they still wouldn't give me the time of day because of the way I looked, and to all but a few of them I haven't said two words to this day."

"You never got the appreciation you deserved, did you?"

"No, none of us did. There are still some vets who don't get proper treatment, especially mental treatment, and still think there are some soldiers held prisoner over there and this government has not done their part making sure."

"That's awful," Mona said slowly with half-closed eyes, "I appreciate you Henry. I'm grateful for what you did."

"Thanks."

"You want me to show you? It's the least you deserve."

"How," Henry said a bit uncomfortably.

"I'll sleep with you," Mona said with confidence.

"I'm not quite sure what to say to that."

"You're not interested?"

"I didn't say that."

"So you are interested? If not, that's cool. I won't take it personal."

"What about James?"

"What about James? James and I are hanging out for a while

until we both figure things out. Don't worry about him. It freaked you out that a nineteen year old came right and made that offer, didn't it?"

"I'd be lying if I said that it didn't catch me off guard."

"I told you I'm nineteen going on thirty."

"I wish you were thirty right now. I was probably about a senior when you were born."

"So?" Mona kept her gaze. She realized that she had made Henry so nervous that it had frozen him. "Listen, I'm not a whore or a slut. God, I hate those names anyway. Why don't boys get them? I'm so done, so far beyond that. I don't offer this all the time."

"Trust me, I don't get offered this all the time," Henry said still in disbelief.

"Believe it or not, I've only slept with one other person."

"James?" Henry said with surprise.

"Nope, and I bet you're surprised. I slept with a teaching assistant of my father's. I lied to him and told him that I was eighteen. My father talked about him at the dinner table and said that he was brilliant and that he was going to be a famous scholar one day. When he came to the house looking for my father he was so nice to me. Just for fun, I did it while he was lying on my parent's bed. I found out a few days later that he was engaged and that he was married a few weeks later. That told me a lot about men. I figured if this guy would do it, any guy would, any guy without big time hang-ups that is. You know guys afraid of Hell and so forth, like God doesn't have more important things to worry about."

"Are you really only nineteen? I knew a woman once that you kind of remind me of, only as far as you view the world though. But she was in her mid thirties."

"I told you I felt like I was thirty. So, do you want it or not?"

"Of course there is a part of me that wants it but…"

"Listen, I'm not going to start hanging around waiting for you.

I have not nor will I ever fall in love with you. I'm not going to try to move in with you next. Let's see--Oh, yes, I'm not going to start wearing your Army jacket and all of a sudden inexplicably start listening to your freedom rock or classic rock or whatever you call that dinosaur. I'm not going to tell anybody. I'm not going to make it my goal to do it again before I leave this place. I won't banish the idea if the right circumstance arrived. In other words, I'm not going to avoid you after. I'm going to act the same whether I do this or not. I'm not going to save the tape from the phone machine with your voice on it when you call James."

"You would make a good lawyer, and by the way, I don't even have a phone, when I want James I just tap on his door," Henry said, still nervous. "What do you get out of it?"

"It's exciting. You're a cool guy. Interesting, mysterious and I'd like for you to remember me. You've been wronged and while I can't make up for that, I can do my part. Listen, you should be the one trying to talk me into it, not vice-versa. If you aren't interested it's no big deal either way. I just thought I'd offer, if it felt right."

"No, don't move," Henry said falling for Mona's bluff as she started to move away. "If everything you say is true, it's one of the kindest gifts offered to me. I find it hard to believe." Henry pulled her close to him. "What if I want more?" Henry began feeling her body, rubbing her thighs and putting his hands down her blouse.

"This is it. No offense, and don't take this the wrong way, I picture myself ending up with someone great: An ocean explorer who makes great discoveries and delivers a paper to a national conference with me by his side or something like that. I know that sounds weird but that's what I have in mind..."

Henry kissed her full on the mouth for several seconds and then laid back. He did not care that she did not consider him a great man; it was enough for him to be worthy of what she was offering now...

"Well, aren't you going to say anything?" Mona asked as she stood up and adjusted her clothes and threw him a Kleenex to clean himself.

"Thank you?" Henry said, more of a question than a statement as he pulled his pants up and buttoned his shirt.

"You're welcome," she said, smiling as if to reassure him that all she had told him was true.

"I really appreciate it."

"I'm glad to have made you happy. You seem so sad so often."

"I'm happy now," Henry said, "and if I get sad maybe if I think of this it will make me happy."

"I hope so." Mona looked through the shades and could tell the afternoon had become evening. I probably should be getting back. James will be up soon."

"I would never want to hurt that kid's feelings. I consider him a friend."

"Don't worry. James and I owe each other nothing. We're using each other for a while. I'm hiding and he's trying to figure out what he's going to do with his life."

"And what are you going to do with your life?"

"When I'm ready, which I think will be soon, I'm going to college. In a big city somewhere, lots of different types of people and different experiences. Somewhere where the bands play good progressive music for starters. You won't forget me will you?"

"Never. You've made sure of that. You can count on it."

Mona walked back through the yard still stoned. She walked into the trailer and looked at James still asleep. She examined James and her own feelings. She liked James but did not respect him. She was staying with him and in return she was trying to teach him. She deplored the naïveté in him that she either lost years ago or perhaps never had. She knew that she was mean to him at times but once in a while she was prone to bad moods and when he tried to cheer her up he went about it in such an awkward way it just made her mad. Mad enough to want to punish him. Mad enough to throw a chair. Yes, she had told Henry that she felt like she was thirty but she threw a temper tantrum like she was ten. She was a paradox. No, she was too complex to be a simple paradox she thought to herself. She lay on the couch and ran the day through her head again and she had no regrets. Her decision made her smile and she drifted off to sleep feeling light, and as she came in and out of wakefulness she felt as if she was floating over the furniture, almost flying. And fly she would, very soon.

Chapter 12

Dear Jason,

I have to admit I am running a little behind. To be honest, I have been a bit sluggish, a bit under the weather. I am sure that you are aware from your father that I have been known in the past as one who can be quite prolific when I need to be. Unfortunately, because of a series of illnesses sometimes months pass without a word produced, which not only fills me with anxiety but a bit of despair too. With my energy all but zapped I feel that I have stalled, hit the wall, to employ an apropos cliché'.

I know that this sounds unorthodox but if you could find a few people to send to me to interview, I'm quite certain I could get the ol' glacier moving again. Preferably someone within traveling distance, if it's no trouble to you. They could come here to my humble flat or I could make my way there if possible. I would prefer, of course, with my nagging gout and rheumatoid arthritis that they could come here. I have a man who comes around to help me and he is quite good with coffee and cakes, so I can still entertain a bit.

Here are the people that I would like to talk to. Males: A Vietnam vet, a male college student, someone around the age of a student who did not go to school, and if possible someone who would be around the age of a Vietnam vet who is bright but floundering a bit. Female: college student, bright, well traveled, bilingual perhaps. I have met a few people in the city who meet this profile but I don't get out much and could use a few more, just to get their ideas on a few things. And of course, I could always write a few letters if anyone matched these descriptions. This reminds me, if you know, or maybe someone you are associated with knows, anyone from the rural Midwest who would be willing to answer a few questions for me that would also be much appreciated.

I know these requests sound strange but I have put many hours of thought into fixing this problem and I don't know what else to do. I'm not looking to use anyone's story directly, that is not how I operate, but talking with people who have been in similar situations give me ideas, and it is the ideas that I seem to be finding elusive lately.

I know you have asked me to send three chapters but, with all due respect, I would really like my request granted and a little more time. I can only imagine what you must be thinking; "the old man has nothing for me." Ah, but you would be so far from the truth. I do indeed have much done. Yes, perhaps not as much as I would like to. I had planned on having not only the first draft completed but also a few rewrites by now but my health prevented it. I can tell you that I have created a most detailed outline from start to finish. In the past, I have worked from an extremely skeletal outline. Sometimes in the past, like some of my favorite jazz musicians, I have totally improvised the first draft. So you see, I hope, that in one respect the book is finished! I just need some assistance from real people to inspire me.

I am well aware that you will be disappointed when you receive this letter and only this letter, but, in three or four months, I believe that disappointment will dissipate. In fact, just writing this letter has filled me with resolve to work with all my might to complete this project. I have my own reasons for completing this project. I wish you the best, sir. I thank you in advance for your understanding and in your assistance in this most unusual but utterly important request, and, most importantly, I ask that you give your most wonderful mother my best. I think of her often.

Sincerely,
E.Palamountin

P.S.
To show that foolish consistency really is a hobgoblin of little minds, I have changed my mind and enclosed roughly twenty-five pages. This is a framed narrative that is consumed largely, after introducing a few of the main characters, by a historian's retelling of the life of Lorenzo DaPonte.

CHAPTER 13

"Just a moment," Hank said as he sprayed an air freshener around the circumference of his trailer, while fanning the air toward a cracked window behind his couch.

"Hi Hank," said James, smiling as if to tell Hank that he just went through a lot of effort for no reason. But although his smile was meant to tell Hank one thing it was actually telling Hank quite a different story. In Hank's high mind, he was about ready to be called out and maybe even challenged by a kid who was one of the absolute last people in the world whom he would use violence against. Hank had prepared a speech but he didn't think he would need it. He was convinced that Mona was "cool" and that she had meant everything she said. Hank was going to tell James that it meant nothing and that if he wanted to hit him go right ahead; Hank didn't think that it needed to come to this point but if it would make the kid feel better in all his immaturity then he hadn't a problem with it. He was going to tell the kid that he wanted it in the jaw or forehead; he didn't want to lose any teeth or have his nose broken. He took a deep breath and opened the door and stepped outside with a serious yet empathetic look.

"Hey man," said James, smiling but noticing the odd look on Hank's face. "You O.K?" he continued with a note of caution.

"I'm just fine, and you? Actually, I've had a few drinks. Been a long time," Hank replied still waiting for a potential scene.

"I'm great, I was just wondering, if you wanted to play some cards. We have three players and we need a fourth." Hank just stared. "Oh, yeah, and I picked these up for you." James tossed Hank a carton of Kools. James knew that Hank had very little money and that he received some money from the government but he wasn't sure why or how much, or, for that matter, if it may not just be a rumor that he received monthly checks. All he knew is that Hank got by with very little money, and now that he had a steady stream of income, it pleased him to buy Hank a pack of cigarettes from time to time. Hank looked at the cigarettes and thanked James. It had become readily apparent to Hank that James knew nothing of what had happened between himself and Mona recently. Hank was also surprised that James didn't even give a second thought to the fact that Hank was drinking. James had never seen Hank drink; He had quit long before they had met.

There was still something bothering Hank. He always appreciated when James would pick up a pack of smokes for him, but this was a carton and, while he appreciated the gift, under the circumstances the gesture seemed excessive. Did a guilty conscience make him less acceptable to charity? No, he didn't believe so. He had no problem picking up other people's loose change for cigarettes or even "bumming" one from many of the neighbors from time to time. He knew that this kid did not have much money and he also knew that James's financial status was a constant concern. He also knew--or at least he heavily suspected--that it was precisely because of this poor financial status that Mona came into the picture in the first place. Mona was too educated not to have come from money, and somehow, she was proving a point to someone, perhaps herself, perhaps someone else, but Hank had little doubt that there was a game being played somewhere, and this is what made him feel a tinge of shame when he took the carton of cigarettes from James.

"You really shouldn't have. This is a lot of money; I don't know how I can thank you." Hank said.

"Well, first, you can agree to be my partner. If I go back home without a partner Mona and Gus are going to be very disappointed. Beyond that, don't worry about it. Things are starting to happen for me." James replied in a way that dared Hank to ask him to explain.

"You got that job, I take it."

"Yep, I did. And I'm going to make more money that I ever thought."

James's confidence built with his interview. He had read a few articles on how to handle himself, what questions to ask and how to answer the questions that were asked of him. He now believed that he had found a skill that he never knew he possessed. He was a natural businessman. From all he read it was an extremely tough job market, with an endless recession. He knew many people who were out of work, so when he was offered the job during his first interview, his confidence swelled to a higher level than it had ever been before.

He didn't have a suit. In fact, there were only a few times in his life that he had had to wear a tie. He wore one to his grandmother's funeral. His aunt, while periodically bursting out in tears, first tied the tie, and then continued to retie the tie until the length of the tip fell to the top of his belt, and now he measured Mona's ability maneuvering the tie, with his memory of that moment. Whereas his aunt had struggled with the tie, Mona, as if she were performing a magic trick, after a half a dozen quick, un-thoughtful moves, had the tie falling perfectly down his shirt to the top of his belt buckle. He stared in the mirror feeling foreign but important.

He drove his parents' van fifteen miles to a nearby town for his interview. He only asked to borrow it when he absolutely had to. Soon he would have his own car, a Camaro or Mustang. He looked down again at the directions making sure he had the right street, and the brick buildings with matching brick-colored doors and shutters added to his excitement. Men wearing suits and carrying brief cases walked down the sidewalk as if they were carrying out a mission that only they alone could complete.

He had to drive down the road a few times because the number went from 112 to 116. He finally parked and walked down the street. Thinking the impossible that he could be late, he started scolding himself under his breath, a habit where he let himself be the abused and the abuser, the teacher and the student. On a hunch he walked down a brick walk between two of the office buildings that lead to a parking lot. At the end of the parking lot he found 114. 114 was a gray-sided building with a tin roof with small windows and shutters that must have been hung in the '50s. Locust Vacuum was painted with yellow letters on an all-glass door and below the name hung a sign made of cardboard that had "help wanted" written with a black magic marker.

The secretary, an elderly lady, graying, her hair still held up with pins into a beehive, probably the same hair style she had when she graduated from high school, asked him if he was a walk-in or had an appointment. He affirmed the latter. He sat down in the waiting room on a gray chair that sat on top of gray industrial carpet. He looked through a stack of magazines and noticed that other than a few *National Geographics*; most of the magazines were company rags, touting individuals throughout the nation who were the top producers. Most of these top producers made six-figure incomes by simply implementing the Locust philosophy. They really didn't give specifics but John from Colorado, Althea from Minnesota, or Lou from Florida had the same caption underneath their picture, "I was moving six units a month before I implemented the Locust philosophy, now I am moving 600 units a month!" James wondered if Locust had one photographer whom they sent all around the country to take similar pictures of these "superstars of sales." James imagined himself a sales superstar: blue suit, thick tie, broad smile, head slightly tilted and turned toward the camera.

A man around forty who was just beginning to have sporadic gray hairs mix with his black hair came out with a huge grin on his face.

"James Geld?" The man said, rhetorically, holding his hand out toward James.

"Yes," James said, standing up, resisting the urge to take a step back.

"How are ya?" The man said pumping his arm up and down.

"Fine, thank you."

"Come on back, whadda ya say?"

Without waiting for an answer, he led James down the back hall to an office. A lady in a gray tweed skirt, yellow blouse, with her hair combed back straight over her head sat with her feet upon her desk, displaying her black stiletto heels like trophies, reading a newspaper, looked up at him, in a way that acknowledged his presence, without any indication that she was ready to begin the interview. James sat down in a chair by Mark Johnson. The woman removed her feet from the desk but did not yet look up from her paper to acknowledge James. Though he felt awkward, he kept his composure, looking at his briefcase, occasionally staring at the Ansell Adams and Patrick Nagel reprints on the wall, and looking at Mark Johnson, who no longer had his head tilted and turned but would still flash a smile at James when he took a break from whatever report he happened to be filling out.

"Do you have any idea," the woman behind the desk said, finally breaking the silence, "why it took me so long to start this interview?"

"Because you were reading the paper?" replied James.

"No Jim," the woman continued, addressing James with the nickname "Jim", a nickname that James had never used, "I wanted to see how you would react. Would you squirm, look nervous, or remain confident? So far, so good."

"Thank you."

"Jim, it says here on your resume that you graduated a few years ago and have worked various jobs, most recently a factory job."

"Yes, but I have always wanted...."

"Jim," the woman interrupted, "let me ask you a question. Do you love to win, or hate to lose more?"

James thought about this question while the woman looked on. He stared down at the nameplate on her desk "Tina Winner--Vice President of Regional Sales."

"It's a relatively easy question Jim. Are you more elated with victory or more depressed by defeat?" Tina asked with an increasing amount of theatricality.

"I guess I hate to lose more." James answered as if he were on a game show and was now waiting to see if he had won a prize or not.

"Great, me too. The only difference is, Jim, is that I don't guess. I know. I know I hate to lose more. Jim, do you want me to teach you how to make a thousand dollars a week?"

James was silent for a moment trying to figure out if this was a trick. A thousand dollars a week was more money than he could imagine. In fact, he wasn't sure that he even knew anyone who made a thousand dollars a week. One of the press operators that James had had a few early morning drinks with had confided to James that he made $14,000. a year.

"No," answered James cautiously, replying in a manner that made his comment seem more like a question than an answer. "I want to make two thousand dollars a week?"

Tina Winner looked over at Mark Johnson and when she started to smile he reflected a smile right back at her.

"He wants to make two thousand dollars a week," Tina said

addressing Mark Johnson as if James were no longer in the room. "I like it. I like it."

"Jim, ask me if you can have this job. There is only one opening, mind you, so there are no guarantees. But, go ahead, ask me."

"May I have this job?"

"Absolutely not," Tina Winner fired back and then just stared at James. James kept quiet not sure if he should now leave.

"Well, is that the end of it?" Tina continued. "I say no and you leave it at that?"

"I'm a bit confused," James said before the idea of this game finally came to him.

"I really want this job. May I have this job?" Tina started tapping her pencil and looked up at the ceiling.

"Wouldn't you like an employee that was going to sell a lot of vacuum cleaners?" James asked, going through the closing strategies that he had read in a book to prepare for this interview. He continued on with six more questions that Tina Winner had to say yes to.

"Then I don't see how," James continued filled with excitement and confidence, "that you could possibly pass up this opportunity that I am offering you to hire one of the best prospects around, do you?"

"No, I don't," responded Tina extending her hand toward James to seal the agreement. "Can you start today?"

"Today," James said, a bit surprised.

"I just happen to have a training class starting today, which means it's your lucky day".

"Well, I kinda need to know about the pay. See, I know my girlfriend will probably ask."

"Oh, that's why we like to hire single people. Spouses can be tough with commission jobs. Perhaps Mark would like to give his two cents here." Tina Winner pointed to Mark.

"Well, James, you need to be a saver when you work on commission."

"Commission?" James said without being able to hide his surprise. "The ad said twenty-two thousand a year plus bonus."

"Well," continued Mark, "true, but we have identified you as a plan A person who would make Twenty Seven and One half percent commission on each sale compared to a plan B person who would only make 16 percent if they were guaranteed that money. It's an exciting opportunity to be let in at this level."

"I see," James's excitement began to wane. "To be honest though, I don't even have gas money to make it over here every day."

Tina Winner communicated with nothing more than a look that she would be dominating the interview again. "Jim, I have maybe done something like this twice over five years, but I am going to authorize that you can receive a 100 dollar qualified draw, at least for," she added as if rethinking her offer, "the first couple of weeks." When James did not seem to agree instantly she continued, "and I can guarantee you that with our training you will far surpass that and your draw won't even be needed because we are going to have you out there knocking doors in no time. In fact, I am going to make it my personal mission that you will be a top producer out of all of our new people."

"How many new people are there?"

"Including you, six."

"Out of ten?"

"Yes, we've had a bit of a shake up here and now we are committed to having only producers, producers who are going to take control of their own destiny. It's up to you Jim, are you going to be the driver of your own car or the passenger in someone else's?"

Having no other prospects, James decided that he would try to become the driver of his own car. Mark Johnson brought him back into the training room, and this was not the type of training room that James would have imagined. There were four men and one woman, all apparently in their early 20s, playing various games, including foosball, ping pong, and pinball. Mark explained to James that it was the philosophy of The Locust Vacuum Sales System to simultaneously build teamwork while fostering healthy competition, so, before the van drove any sales team to a neighborhood to "knock doors", the team would compete using the various games. Every one of the men wore a tie and the young woman wore a gray blouse and skirt. James looked down at his own ensemble, which he had bought on an extremely limited budget: Dockers, white shirt, plain tie, soft brown shoes, and noticed that every guy in the room was wearing something very close to his own outfit--a different tie here and there, and blue shirt instead of white, blue Dockers instead of tan, anyone of the five could have easily traded any part of their clothing with each other without making a difference.

James's training period, for reasons never fully explained to him, was cut from two weeks to two days. The managers of the Locust System always stressed how malleable the system was. Now, the system was changing to more of an "on the job" training approach. James attacked the streets with much vigor and much of his two-day training was simply to prepare him, first, for rejection, and second to develop some perverse affinity for the rejection that once made him reticent. He began to understand through his training that rejection was a positive because it brought him that much closer to a sale, so when he arrived at his forty-first door of the day; he still had an ample amount of enthusiasm when he knocked on the door. This house looked like the rest on the street. Three thousand square feet with a large bay window, expansive lawn cut through with a turn around drive. A few people were nice enough to let him finish his canned solicitation but this particular house, tan siding, swimming pool, exterior lights that lit up the brick façade, would be the first one that invited him in.

The man introduced himself as Dr. Gardner and called for his wife who seemed to be delighted to have a guest. Dr. Gardner wore gray slacks, white shirt, with a red sweater vest, and his wife looked like she was dressed for an evening out. James finished his canned presentation and was so surprised that the presentation was having such an effect on the Gardners that he wasn't quite sure what to do next. So, after a few banal compliments regarding their beautiful home, James decided to start a string of closes that he learned during his training.

Would you like for me to give you a demonstration in your living room or dining room? This strategy would give the Gardners a choice between two yes's, but, oddly enough, they declined both choices but still gave James a third choice by offering the sunroom couch. James removed his blue blazer, rolled up his sleeves, loosened his tie, removed the cushions, and applied the vacuum nozzle to the couch and methodically vacuumed while pointing out all of the features and benefits over the low hum of the machine.

When he finished, he triumphantly showed the Gardners the filth that had been silently lying beneath their cushions. While they slept at night similar filth accumulated on their mattress and floor, dust mites and microbes that were undetectable to the human eye but led to allergies and disease all the same.

"Do you have children?" He asked Mrs. Gardner, as if somehow the customer was able to overlook the invisible threat that they cohabitated with, they must then be made aware that their children may be at great risk. James was told that the Gardners did not have children living at home but they had grandchildren who stayed with them occasionally. James could see that the grandparents were obviously concerned with the health of their grandchildren.

"The nice thing about this incredible investment for the health of your family, M'am, is that you can finance it. No need to pay for it all at once. All I need is a check made out to Locust Vacuums for twenty percent of the total."

"We finance nothing. Everything you see is paid for. Now, how much for that machine?" ask Dr. Gardner. James felt his heart flutter. He imagined Tina Winner and Mark Johnson's approving smiles when he walked in with the application and the check, not a deposit either, but a check that had "paid in full" written in the memo. The first two days Tina Winner had shown him encouragement when he came back empty handed. The first day, she left a quote about *success*. The second day she left a card on his desk that let him know that by working together they could fly like eagles, whatever that meant. James still wasn't quite sure. But the third day she was clearly frustrated with him and not only would she not make eye contact with him; she acted like he wasn't even there. She seems like a completely different person, James told Mona later that same night. This would set everything right though.

"So, how much?" asked Mr. Gardner, test-driving the machine on the chair in the sunroom.

"Fifteen," James said, staring into the old man's eyes, holding his ground. He had an artillery full of phrases that could overcome any objection the doctor might have. He was ready. But none came. The Doctor just nodded to show James that he thought that was fair enough. After a slow start, James was evidently starting to become the salesman that Tina Winner thought he would be during their interview.

The doctor excused himself, promising to be back in a moment. Mrs. Gardner sipped a whiskey on ice and offered a drink to James who declined but thanked her all the same. The Doctor was gone for longer than James expected but James was put at ease when he saw the doctor come out of the next room holding his wallet.

"Fifteen right?" The doctor confirmed.

"Yep, that's it."

"Well, you got change for a twenty?" the doctor asked as he

handed James a twenty-dollar bill.

"What's this?" James was momentarily confused.

"It's a twenty dollar bill." James said nothing. The Gardners looked stoic until one looked at the other and they both burst out in laughter.

"You really think we would pay fifteen hundred dollars for a vacuum cleaner?" The doctor was laughing so hard that he had to sit down on the newly vacuumed couch. "Any way, you guys stop by here so often, we eventually get everything cleaned for free anyway." Mrs. Gardner could see that James was hurt.

"Oh, c'mon now, no hard feelings, we just like having a little fun with you guys. At least we don't slam our door in your face like everyone else on the street does. Howard, fix the boy a drink."

Tina Winner would not even come out of her office to look at James's address list. She could tell by the way Mark Johnson shook his head in disapproval while talking to James that the kid still hadn't made a sale. James looked up and saw Tina but she abruptly avoided eye contact with him and disappeared from sight. James had not received the draw check that he had been promised and when he had inquired about the money all he received was a very convoluted answer from Mark Johnson about policy changes.

When James entered the trailer that evening he was already feeling defeated. The final blow to a bad day came when he noticed Mona sitting in the kitchen, staring ahead saying nothing. Usually, he would become a laborer and hoist the third of her scale up a half step trying to change her mood from minor to major. Such a move of only one half step although being only 1/24th of a scale left him exhausted, and sometimes his effort failed, as he watched helplessly as the third sunk a half step down into darkness. His inclination was to begin the back breaking, mind numbing work but the experience at the Gardners' had broken him. His legs would wobble and give under him as he tried to push the third up into a major chord, full of brightness and possibility.

He also felt betrayed. He thought to himself how it was no time for her to fall into self-pity, not after what he had gone through during the week. He resisted the urge and went into the bedroom and lay down without getting undressed. He heard the door slam. He had a moment when he started to rise from the bed, intent on following her but the moment passed, and after a fitful night with uncertain dreams, he was woken by a shining sun unhindered by any of the sporadic clouds, still fully dressed. James looked at himself in the mirror and, although he didn't see the point in changing, he put on a new shirt and tie, washed his face and ran a wet comb through his hair and started toward the door, but right before he reached for the handle he stopped. Had he only been through this routine for five days? At that moment, for reasons that he may never know, memories of mornings with any other rituals seemed too distant to be a part of his experience. He opened the door to a chilly morning with hard rain, the sun that shone brilliantly just a quarter of an hour before now hidden, and by judging the sky, the rain had no end in sight. He closed the door and lay back down on the couch and closed his eyes.

Mona woke him. The telephone was for him. He went into the kitchen and Tina Winner, sounding much like she did in the interview, was calling because she was concerned that perhaps he was sick or in an accident. No, he was much braver over the phone than in person, and he confessed to her that maybe this wasn't for him. A positive attitude wasn't enough to carry him through rejection and humiliation. Tina made a personal guarantee--something, she assured him, she rarely ever did, but, for him she would make an exception--she would personally make sales calls with him. It was a matter of tweaking, she said. He reluctantly agreed to come back to work, though he did not hide his reluctance; the time for irrational exuberance, he told Mona, had come to an end.

Unlike the previous night, Mona was in a good mood. She was asking him questions and giving him a general feeling of support, which included a response from time to time that made him stop and think. Not once since she started staying with him had she made a breakfast like this. She had eggs, bacon, biscuits, and coffee ready for him. He had not eaten supper the evening before so he was hungry and quite pleased that she had gone to the trouble. Maybe things were not so bad after all.

He entered the office and the crew had already left in the van. No problem, Tina Winner said, today he was going with her. She was going to do something, she said, that she rarely did; she was going to show James how it was done. "It" went way beyond sales. The meaning of "It" for Tina was nothing less than taking control of one's own destiny.

The rain still slammed hard against the pavement. Tina had brought Locust Vacuum umbrellas for both of them. Tina drove out of town and James didn't ask questions. She drove for about twenty minutes until they entered another town on the county line. This town looked, at first, much like the town they just left, but Tina kept driving down the main drag of the city until they reached the courthouse. She drove through downtown and took a few turns and parked. James looked at the neighborhood. Was this a test? The houses were small and looked run down, cars were rusted, and in some cases the houses looked abandoned, the windows boarded up, the porches full of junk.

"I can see you're surprised. You've working all the high-dollar neighborhoods where you think people can afford an expensive vacuum cleaner. We're going to make a lot of sales today. I'll warn you, though, don't get your hopes up. We are going to leave with a stack full of applications but we will be lucky if one maybe two of them have the credit to purchase. You throw enough shit against the wall and some of it's bound to stick."

143

James was amazed at how easy she made it look. She used humor first and then became personal. Asked them about children and grandchildren and always related something of what they said back to herself. It didn't matter if they were white, black, or Latino, Tina was one of them, understood their plight, made them understand how this vacuum cleaner could bring them closer to God.

In the fourth house she encountered a bit of a problem. The elderly black man was intrigued by the machine but wasn't willing to sign anything today. Tina told him that there was a special today. If he signed today, she could knock 100 dollars off of the machine-- after today, she would have to have the full price. After a little hesitation, the man looked at the filth that had been vacuumed from his mattress, a mattress that he had slept on, and until that moment he had always assumed to be clean. Now, he wondered what type of invisible filth lay elsewhere. He didn't want to lose out on the one-day special so he signed.

Tina drove the car down toward the end of the street. She parked and looked over at James and paused as if she wanted to choose her words carefully. "You have about ten houses here," she said looking up and down the street at the dilapidated homes. "It's simple: you, all by yourself, make a sell, then you have a job on Monday. If not, well…"

She watched him knock at a few doors. When no one answered he looked through the windows, thinking that maybe someone was slow to answer. He popped open his umbrella and jogged across the street. She watched him stand at a door in the rain talking to the apparent homeowner. If she had to make a guess, he wasn't going to get through the door. She had an impulse to jump out of the car and get him into the house but she resisted. She nodded as he left the rain and entered the house, the door closing behind him. That's half the battle, she thought. She waited, filled out forms and made a to-do list for the next day, and after intervals of more waiting and listening to talk radio, she completed more to-do lists three days out. She wondered what could be taking him so long, and, as before, resisted the urge to go in and close the deal for him. She would give him fifteen more minutes, which would mean that he had a solid hour. She whispered to herself: five minutes, maybe ten. That's all it should take. Fifteen more minutes. More than enough.

He couldn't believe his luck; it was about time. The woman, who was only fifty but looked ten to fifteen years older, led him back a dark hall and opened the door. The young child had nothing but a diaper and shirt on, laid on its back taking large, deliberate breaths. The machine covered the child's nose and mouth and a hose ran down to a small canister. James shook his head with sympathy. The woman closed the door and walked James back into the main room and asked him to have a seat. James set on a couch that reeked of tobacco smoke. James went through the stack of papers and pulled out a sheet that had testimonials of people with asthma. He sat the screen that had the dirt from the canister in front of her while he went over the material, just as he had been taught. Always display the dirt. Also, as he was taught, James only ran his vacuum over the cushions after the lady ran her own. He wanted to show her how worthless her machine was.

"All this debris," James said looking up from his folder "is the enemy of people with breathing problems. M'am, you need this for your granddaughter. I know it will help."

"Sure seems like it will. You say she is sleeping in that?" The woman pointed toward the screen with all the dust.

"As we speak. Her little lungs are filling up right now. The HEPA system in this machine will remove not only 99% of the dust but also 99% of other allergens, like pollen and cat hair. Would you like the machine delivered on Tuesday or Thursday?" James was closing.

"Tuesday I guess," said the lady, picking one of the two options that was made available to her.

"That's good, because with your granddaughter's problems…"

"But how much is it?"

"Mrs. Davis, we are running a special and I can get this machine to you for less than 50 dollars a month. I know it sounds too good to be…"

"What's that come to though?"

"If someone had to pay cash for this machine today. They would have to write me a check for sixteen hundred dollars."

"Sixteen hundred dollars!" The woman eyes darted from side to side.

"Does that sound like too much to spend on the health of your granddaughter?"

James sat the application and the pen in front of her.

"I want to speak with my son first?"

"Why, Mrs. Davis, you didn't tell me that your son was a doctor?"

"He isn't. He works at a body shop."

"So, would you have a doctor fix your car if you were in a wreck?"

"No."

"That's what I thought. If your son isn't an expert on asthma and vacuum cleaners, it seems to me that it doesn't make a lot of sense to ask him about this machine."

The lady nodded in agreement. "It's just that…that's so much money."

"O.K., here is what I am going to do. I'm probably going to get into a lot of trouble but you are a very nice lady and it's been a long time since I have come across anyone who needs this machine more than you." James looked down the hall to convey his meaning. "We had a special that ended yesterday. I can backdate this application and take $75 off if you sign today."

"Could you do that if I talked to my son and you came back on Monday? I'm probably going to do it. I just want to speak with my son first."

"I'd love to," continued James. "But I can't. I'm really pushing it as it is. I'm putting my job on the line for you Mrs. Davis. I'm going to be really honest with you, Mrs. Davis, with all due respect it seems to me that you should be worried a lot more about that little girl back there instead of your son right now." James was hoping that his desperation wasn't starting to show. "I can only give you the $75 off if you sign right now." He picked the pen up from the top of the paper and laid it down right by the signature line and then remained silent. The woman stared down at the paper for only a few seconds but to James it seemed like minutes were passing. She picked up the pen, steadied the paper with her left hand, and signed.

Tina could tell by the way he ran to the car in the downpour that he had made a sale. "How much did you have to go down," Tina said,

"I didn't," he grinned.

"No! You hit a home run?"

"Better, I sold it for twenty-five dollars over!"

"I knew it. I knew you were going to be good at this."

"I kind of felt bad though. I started thinking I was going to have to cut more and to tell you the truth, I was competing against you. You took a hundred off."

"That's great. Great job, but I," Tina added as if she had to defend herself, "sell them at list all the time. And don't feel bad. So you soaked her for twenty-five extra. If you wouldn't have done it somebody else would've...can't protect people from being dumb." She could see he was proud of himself. "Don't get carried away," she cautioned him, "we still have to run credit to see if she qualifies."

He knew it as soon as she walked out of her office with the report. There could be no other reason why she would be carrying a bottle and two glasses.

He felt woozy as Tina Winner topped off his glass. He listened as she shared with him all of her motivational philosophy. He had tried not to notice, but, now that he had whiskey flushing through his veins, he tried to formulate in full thoughts that up until that point had only been vague impressions. Yes, she looked good. Not really attractive in the conventional sense, like Mona, but attractive all the same. She was using words like *determination* and *perseverance* that much he knew, but he was too distracted to really know what context in which she was using those particular words. What is it? He thought. It's her attitude. It's the way she walks as if she knows exactly where she is going. It's also what she walks in that makes the effect. Those heels and that business suit…professional but still shows off her legs. Tina crossed her legs and James looked and then diverted his gaze. He held his gaze long enough to test to see if she liked the attention but not long enough so that she would know for sure if the gaze was deliberate. The sale had made James confident and ready to assert himself more if the opportunity arose.

"I said are you prepared to create your own reality?" Tina was obviously repeating herself.

James didn't answer but he did notice that when she had her legs crossed that her skirt rode up exposing much of her right thigh. For reasons unknown to him, he first calculated that she must be five or six years older than he was, and then he put the palm of his hand on her thigh and rubbed it like it had a small muscle cramp; his expression alternated between hope and fear. Tina Winner looked down at his hand and then back up into his eyes.

"I've been giving you advice all day and I'm going to give you some more. If you don't get your hand off my body I'm going to kick your ass," she said matter of factly. "I've worked way too hard and been through too much for any man to touch my body without an invitation." She let the silence invade for a few seconds. James cast his eyes toward the floor like he was being scolded by his first grade teacher. "Do you understand?" James nodded yes and said he was sorry. Tina continued as if James had said nothing, "because if you don't understand and we are not completely clear then you can leave and never come back. I don't care what kind of potential you have. I demand respect from all of my crew."

"O.K., I'm sorry. I just thought that…"

"Save it. I don't care what you thought. It doesn't matter. If and when I ever want you to touch me you'll know. Until then, don't."

"O.K., I'm sorry." James apologized for the third time.

"Now that you've made a sale, I'll go get your draw check."

***

The first thing that he bought when he cashed his check was a carton of Kools for Hank. Now James watched Hank as he lit one of those cigarettes and stared intently down at the cards he was holding. The trailer was filled with smoke but the booze eased any eye irritation. Gus was drinking whiskey straight on the rocks; James and Hank were drinking a beer, and Mona, wine coolers. The sun had sat and the stereo had been turned up in increments as the evening progressed. They played Hearts, Pinochle, and Euchre, and now had gotten chips out and begun a poker game. James was still feeling very good about his sale and the breeze coming through the window added to his contentment. He got up to use the bathroom and noticed that he was drunker than he thought. Hank smiled at him as if to say, "I know exactly what you mean. I'm right there too." Mona was saying something to Gus in German that always seemed to make Gus a little uncomfortable.

James put his hand against the wall to steady himself while he

149

urinated. He watched the stream bombard a piece of toilet paper that floated in the toilet. As he was finishing he heard voices grow loud, and he could tell, intuitively, that this was no longer the loudness of laughter, spurred on by alcohol, but the loudness of rage spurned on by alcohol.

James jogged down the hall only to find that Mona had her hands against Hank in an effort to calm him down. Once that it became obvious to her that calming him down was an impossibility, she then began to convince him to go home and cool off.

"What in the world is going on out here?" asked James.

"That fat ol' fuck is a cheat that's the problem."

"I did nothing wrong," Gus replied defensively.

"He dealt himself an Ace. He's either the luckiest fuck alive or he's a cheat."

"Jesus," said Mona, "he could have just gotten lucky. Will you relax or go home."

"We're only playing for chips Hank, what's the big deal." James said as he got himself between Hank and Gus. James had never seen this side of Hank but he also never had been around him when he had drunk this much.

"It's the principle." When Hank said this James looked at Mona. James and Mona had often discussed the impossibility that Hank could have ever killed anyone. They would often say things like, "How could someone so gentle shoot somebody under any circumstance?" Now, though, as they looked at Hank look at Gus, they understood that maybe he did, at one time, maybe even now, have the ability to kill. Mona now realized that this altercation could get out of control, but something about the way James and Mona now looked made Hank calm and he sat down in his chair.

"I'm very sorry Hank if you think I was cheating. I'm an honorable man." Hank didn't reply and Mona and James sat back down too. Hank got up which made Mona and James rise too because of the uncertainty but Hank just grabbed another beer.

"You sure you need that, Hank?" Mona asked.

"What are you my mother now?" Hank said. Mona, while knowing the question was rhetorical, answered anyway.

"Someone needs to be obviously," James was suddenly enjoying this too. He thought he was the only one that Mona would take a sarcastic tone with, and seeing her sneer at Hank made him feel less deficient somehow. Hank just kept repeating "you gonna be my rich mommy...my rich mommy...my rich mommy." His voice became softer as he repeated the line until he was just moving his lips back and forth while looking at his cards, knowing how much that it was irritating her.

Mona deliberately began to deal the cards. Every time she would throw a card down it would spin and either separate from the pile or fall off the table. Gus had a look of exasperation on his face when he said, "I'll tell you Hank, I have some extra time. How about I fix your trailer up for free. No problems--I just paint the outside, clean the gutters, repair the dents. I'll be glad to do it. Three days, four at the most and you won't even recognize it." Gus sat there smiling, his two bottom teeth missing. His thick forearms covered with graying hair placed on the table with his palms up in a gesture of giving. Gus was a fixer and now he thought he had fixed the evening.

"Something wrong with my trailer, Gus?"

"No, I just have the extra time. I could repair the spouts, paint, make it look real spiffy."

"Spiffy? You want to make my trailer look spiffy?" Hank's expression and tone made Mona and James return to alarm mode.

"Yeah, you know, nice and spiffy," Gus said, his smile fading.

"Yeah, nice and spiffy," mocked Hank. "You embarrassed of my trailer Gus?"

"Ahhh, I give up," Gus said swatting his hand as if he were

swatting a bug in front of his face.

"Do you ever think that all this charity work you do isn't wanted by everyone? I for one like to take care of myself. Or is it charity work, Gus. Or are all these ol' ladies that you service servicing you, Gus?"

"C'mon, Hank," James said, trying to contain his own laughter.

"You have a filthy mind." Gus replied, wiping the moisture from his forehead. Though Gus was the last person on earth that Mona would hurt, she could not hold back her smile, as Gus turned crimson with the accusation.

"You bangin these ol' broads after you mow their lawns or shovel their sidewalks, Gus?" Hank asked turning toward Mona and then James, smiling as if he were about to have his picture taken.

Mona took Gus' hand and said, "I know if I were one of these old trailer park ladies..." then she made two clicking sounds by pressing her tongue against the roof of her mouth and winked. It was only when she realized that this wasn't fun for Gus, that in fact the teasing was making him increasingly uncomfortable, that she began to defend him. "Gus operates from pure altruism. He helps people because he's good. He's better man than the two of you could ever hope to be. It would behoove you to try and be more like him.

"Behoove...behoove, what a pretentious word. Where do you think you are girly? I don't let anybody behoove me to do anything."

"You're the one with all of the religious books and Buddhas and whatever else you have over there. Get rid of all that and just watch the way Gus lives his life. Selfless, isn't that what so many religions are about, East and West."

"Really, I'm not good," said Gus, still with his head down. His large brown-framed glasses had slid to the end of his nose. Small drops of sweat ran from his balding head and fell onto his rounded belly.

"You don't do things for the sake of goodness. You do them because you're good."

"Thank you, my dear."

"And he's keeping all the blue hairs happy. No wonder all these ladies walk around this place smiling all the time." Hank wasn't smiling anymore. Mona's praise of Gus irritated him.

"Enough of your filthy mind," Gus said calmly.

"My trailer's filthy, my mind's filthy, maybe you need to watch who you are calling filthy, fat man," in one swift move Hank picked up Gus's glass and threw the whiskey and ice at him. The ice knocked Gus' glasses off of his face and they fell to the ground. No one moved for a moment until Mona marched over to the door and opened it and told Hank it was time to leave. Gus picked up his glasses and made no attempt to defend himself; he accepted the assault as if it were punishment that he deserved.

"Go!" Mona repeated, pointing toward the door. Her voice trembled and her eyes watered. Hank and Gus were probably her two favorite people that she had met since she started her self-imposed exile from the life that she had always lived--since she had started "hiding out" as she called it.

Hank picked up his carton of cigarettes and left, causing no further commotion, nor offering any defense for his actions. Mona went over to Gus and started to wipe his forehead with a paper towel. She told him how sorry she was as if she had thrown the drink herself. Gus, in his typical self-deprecating way, told her not to worry about it and that he was fine. He told her that he knew that Hank meant nothing by it. Hank was too drunk and once he sobered up all of this would pass.

"Ah, intoxication is no excuse for behavior like that," Mona said, pacing back and forth across the kitchen floor, unable to find a suitable outlet for her confused emotions. "I can't believe what a jerk he became. I've never seen him like that. Damn it." Gus hugged her goodbye and tried to reassure her again in his gentle way. James was still fighting a combination of too much alcohol and fatigue from a day that had started at 6 A.M. the previous morning to show much reaction. Before he closed the door behind him, Gus looked across the dark trailer park just to make sure that he wouldn't be attacked on his way home.

Mona turned around and said nothing to James but he could tell that he was supposed to understand that she was not happy with him. She started to clean up deliberately, raking an empty beer can across the table, pounding an ashtray against the garbage long after any loose ash had fallen into the canister, and the move that irritated James the most, slamming cabinets.

"What!" James said more forcefully than he was accustomed to. She ignored him except for a quick look meant to convey that he'd better back off. Tonight, no matter how tired or how drunk, he was not willing to go to bed wondering what had gone wrong, or rather, since he was quite aware of what went wrong, what *he* had done wrong. He had never known Hank to act so irrational, he hadn't put him up to it, he hadn't coaxed him on, but he was determined to find out what he had supposedly done wrong, no matter the consequences. He opened the guest room door with force to make sure Mona had no doubt that he would not be bullied tonight, but she instinctively trumped him and did not rise to the bait. She stared straight up at the ceiling, lying on her back, as if nothing were bothering her anymore. James had shown his hand and he wasn't willing to back down now.

"What was your problem out there?" James said standing over her, feeling more confident by the minute. He somehow drew on his victory as a vacuum cleaner salesman earlier in the day to help bolster him for a confrontation.

"Nothing," Mona said simply, changing nothing except for an exaggerated chewing of her gum, its clicking and popping communicating her meanings.

"Wasn't my fault. I didn't do anything to Gus or coax Hank at all. Him and I were just having fun when he started acting like that."

"He and I."

"What?" James asked.

"He and I were just having fun, not him and I. He and I is the subject--him functions as an object." Mona chomped on her gum to celebrate her small victory when she decided to throw in for good measure: "Dumbass."

"Get out."

"Yeah, whatever. I'm not going anywhere. For now at least. But don't worry," she said standing up to face him, "I'm leaving very soon. What? You didn't think I would stay here with a *dumbass* like you. Since you're the only one that hasn't figured it out I'll tell you; I'm using you, James. Do you really think that a girl like me would possibly stay around a small town like this--a trailer park no less? You have to be out of your mind. Him's out of his mind," she said to the cat that entered the room. "Him were not even able to speak proper English to tell that crazy Vietnam vet not to abuse our poor Gus."

"Is this what this is all about? I didn't do anything."

"That's the problem dumbass, you didn't do anything," Mona had elevated her voice and now spoke slowly with exaggerated gestures as if she were talking with someone who was hard of hearing and mentally slow. "You sat there and didn't do anything to defend Gus or me. You showed absolutely no emotion. You couldn't care less that Hank was humiliating Gus and you couldn't care less that he was upsetting me. You just sat there and since you asked, that's the problem....dumbass."

"They're big boys."

"Yes, but you're not and that's yet another problem." Mona always had a comeback that outmatched anything James could come up with.

"What, am I supposed to guess the right thing to do? If I would have done something it probably wouldn't have been right."

"Probably, dumbass."

"Mona, this is my place…."

"OOHH, and what a place it is."

"This is my place, and if you don't start treating me with the respect that I deserve then I'm not going to let you stay here any longer."

"Whatever you say dumb…" James meant only to pick her up and throw her over his shoulder but his shoulder hit against her knees harder than he had intended which sent her back onto the bed as he fell on top of her. She screamed and dug her nails into the side of his face and cut across to the corner of his eye. With much more determination he brought her up from the bed and picked her up successfully and began to carry her out of the room. For the first time, Mona was scared of James and she fought against him in every way she could, plunging her knees into his side and landing blows against the back of his head. The pain that seared through his skull only motivated him to remove the source of that pain. He fell to his knees twice before he pushed open the front door and carried her down the steps. He wanted to lay her down unharmed onto the grass but twisting her own body into convulsions he dropped her with all but her left elbow landing in the grass. She was crying hysterically and James wanted to look back and make sure she was all right but he was infuriated. He ascended the stairs, shut the door, and latched the lock. It didn't take long for her sobs to work on his conscience, but he would not be the first one to communicate. It was up to her to apologize. If he made the first move nothing would ever change, he thought.

He peeked out into the yard and watched her. He could hear her sobs so he expected the neighbors could also. He would soon find out from the approaching sirens that the neighbors, at least one, had heard or seen much more.

The first police officer who entered the door took James by the arm and brought him back into the bedroom and closed the door. James got the distinct feeling that the officers wanted to talk to Mona without him around. The officers were experienced enough in "domestic situations" to know that if the male could hear or even stare at the female then they wouldn't get the facts. James waited apprehensively as he strained to hear the conversation in the living room but he could make out nothing but mumbles.

When a short, heavy officer came through the door he was expecting to be taken away to the county jail. Instead the officer wrote as James told his side of the story. In the other room, another officer, maybe twenty-two, was checking the facts of Mona's story and making sure that she did not want to press charges. The officer explained to Mona that though she was not struck, she had been handled physically, and that was enough for assault charges.

"Do you know how many men I would have put in jail by now if that were the case?" Mona smiled and touched the officer's arm, which only gave the police officer more incentive to have James spend the next day or two in the county jail, though it soon became obvious that Mona had no intention of filing anything against James, even though the thought of a lesson learned crossed her mind.

"O.K., but I'll need your phone number," the officer said, "just so I'll be able to follow up on the situation."

"Oh, I see. Just to do your civic duty?"

"That's it. Well, I'm just very concerned about you."

"You seem to be," Mona said before her attention was diverted

157

by the older officer coming back into the room.

"Whata we got here?"

"Nothin," said the young officer, "she don't want to do any-thing."

Doesn't want to do anything Mona said to herself, still making eye contact with the young officer.

"You sure little lady?" The older officer said, "I've seen these things end badly."

"He's no threat to me. Nothing more will happen."

After a few more reassurances the police officers left the trailer. The young officer looked back at Mona and nodded one more time before he closed the door. Mona grinned at him as he left and then whispered "dork" to herself.

James emerged cautiously from the door, making sure the cops were gone. Mona was sitting on the couch looking through a maga-zine.

"You have no interest in making this thing work for the long run, do you?"

Mona looked at James with a tinge of sympathy. "No, but do we have to worry about the long run. Look James, there isn't even a 'thing' to make work." She could see the hurt spread across James's face. "Listen, you're a good guy. In some ways, way too good for me. You deserve much better. Do you want me to leave? I'm not quite ready but if you want me to leave, I'll leave, I have plenty of other places to stay."

"No, I don't want you to leave. Stay as long as you want. You're lucky," he continued, repeating something that Tina Winner told him, "lucky is when preparation meets opportunity."

"I have no idea what that means."

"Goodnight. I'm beyond exhausted." James went into the bath-room and dabbed a cotton ball with peroxide and ran the cotton ball across the cut on his face. He watched his face wince in the mirror with detachment--he was aware of the burning but he couldn't feel it.

He lay down in bed too tired to get undressed. He replayed the day's events. The last image he had was of the child lying in a dark room using a breathing machine to calm her asthmatic condition. He felt his lungs tighten and soon he was forcing air down into his lungs. He began to hyperventilate; it's all the stress, he thought. He cupped his hands around his mouth and tried to relax his breathing but his chest continued to tighten. He briefly considered running into the other room and pleading with Mona to help him breathe. Take him to the hospital or call an ambulance. This thought left him feeling too vulnerable so he decided to lay still and try to get whatever was happening to him under control. Use the mind to control the body. Relax…relax….relax…the mantra seemed to be working as he gulped a breath of air that finally seem to filter through to the bottom of his lungs. Relief. He fell in and out of sleep, waking up occasionally to monitor his breathing, marking a vivid sequence of a dream, something oceanic and terrifying, morphing experiences, becoming forever and paradoxically actively dormant, altering his being, possessing thoughts that would never again be known to his waking mind.

Chapter 14

When James emerged it was almost noon. Mona was watching cartoons and, much to James's surprise, she looked up at him and said good morning before she returned her attention to the T.V. James sat at the kitchen table eating cereal when Mona, cup of coffee in hand, sat down in the chair next to him and starting talking. She talked about a newscast that she had watched earlier in the day, she talked about what was happening in the neighborhood. For example, Gus planting Mrs. Garvner's flowers. Kids' riding mini-bikes in the field across the road. A factory laying off 200 people. She talked about the taste of the generic coffee that she had purchased the day before. She talked as if nothing out of the ordinary had happened. James was prepared for a day of silence but Mona not only didn't acknowledge the trouble of the preceding night, she continued on in a way that suggested that there was no problem at all.

Mona looked at the past as something distant, even if it was the immediate past. There was little difference between two days prior and two months prior; she could just as easily bring up a fact from six months ago to prove her point, while remaining totally unaffected by an event that happened six hours ago. James was different, unsettled. To ignore last night would mean that he would have to carry it around, analyze and reanalyze it like a conspiracy theorist over the Zapruder film. A particularly warm, sunny day was not enough for him to simply cast any worries aside. Issues had to be resolved. He would wait, though, for the right moment to bring up a litany of defenses that he had worked out while lying in bed during the morning, in no hurry to face what he wrongly expected to be another meltdown. For him to reintroduce any dialogue that could ignite another scene would be like reopening a healed wound. He would wait, constantly gauging her temperament, and then he would make a pitch for justice, vie for an admission of wrongdoing, and ideally, an apology. Not just an empty apology, but also an apology that would admit mistakes, a sincere commitment to *permanent reform*.

Why would he want to ruin the moment? She was now as he hoped she should be and would remain. Joyful, optimistic, sociable. No, he would not let the unfinished business between them go unresolved only to be relived in some cycle of the psyche, but he would also not deny himself the fruits of the present truce.

"Let's go over to the courts and play tennis," Mona said, rising up from the chair.

"Ahhh," the very idea of physical exertion reminded James that he had drank too much the night before and slept too restlessly. "I don't know if I'm up to it. I have problems giving you a game as it is."

"All the better." Mona disappeared and when she reemerged she not only had her racket but she had on a striped polo with a white athletic skirt. She was ready for competition.

James rose from his chair and put his dishes in the sink. When he came out of his room he had a wrinkled, black tee-shirt and was wearing cut-off jeans that still had jagged threads hanging from an amateurish trim.

James and Mona walked across the lawn onto the road and Mona bounced the ball with her racket. James, still working over the preceding night's events, was thinking about all the issues that he wanted to address. A woman, who lived nearby, fifty-five perhaps, was walking her dog; she worked at the same plant that Gus had retired from and had a mysterious illness that made her take an extended leave of absence from work. Her left arm became paralyzed, and though she showed no signs of stroke, she went through periods of immobilization on her left side, including a drooping of her left eye and the left side of her mouth. Her name was Jane Geld but she was no relation to James even though they shared the same last name. Gus had taken care of her including walking her dog on days that she could not use the left side of her body, but today, perhaps because of the agreeable weather, she was walking her dog, even though she limped every time she put her left foot down and her left arm hung at her side while she controlled the leash with her right hand which appeared to be unaffected. Jane smiled at Mona and James and said good day, and the two nodded back to her, and then turned to watch her limp from another view, commenting on the unfortunate, unnamed illness that had stricken her, possibly some virus Gus had explained Mona.

The ball sailed into the air and Mona brought her racquet against it with a force that still surprised James, even though they had played a couple times a week during her stay. However, he had improved from the days when he could barely get his racquet in front of the ball. He returned the ball determined to finally beat her. He had come close lately and today, he thought, was going to be his. The sun warmed the day and James felt the sweat start to drip off his face. He smelled the beer from the night before as he wiped his eyes, but the more he perspired the cleaner he felt, and the more energized he became. Mona sensed his determination and she was impressed but even more determined herself. Her serves, lethal from six years of private lessons, made her, to this point, undefeated against James, but if he could keep her aces to a minimum, and get her into a long volley, he could keep it close by wearing her down. James was tall and strong and if tennis were only a game of strength and not touch, Mona would be no match for him.

James seemed destined to win his first match when Mona abandoned her power game and started concentrating more on ball placement. Using this strategy she took the lead and was one point away from securing the match. She wiped her forehead and bounced the ball a few times against the court, and prepared to throw the ball into the air when James signaled for a timeout and started walking toward the net.

"What's up?" she said standing across the net from James.

"You know and I know that you are leaving soon, correct?"

"Well," she said looking around, "I'm not going to stay around here forever."

"Are you still going to go with your Mom to Columbus?"

"Yes. I am. There is a good chance that I could enroll. I haven't kept that a secret though have I?"

"I'm ready."

"For what? For me to serve?"

"No, I'm ready for you to go."

"Because of last night?" Mona said.

"No. That's not what I mean. I'm ready for you to move on when you are ready. I'm not asking you to leave. As I've said before, you can stay as long as you want. I'm just telling you that you don't have to worry about me when making your decision. Not that you were worried about me anyway." James said forcing a small laugh. "Let's face it you won't even do anything with me."

"Maybe I will before I leave." She said.

"Really?"

"Maybe."

"No pressure but that would be something very special for me. I would really, really like that," he said, looking down at her legs.

"Ah, that's good to know, James." Mona said reaching her hand over to touch the side of his face.

"We can stay friends."

"Of course."

"I could even come down there to visit. You can stop by when and if you ever go visit your parents."

"Absolutely. In fact, let's swear an oath on it. Right here and now. I pledge that Mona and James are going to keep in touch and remain friends." Mona stuck her hand out and James took it to complete the oath. Mona returned to the back of the court, threw the ball high into the air, and came down on it with the most force that James had seen yet from her. James attempted to lunge toward the ball with his racket as the ball sped by him bringing an end to the match.

CHAPTER 15

Perry had made plans to meet Graham on the oval to pass the football around. Perry was on time but Graham was late. Perry kicked the football as high as he could into the air and then proceeded to see if he could catch it on the way down. On the edge of the oval stood the village idiot, watching Perry as an ape might watch a toy train. The village idiot was a well-known, apparently homeless man known by the name Michigan Mike. Michigan Mike would roam around town with a blue hat that contained an M on it, a blue and maize shirt that was more maize than blue from Michigan Mike continually wiping his nose on his sleeve. Though Michigan Mike would continually walk the streets he would often come stand at the oval for hours at a time. He would stand there with his mouth gaped open, his tongue wagging out of his mouth, and his hands stuffed into the pockets of his pants, pants that rode up about two inches above his ankles.

Graham was about fifteen minutes late. He had gotten sidetracked by some coeds who needed help moving a couch up three flights of stairs. Perry was skeptical. Graham looked hung over and in no shape to carry a couch up three flights of stairs. The two men passed the football around for about twenty minutes, and then Perry ran a series of patterns into an imaginary end zone. Perry tried to get Graham to run patterns but he refused to do anything other than play the quarterback and even that exertion was starting to take its toll.

"What are you doing with music these days?" asked Perry as they walked back toward High Street.

"Ah, man, I got just a fantastic gig going. I am playing with some guys who I used to idolize. I used to go see them all the time and now I'm jamming with them."

"What's the name of the band?"

"The Buzz Fazio project?"

"Who's Buzz Fazio?"

"Uh, that would be me," Graham said proudly.

"I'd like to see you," Perry replied. "When are you going to start playing out?"

"Well, it will be a few months." Graham said this in a way as if to imply that Perry should be patient.

"When did this band start?"

"Last Tuesday was our first practice."

"How long did you practice?" Perry was not going to let this one go.

"The problem is," Graham now looked up into the sky, "only the bass player showed up for the first practice. You know how these things go sometimes. The guitarist had to fill in for somebody and the drummer's girlfriend was peeved because she didn't want him to get into a band again. She's the jealous type. Know what I mean?"

"I guess." Perry paused. "So you don't really have a band yet then?"

"No, no, it's not like that at all. I talked to them all. They're still game. It's just one of those things, that all. In fact, when I first approached Donnie the drummer he said he wished that I wouldn't have waited so long to invite him to join one of my bands. Trust me, these guys can flat out play."

Perry shook hands with Graham and told him they would meet

again in the evening. He walked by a used record store and stopped in front of the window, surveying all of the band flyers. There was no shortage of music: Rock, punk, jazz, and folk were all within a few blocks of his apartment. A small rectangle flyer caught his eye. Now, there is something interesting to do, he thought. A poetry reading. Perry was taking *Introduction to Poetry*, and had developed enough appreciation for the art that he had of late tried his own hand. Though he had no confidence in either himself or his work at this point he was curious to see other people read their work, and he was certain that Graham would come along, at least before a possible visit to the Governor's mansion.

As soon as Perry opened up his mailbox he recognized the large purple envelope and knew instantly that it was from Reinbeck, Iowa. He set his mail on the counter, walked over and sat on his couch and opened the envelope:

What is this?
Some sort of prisoner's dilemma!
The question is amoral
And I refuse to answer.

Now, here is my question:

Does mind refer systematically to an entity per se? Or merely a collection of mental events experienced empirically by a person?

Perry closed his eyes and considered the question and picked up his pen.

For the last three months or so, I have considered myself an Existentialist so I am going to say the latter.

Every time Perry answered a question from Reinbeck Iowa, he seemed to consider it more thoughtfully. On the other hand, every time he wrote his own question, the answer seemed more ambiguous until this time there was even a refusal. This did not deter Perry, and he decided to keep asking. Perhaps he needed a radical paradigm shift with regard to his questioning technique. Just possibly he needed to put more thought into his questions and research the question himself first, and then provide possible answers, or he needed to enlist the help of others, including Graham, building the question through a series of votes, dismissing parts that do not meet with the majority, and accepting those that, say, at least four out of seven approve. This very well could be over thought. Perry eventually decided to pose his next question through a Brentonian automation, clearing his mind to tap into his subconscious, getting at the issues that really mattered to him. After a deep breath, letting his mind think only of gray clay, he wrote:

If Ted Williams could have batted ten times against Cy Young,
would he have had four hits?

Perry addressed the envelope, sealed it, and placed it in his book bag. He took out his list and added "mail envelope to Iowa." Other items on his list included: laundry, groceries, research paper on *Mayor of Casterbridge*, go to Astronomy department, meet with Kathleen on Hebrew Bible project, finish truth tables and Venn Diagram circles for logic (O.K., if not done to complete on Sunday.) This would take him more than one trip. He figured he would do the laundry next to last and finish with picking up some groceries on the way home--mostly Ramen noodles, soup, macaroni and cheese, and various other college staples.

Perry cut through the English department on his way to the library and stopped in front of a glass case that usually featured various publications from faculty. Usually because of the size of the English department and the large amount of works, be it monoliths or articles, the department would set up a new display every few weeks. As he looked through the publications he recognized a book written by Jon Erickson among other books written about Shakespeare, Wordsworth, Austen and articles on Barthe, Buchner, and Pynchon. One book that stood out was a huge volume titled *Asimov on Shakespeare*. How odd, thought Perry, I wonder if he is going to be a guest lecturer of the department or something. Perry knew little of Asimov except for the fact that science fiction junkies were really into him and that he wore a cool bow tie and that he looked a little bit like the current surgeon general. It seemed peculiar, to Perry, that he was also an expert on Shakespeare. Perry's curiosity was peaked so he got out his notebook and wrote down the exact title so he could examine it in more detail at a later date.

Perry disliked doing research in the library so he photocopied enough articles on *The Hebrew Bible* to get by. He probably could have used a few more references but stopped at five because of the price. He pulled his list from his book bag and scratched off another item and then proceeded to walk toward the religion department to meet Kathleen. Once again he stopped by the showcase of faculty publications, and this time it did not take him long to spot another book that was roughly the same size titled *Asimov on the Bible*. Surely there was something going on with Asimov. Once again, Perry shook his head that a scientist/science fiction writer wrote such a large volume of work in yet another area of the humanities. He jotted down the exact title next to the title of the first book.

Kathleen stared at him with a matter-of-fact expression. He greeted her and sat down and pulled out the instructions.

"I have some ideas and I have a few of those ideas outlined," Perry said, proud of himself for being prepared. The fact that Kathleen was so smart and always seemed not only to be prepared for class but also to have all the answers, gave Perry extra motivation not just to do the minimum to get by, as was his habit. He had watched Kathleen's expression, or rather lack thereof, when the professor announced the partners for the project. When she said, "Perry and Kathleen" Perry looked at her, Kathleen stared stoically, which kept Perry uncertain of whether she was disappointed or not; he would have his answer soon enough, though.

"The one I like," Perry continued as he slid the outline in front of Kathleen, "is this idea about how Abraham negotiated with Yahweh." Perry gave Kathleen a chance to look it over and give her comments but she seemed distracted. Perry assumed that she was not impressed with the idea, to say the least. "Well," Perry said.

"Excuse me," Kathleen replied, breaking out of her distraction.

"Abraham, do you like it or do you want to see something else or do you have an idea."

"Here," Kathleen said, handing a finished paper to Perry, "it's done. It's about Ruth. We'll get an A. I researched and wrote it in a day." Kathleen rose and put her book bag around her shoulder but before she turned to go she said: "Your part is that you have to either retype it or pay to have it retyped. It's in perfect MLA with correct bibliography and I have marked any corrections." Without giving it another thought, Kathleen turned and walked away.

Perry looked at the paper and grinned as if he were a 49er who just discovered gold. He couldn't believe his luck and endorphins rushed through his body creating a natural high. He even felt his scalp tingle.

There was a bit of a dilemma now. He certainly was going to have more free time over the next few days than he expected and no he was certainly not going to retype it himself, but if he paid a dollar a page that would also eat up his grocery money or leave him penniless to go out over the weekend. What to do? There was only one choice; he would go sell his plasma.

***

Perry lay on the couch, leafing through a book, periodically looking at the band-aid that lay across the crux of his arm when he heard the knocking at the door. He looked down the eyehole and saw Graham and was about to open the door when he saw somebody familiar standing just to the right and behind him. It only took a fraction of a second for Perry to figure out that it was Ness.

Perry yelled out the door that he would only be a minute and then he frantically started to hide his books. He slid them under the couch, piled them into his closet and with a quick run through his bedroom tossed the remainder under his bed. After one more quick look over just to make sure he didn't miss anything he opened the door.

"What's going on in here--are you stashing dope, girls, or both?" asked Graham looking around suspiciously.

"Neither, I was just tidying up the place. You're a bit early," replied Perry regaining his composure. "Hey, you got a hair cut."

"Yep, it was time. Let's not make a big deal of it. I'm still trying to get used to the whole idea. You know Ness, right," Graham said, pointing a thumb back toward Ness.

"Yes, of course, we've met briefly," Perry said, extending his hand, and, only after Ness looked at his hand did it come back to him that Ness was not only a germaphobe but he had a philosophical basis to not shake hands. "That's right, I almost forgot," Perry said bringing his head back to his side and giving a short nod instead. Ness nodded back in return but said nothing.

"Well, we ready to rock and roll?" Graham said, breaking the silence.

The three headed toward where the poetry reading was to take place. Ness finally spoke his first words of the night. "Are you recit-

171

ing a poem Graham?"

"Of course," Graham said, surprised by the question.

"I hope something original."

"Of course," this time Graham sounded a bit offended by the question.

"One thing I can't stand is when one of these college kids gets up there and reads somebody else's poetry from a book. Happens all the time. It's why I don't go more often. You're not reading someone else's poetry are you?" Ness asked Perry.

"Huh-uh, I'm just a spectator."

"You should work on something. Self-expression is a good thing--even when it's bad."

The three walked into the dimly-lit bar and a young girl was reading a diatribe about the loss of her virginity. She had cropped-off brown hair and thick black glasses, and she wore badge baggy pants with a torn black T-shirt that had the word *PRISONER* in large white blocked letters. Perry liked part of the poem but found that the girl jumped around too much making words like *global warming* sound like *global horming* and words like *the homeless* sound like *omlessness* and the angrier she got the more jumbled her words became until she was out of breath. She paused, took a deep breath, and ended her poem by sticking out her chest and whispering: *prisoner*.

About a half hour later Graham approached the microphone and, being much more serious than Perry was accustomed, leaned over to the microphone and began in a dramatic cadence:

So long
My dear friend
The sheer thought of
Cutting our relationship short
Seeing you lay on the floor

Only to be swept aside
And discarded by
Irrational forces
Mystery
Loss
Foreboding
Regret

...

After a tepid applause Graham returned to his seat and Perry smiled and nodded his head in approval. All the other poets had been so heavy and serious; he liked the fact that Graham's poem amused him. Next it was Ness's turn. Ness approached the microphone and pulled several handwritten sheets from his pocket, unfolded them, and announced: "This poem is called An Ode to Isaac Asimov," and, after the coincidence that Perry had experienced earlier in the day, his head shot up in surprise. "Ode to Asimov," Ness repeated clearing his throat. Then he proceeded to narrate his poem that consisted of every title of every book that Isaac Asimov had ever written. And, as the minutes passed, the crowd became more engrossed and amazed. The following is just a sampling of the over eight minute poem: *Asimov on Science, Asimov's New Guide to Science, Asimov's Why Is the Air Dirty?, What Causes Acid Rain, The Moon, Mars, Stars, How Did We Find Out About Black Holes?, How Did We Find Out About Neptune?, How Did We Find Out About Coal?, Inside The Atom, A Short History of Biology, Is Anyone There?, Asimov on Chemistry, Asimov on Biology, The Roving Mind, Asimov on Science Fiction, The Roman Republic, The Roman Empire, The Shaping of France, The Birth of The United States, Asimov's Annotated Gilbert and Sullivan, The Sensuous Dirty Old Man, Limericks: too Gross; or Two Dozen Dirty Stanzas , Isaac Asimov's Book of Facts...*

The poem concluded with *Futuredays: A Nineteenth-Century*

Vision of the Year 2000. And as Ness accepted hearty applause, he ceremoniously held the papers containing the poem high over his head and displayed them front and back first to the left, right, and then center of the audience, like a conductor lifting a score. He then took a lighter from his pocket that was set on high and with a flick it shot a flame into the air, and for a good ten seconds he held the poem in one hand and flame in the other, triumphantly watching the fire as it devoured the poem dropping the charred stub into a trash can until the fire lost its energy and smoldered.

"Because the work of art had been presented, and it's time has come and gone, and now it needs to be destroyed," Ness answered Perry. "Also, who needs a museum, an anthology, a canon for that matter? The museums are full, metaphorically speaking. There is no more room."

"What would stop someone else from just reading Asimov's book titles again?" Perry asked.

"Nothing. But they won't be able to do it like I did it. If you noticed, I didn't read it alphabetically; I wrote them down at random, there is about as much chance of somebody repeating my poem as ink spilling into *Prufrock*. If you named every title randomly, the chance of doing it again the same way is 200X199X198...."

"But as long as all the titles were read isn't it basically the same thing?" Perry was not letting this one go.

"See that tree there," continued Ness, "Isn't it basically just like the one beside it?" Ness waited for a yes or no answer.

"I guess," answered Perry.

"But the two trees are not the same tree are they?" Ness stopped and waited for an answer but nothing came to Perry right away.

"Perry," Graham said, breaking the silence.

"Yeah."

"Don't mess with the Ness. You will be pulverized."

Perry made no reply but he was not without a thought. At some point, he would have to revisit the discussion.

***

The three decided to at least start the night at the Governor's mansion. They walked along down the street past the record stores and bars until Ness suddenly stopped in front of a restaurant.

"You know what?" he asked. "I just realized that I haven't eaten anything all day. I'm starved. Anyone else hungry?"

"I could eat." Graham said.

Without waiting for an agreement from Perry, Ness opened the door and let the smell of chicken wings greet him as he entered. The three stood at the counter surveying the options. They ordered twenty-four barbequed wings and a pitcher of beer, and while Ness and Perry waited in silence, Graham sauntered in to the next room to explore the scene, especially curious about the music.

He had Ness and Perry's attention upon his return before he even said a word. His eyes were lit up and a broad smile stretched across his face.

"Holy shit, you gotta see this…"

They went into the next room to see a crowd of people listening to a performer.

"That is one tall sonavabitch," Graham said, shaking his head back and forth, showing a mixture of disbelief and delight.

"What do you think he is?" inquired Perry.

"I'm not sure, but he sure is huge. Looks like he has a darker complexion too."

"Man, he sure can sing," Ness added.

Conway Jones Jr. continued his set. He happened to be really feeling it tonight and he held nothing back. He closed his eyes and put his hand a few inches above his mouth and held it down at a forty-five degree angle, occasionally gesturing to show a moment of strong emotion.

> Today, I started lovin' her again
> Now I'm right back to where I've really always been
> I got over her, just long enough
> To let my poor heart mend.
> Because today, I started lovin' her again.

The guys joined the rest of the crowd in a chorus of enthusiastic applause. Graham bent over and increased the volume of his voice so the other two could hear him through the applause of the crowd and said, "I like it but if you think about it 'today I started lovin' her again. Now I'm right back to where I've really always been' I mean, that doesn't quite add up...doesn't make sense somehow does it? I mean there's just no way both of the premises could be true. Fails the logic test." Graham had made his point and now he started to alternate his applause making a circle with thumb and middle finger, inserting the circle into his mouth, and producing a piercing whistle.

***

They started the steep, slow climb to the Governor's mansion. Graham continued to talk about the irrational lines of the song, interspersed with whistling the melody, but both Ness and Perry had tuned him out minutes into the trip. Their detour by the Wing Palace had made them late and a line had formed at the door. They had no idea what the hold up could be. Could the house be full? As huge as the house was that seemed doubtful. In fact, the house was so large neither of the men had even seen it all. Once in a while certain men and women would walk past the line to the front, open up a folder to show the doorman, and then would gain admittance.

"That's bullshit, boss," Graham barked at the doorman with the bowtie. The man didn't answer but kept looking straight ahead. "That's discrimination. This may be enough for me to make a call to the ACLU and don't think I won't." It was obvious that the doorman was not going to acknowledge Graham.

"Sir," Perry asked respectfully, "what were the men and women showing in their folders that got them preferential treatment?"

"They were showing their PhDs of course," the bow-tied doorman replied.

"What!" That's not fair."

"Life's not fair," the doorman said cracking a smile, evidently amused, if not delighted, at Graham's disgust.

"Well, I wish I had known," Graham exclaimed to the line behind him, giving a wink to Ness and Perry, "I would have brought mine in that case."

After gaining admittance to the mansion, Graham delivered a Fiesta Liebermich to Perry and Ness. They elaborated on different aspects of the day--the poetry reading and the crooning of Conway Jones Jr., mostly. Ness suggested, without coming right out and saying so, that he was going to take a trip upstairs to the red room, mostly just to observe. As Ness climbed the violet-carpeted winding stairs, Graham and Perry watched him until he disappeared around the corner, and then they both took the opportunity to scan the massive bookshelves.

Perry came across two burgundy leather bound books that caught his eye. The Great War Part One and Part Two. Something about the titles of these two particular books hypnotized him and he had no idea how much time passed before he finally picked up Part One. The titles struck him as odd. He opened up the cover and saw that they had been published in 1923, so as he had expected, the books were a complete history of World War 1. Something about seeing World War 1 referred to as the Great War at once disturbed,

177

fascinated, and depressed him. Perry understood that *great* did not mean better than *good*, it meant *massive* and *horrific*. He thought about not only the author of the book but of also the world at that time. Calling World War 1 *The* Great War was a mixture of optimism and naïveté, but the author realized neither ingredient of the mixture. He, and the world around him, were neither consciously or subconsciously being optimistic nor naïve. No, they believed they were stating a fact--an historical fact—resonating hundreds, perhaps thousands of years, and this was much more of a reality for them than a meager fifteen to twenty years when Hitler's tanks would roll across Europe, starting a conflict that would only end when of scientific research of the age would unleash its wrath on Hiroshima and Nagasaki, along with other horrific slaughter, not the least of which would be the scourged skeletons in the Nazi gas chambers.

But Perry was not able to sort out all of his feelings yet; he was not able to attach words to his emotions but that didn't in any way negate the emotions that those two books instilled in him. All he knew is that his own ground of being, his own beliefs about the future were as suspect if not more than the person who wrote those books.

"Hey, where ya goin?" called Graham as Perry rushed by him toward the door. "You're going to miss the historian," he continued, shaking his head in disgust and disbelief when Perry didn't even break his stride until he was standing in the doorway, only looking back with a gesture, meant to convey that there was nothing here for him.

**

Perry considered going home and reading a book but decided instead to get a drink. He walked along the street on the crowded sidewalk, trying to make a decision about which club to enter. He saw two young men roughly his age enter a bar. One had round, black, wire-rimmed glasses wearing a T-shirt with "The Ramones" written in large black letters across the front. The other young man had on leather pants, a Jonathan Richmond shirt, and jet-black hair teased up about eight inches above his head. Perry didn't know why but he instinctively walked through the door behind them. The bar was dark except for strobe lights that flooded the dance floor. Perry ordered a shot and a beer and quickly drank both while standing at the bar and then ordered another beer. He felt his head swoon and remembered that he was feeling the effects of the alcohol so soon because he had given plasma earlier in the day.

The strobe lights added to his intoxication as he sat his drink on a small board that ran across the back of the dance floor. The dance floor was packed but people were making room for two people in particular. Perry watched the two young men whom he had followed in jump up and down at a furious pace, stopping only to slam into someone who dared come into striking distance. Occasionally a body would fly in from the outer regions of the dance floor and deliver a body blow that could easily send another flying to the ground. A slam didn't even seem to faze the dancers; in fact, it seemed to energize them more, making them sacrifice their own bodies back across the war zone. The DJ played one high-energy song after another: Fingerprintz, Fugazi, The Cramps, The Misfits, The Cult and Uncle Sam. But it was when Tav Falco started quoting Ginsburg that one of the young men started whirling like a Sufi paying no matter to any objects within his orbit.

Perry downed his beer and bought another. His head was spinning as he took a large swig of his beer. He put down his beer on the shelf and without a thought ran and threw himself into the pile of humanity. The inertia of the crowd bounced him around the dance floor like a pinball as he felt the energy from the music, from the

179

lights, from the other bodies orbiting and occasionally colliding into his own and for a short time he became a self-contained microcosm, making time irrelevant, left in his own gravitational pull. Occasionally a blow would send him to the floor but with one instinctive move he would bounce right back up into the action, feeling no pain. Sweat first beaded, and then poured off his forehead until his hair was wet and when he shook his head to the music his sweat would fly out around him.

He walked over to the side of the dance floor and put his hand against the wall to try to balance himself. The room was spinning and his head felt heavy and full like a saturated sponge. He looked over and tried to focus on a person who was standing next to him.

"You gonna be alright?" said a young woman with blonde spiked hair.

"Yeah, I just need to catch my breath," replied Perry.

"Man, your eye looks really bad."

Perry put his hand up and touched his eye and winced as the pain shot down his neck to his spine.

"You should put some ice on that. You're going to have a nice big shiner. C'mon over here for a second." Perry followed the girl to a dark corner of the bar. They both had to talk loudly to penetrate the music. "Are you interested in any of these?" The girl shook some pills out onto the palm of her hand. The pills were blue, purple, pink, and black. "Whatever you need. Help for pain, energy, to sleep, very cheap too." The girl spoke loud enough so Perry could hear her but she funneled a hand over his ears so that no one else would be able to make out their conversation.

"No, no thanks," Perry shouted back, making sure the girl could hear, but Perry didn't cup his hands which made the girl nervous so she took a quick look around her to make sure no one was able to overhear.

She looked around again and moved up against Perry so tightly that he could feel her breasts up against him. She cupped her hand over his ears and put her lips right up against his ear and in a mixture of a whisper and a yell asked, "How about coke, you like coke?"

Perry put his arm around her and brought her more tightly against him. "No, I'm chicken." She pulled away from him and smiled. He pulled her back up against him and asked, "Do you wanna get out of here. Go somewhere else and talk where we don't have to shout?" She pulled away from him once again, flashing her playful smile and held up her index finger to communicate to him that she would be right back.

Perry continued to wait for her even after he was convinced that she wasn't coming back. What if I leave and she comes back? He kept thinking to himself every time he started to leave. He thought about looking for her but instead sat down and waited. He stared at the dance floor trying to make out the various shadowy forms, hoping to get a glimpse of her, confirming that she may have just gotten sidetracked. The DJ played one song after another until finally the lights came up and snapped Perry out of his trance. He stood upon a chair and scanned the room as the moving crowd filtered out the exit. She was gone. He did see the young man with the Ramones shirt still moving back and forth to the music and using the drinking shelf as a drum kit. Perry approached him. Before Perry had a chance to say anything the young man turned to him without missing a beat and said, "We're doing gyros tonight you interested?"

Perry watched the drops of sour cream from his second gyro fall to the sidewalk and splat out into a circle. He took a few drunken steps and then would stop to balance himself so that he could take a bite of his gyro. The sour cream slid down his chin onto his hand. There was nothing like a gyro after a night of drinking, thought Perry. He looked at other students sitting at tables eating chicken wings, hamburgers, pizzas, and any junk to soak up the alcohol. Perry's drunken appetite would not be satisfied by any of those American foods; he needed the thick, doughy pita bread in his stomach. Perry stopped and listened to a man sitting crouched over playing a guitar under a blue neon light with his case open for change and finished his gyro, and then he fished through his pocket for loose change to throw into the old man's case before he stumbled back to his apartment.

Oh, please don't be my door, Perry thought to himself as he heard the rapping on his door. He squinted and tried to look out his window but the sun scorched his eyes. He smacked his lips together trying to create any moisture he could while rubbing his sandpapered tongue against the roof of his mouth. He sat up in bed and a pain sifted down from the top of his head, ran across his temples and rampaged into his sinuses. He stood up carefully and looked into the mirror. One of his eyes was bruised and swollen and the other one looked like a county map. He shuffled down the hall to the front door and opened it slightly.

"You're sleeping half the day away," he heard Graham say in a bright tone that he was not ready to deal with. Perry opened the door with a movement to convey an invitation to enter. "What the Sam hell happened to you?" Graham said with concern. "Did you get rolled?"

"No."

"Someone beat you up?"

"I beat myself up."

"What?" Graham now became very serious.

"It's nothing. After I left I went to Mustards and slam danced."

"Slam dancing, seriously?" Perry nodded. "You got that from slam dancing? Really?" Perry nodded again. "Damn, that's hard to believe." There was silence between the two men while Perry thought about what happened the night before and Graham tried to imagine what had taken place. "See," continued Graham, "that's why I prefer the kids who are into the retro hippie thing over the punks. That behavior is ridiculous."

"It was fun."

"Fun?" Graham said, offended. "Why don't you just stay home next time and beat your head against the wall? Say, got any coffee?"

While Perry made coffee Graham sat reading the paper that he had bought earlier in the morning. As if Perry were not even present in the small efficiency apartment, Graham would give commentary on what he was reading without explaining what he was commenting on. He would shake his head and say, "man, this is a messed up world," and "you gotta be kiddin me," and "unbelievable, the stupidity of people."

Perry brought two cups of coffee over and sat across from Graham, sipped his coffee and put a cold beer up against his aching eye.

"Hey, check this out," Graham said, briefly looking up at Perry with curiosity, noticing the beer up against his eye. "These people are going nuts over this silo. Through some sort of oxidation process an image appeared that supposedly resembles Jesus. Wow, I mean, what are the chances that anything would oxidize into any type of image?"

"Is there a picture of it in there?" Perry said.

"Yeah, but it's kind of dark. I can't really make anything out, can you? Graham held the paper out so that Perry could see.

"Not really, but my eyes are a bit blurry today."

"You can say that again. Listen to some of this, man: 'Thousands of people from all over the world have poured into the area. Some just out of curiosity. Others, like the terminally ill, seeking cures.' People are desperate. 'I think it is a sign of the second coming, said twenty-three year old Jenna Black.' Now that's my kinda girl," said Graham smiling and nodding in approval while continuing to peruse the article. "I like it. Oh, yeah," Graham continued, becoming more animated. "Look at this guy with the beer gut and the bucked teeth." Graham handed the paper to Perry folded over to show him a picture. A smiling unshaven man was wearing a shirt and holding a coffee cup with the words 'I saw the image,' and the shirt even had a faded picture of the silo on it. Graham growing more excited as the thoughts raced through his head said, "I got to have that shirt and that cup. We got to go there!"

"I don't have the time." Perry said handing the paper back to Graham. Graham looked at the picture again, which only increased his excitement and determination.

"No, you don't understand. We have ta go there. I have ta have that shirt and cup. Plus it may be interesting to see the image. Ness would be in. C'mon you can't miss this. It's probably only two, two and a half hours max."

"I'm too tired right now to think about it, but I might be into a road trip," Perry said, warming up to the idea. "It would have to be on a weekend, preferably Saturday."

"Of course, of course," Graham said, nodding in approval. "This is great. Well, I'll let you recover." Graham stood up and drained the last of his coffee, preparing to leave. "One more thing, do you have wheels?"

"You mean a car? No, I don't. Don't you?"

"No, I don't. Hmmm, let's see, Ness never bothered getting a license. I'll have to put some thought into it."

"You could rent a car," Perry said.

"Well, I could, but I would need a license to do that, wouldn't I?"

"You don't have a license either?"

"No, well, I had one but the man took it away."

"Drinking and driving?"

"No, not exactly. It's a long story."

"Well, what happened?" Perry inquired, becoming uncharacteristically nosey.

"Huh," Graham exhaled. "O.K., I was caught shop lifting and didn't show up to court and when I did I never paid my fine. One day I got a certified letter stating that my license had been suspended. I can tell you are surprised but things are not always exactly what they seem. I'm an honest person."

"What did you steal?"

"That's the thing. I didn't think I was stealing anything. I took an Ornette Coleman cassette, put it in my pocket and carried it right out of the store." Graham opened the door preparing to leave. "But you see there were extenuating circumstances and that is why with my defense the judge let me off with only a fine."

"And what was your excuse?"

"Defense, not excuse," Graham quickly corrected.

"What was your defense?" Perry repeated.

"It was under a sign that said 'Free Jazz'."

Perry was not feeling well and he was glad to be alone again. He poured another cup of coffee and sat back in his chair. He noticed Graham had left his paper so he began to look through it the best he could, focusing with one eye. He went over the article again about the image and he realized that this is a road trip that he probably did not want to miss. He continued to look through the national news, the local news, and the sports section. He turned to the arts and entertainment section which had a picture of an old man with thick black glasses and a bowtie and underneath the picture was written a caption: "Isaac Asimov dead at 83."

CHAPTER 16

Here are the people that I would like to talk to. Males: A Vietnam vet, a male college student, someone around the age of a student who did not go to school, and if possible someone who would be around the age of a Vietnam vet who is bright but somehow is floundering a bit. Female: college student, bright, well traveled, bilingual perhaps. I have met a few people in the city who meet this profile but I don't get out much and could use a few more, just to get their ideas on a few things. And of course, I could always write a few letters if anyone matched these descriptions but they were too far away to travel. Which reminds me, if you know, or maybe someone you are associated with knows, anyone from the rural Midwest and would be willing to answer a few questions for me that would also be much appreciated.

I know this request sounds strange but I have put many hours of thought on how to fix this problem and I don't know what else to do. I'm not looking to use anyone's story directly, that is not how I operate, but talking with people who have been in similar situations may give me ideas, and it is the ideas that I seem to be finding illusive lately.

I know you have asked me to send three chapters but, with all due respect, I would really like this request granted and a little more time. I can only imagine what you must be thinking, "the old man has nothing for me." Ah, but you would be so far from the truth. I do indeed have much done. Yes, perhaps not as much as I would like to. I had planned on having not only the first draft completed but also a few rewrites by now but my health had other plans. I can tell you that I have created the most detailed outline from start to finish that I have ever created. In the past, I have worked from an extremely skeletal outline to say the least. Sometimes in the past, like some of my favorite jazz musicians, I have totally improvised the first draft. So you see, I hope, that in one respect the book is finished! I just need some assistance from real people to inspire me to "flush out the flesh" for lack of a better term.

I am well aware that you will be disappointed when you receive this letter and only this letter, but, in three or four months, I believe that disappointment will dissipate. In fact, just writing this letter has filled me with resolve to work with all my might to complete this project. I have my own reasons too that I want to bring this project o completion. I wish you the best, sir. I thank you in advance for your understanding and in your assistance in this most unusual but utterly important request, and, most importantly, I ask that you give your most wonderful mother my love.

E. Palamountain

CHAPTER 17

James had had a particularly grueling day topped off by bad news. Not only had he walked miles and knocked on literally hundreds of doors he found out that two of his deals that he thought were "in the hopper" couldn't be financed. When he came through the door Mona sensed his mood and instinctively gave him space. The transition was complete. Now, it was James's mood that dictated whether or not the night was going to be blue or red. Mona knew that she had lost her power over him, and while this caused her some consternation, and she knew that she could recapture her position, she couldn't find the proper motivation to do so since she was going to catch a bus out of town in a few weeks. Though if she had it to do over again, she would have kept her departure a secret until the last possible moment. It was only when James had accepted that she was leaving that he gradually stopped responding to her whims. Now, she could brood all she wanted and he would just continue to watch T.V. She could break a dish or bang the door to her room and he would merely leave without a word, returning many hours later, with no intent of divulging where exactly he had been or what he had been doing.

Once she told him that she just may leave early, and he replied with some cliché such as "suit yourself" without even making eye contact. Not only did he start to ignore any negative comments or outright tantrums, he realized the more he ignored such episodes, the less they happened.

James was often stressed out by his job and when he was in a foul mood Mona saw a side of him that she didn't know existed. In fact, it was a side of himself that he was even unaware of before he started "knocking on doors". Though he began to discover a tool that became quite useful to him--the less amicable that he was, the nicer Mona became. James could mentally document the transition. He even feigned anger coming through the door one night when he was in a great mood. She fell over herself practically trying to cheer him up. Now even if James sensed the slightest discontent coming from Mona he would preempt any trouble by immediately surpassing her darkness with a nasty, dissonant chord of his own. He might even lose his temper so completely (sometimes this was legitimate and sometimes a charade) that he would put his fist through the screen door to which Mona would have a reaction first of disbelief and then acquiescence, but instead of a long drawn-out drama lasting the entire evening, there would be at minimum peace, and sometimes true friendship and pleasure.

So this was one evening when Mona was doing her best not to agitate James, and possibly even change his disposition. She tried to make him laugh and she brought him first a beer and then later a T.V. dinner. James took solace in his new found power so even when he was no longer caring about his bad day and he felt comfortable sitting on his couch, feet propped up on the coffee table, drinking another beer, he didn't let Mona think that he had come around too quickly. Soon enough though he was telling her about his day and things that had seemed like a disaster earlier in the day now seemed to be humorous and the two laughed on and off together through most of the evening into the night.

James told Mona about the different sales people, from young guys who were only concerned about finding a date that night to old men who were forced to try sales because they had been laid off by GM or Ford or some other industry giant. Mona particularly like the stories about a guy named Vincent who always wore suits that were too small for him. Now Letterman was on and they watched the T.V. and only continued their conversations through commercials.

The front door to the trailer was usually kept open until one or both of them went to bed, so when someone knocked at their door that person would knock on their screen door which made a sound of rattling metal. However the raps that hit the door this time not only rattled the screen door but seemed to shake the whole trailer. Both Mona and James were startled enough to jump off the couch, and they became no less alarmed when they saw Hank's expression when he leaped through the door. His eyes were sunken surrounded with dark circles and his face was pale and his hair was matted against his forehead with sweat. "Jesus Hank," Mona whispered though she meant to say it louder.

"Somebody's after me." Hank said, not blinking, alternating his gaze back and forth between Mona and James.

"What?" cried Mona.

"Somebody's after me. Just like last time."

"Hank, what are you talking about," said James, finally becoming more relaxed after the abrupt intrusion.

"You don't understand what I'm saying? Somebody is after me."

"Who?" James and Mona asked simultaneously.

"The FBI."

"The FBI." Mona said incredulously. "How do you know?"

"I know. I recognized one of them. They've been driving around here all day."

"How do you know they're after you?" Mona now took a prosecutorial tone.

"Who else would they be after? It's the same guy who came

after me before."

"You're paranoid." Mona said, sitting back down.

"Don't call me paranoid, man. Don't ever call me paranoid." Though only Mona had said it, Hank pointed his finger back and forth between both of them. "I know the dude. He's older now but his face is seared in my memory."

"Hank," James said, lowering his tone coming closer to Hank, "is it the pot they're after?"

"I don't know. If it is, I just got rid of it. I just came back from the woods. After what I did for this country if they're going to harass me about the grass..." Hank stopped, not quite knowing how to finish his sentence.

"Maybe it's the guns," Mona said looking at Hank as if she were revealing secrets to James about them.

"You have guns?" James asked in a manner that also implied a question to Mona, "how do you know that he has guns and I didn't, when I've known him for years and you only months?" All three of them grasped the implication.

"Yes, and I'm not giving them up. You're going to see a hold-out that you haven't seen since the Wild West if they come after them." Hank had used a similar expression to Mona before about the IRS. He had told her that he had paid no taxes since he had returned from Vietnam. When he returned from Vietnam he did home improvement side jobs, drywall mostly, and when a general contractor asked him if he was paying his own taxes, Hank said no. The general contractor told Hank that was something that he might want to think about. And Hank did. He thought about it that night and he became angrier until he vowed that he wouldn't pay taxes. He had paid this country enough. People who didn't go, and he knew quite a few of them his age, *they* could pay the taxes. He had paid his debt. And though he had gotten a letter or two from the IRS over the years he had ignored them. He told Mona that if they

191

ever came after his trailer or the very few possessions that he had that there was going to be a fight, and that was when he used his "wild west" analogy the first time.

"The bottom line," said Hank, lighting a cigarette, "is that those sons a bitches are going to have to drag me in that car dead as the day is long this time." Hank went over to the window and pulled the curtain aside. James did the same and saw nothing down the alleyway but darkness. "I'm taking off for a few days. I have a tent, a bag--I'm going off into the woods."

"Where in the woods?" Mona asked a bit contemptuously.

"You know enough already. I wouldn't put you in a position to know more. Don't worry about me. I'll be in touch once I have time to figure this all out." Without saying anything else Hank opened the door and surveyed the area and deciding that it was clear he disappeared.

"He's lost his mind," Mona said, once she was sure that Hank had left.

"My God, I know. I feel bad for him. I wonder what we can do. Too many drugs or something. If he doesn't come back from his little wilderness excursion in a day or two maybe we'll try to get him some help. He goes like this once in a while you know. Just takes off into the woods but he always comes back. I've never seen him this paranoid before." James knew the story of how Hank was captured when he dodged the draft, and as far as he knew, Hank had told no one else, so he felt that he would be betraying his trust right now if he went into it with Mona. James had no doubt that the long black car and the man in the sunglasses was some sort of flashback that Hank was having. James knew that Hank had suffered from post delayed stress syndrome after returning home but as far as he knew he had come to terms with his ordeal and he no longer suffered from the affliction. It was obvious to James that something had snapped and Hank was once again suffering from a mental ailment relating to his experience. Somehow, James concluded, Hank was reliving that traumatic experience and if he wasn't reliving the whole experience, some part was haunting him in some way that James couldn't figure out. James once again debated with himself whether or not he should tell Mona that Hank was hiding from the past, threats that ended over twenty years ago. It wouldn't totally surprise James if Hank eventually landed in jail for drugs or guns, and he would have been more inclined to believe that Hank was threatened had Hank not invoked anyone who had been part of his original capture on his father's farm. "I think he is reliving something from his past," James said to Mona, without going into any more detail. He went over to a drawer and pulled out an envelope and handed it to her, and to avoid any further inquiry he shut off the T.V., said he was beat and headed toward his room. Mona looked at the envelope and read the outside first: *The spawn of disorder, I inhabit the ironic realm between an ideally coherent hierarchy and the factual chaos of degeneration away from order. With such chaos, however, I can, being by social definition nothing, be anything my life permits.* Mona opened up the envelope and read a short note that was folded inside: *James, this book is a gem, and I give it to you. I would re-read excerpts while having lived through symptoms of post-delayed-stress syndrome for about five years.*

Mona went back and knocked on the bedroom door. "When did he give you this note?" Mona asked through the door.

"I dunno, bout a year ago."

"Well what book is it from?"

"I don't know."

"What do you mean you don't know?"

"I don't know Mona, I don't remember. He's tried to give me so many books over the years." James was not trying to hide the growing agitation in his voice.

"Do you still have it?"

"I lost it."

"You lost it?"

"Listen," James said opening the door, "I don't have the god-damn book, Mona, and I don't know what it is or was or whatever. I kept the envelope O.K.? I wish I wouldn't have even showed it to you, I'm beat, OK."

Several days passed and James and Mona had seen no sign of Hank. They began their day going over to his trailer and knocking first, and then using a key that James had to check in Hank's room. Since they once again found the room empty, they returned to the topic of the police, a missing person's report perhaps. They decided to give it another day or two; Hank had a general phobia about the police or any other authority figure for that matter. He would be furious if Mona and James contacted the police. But what if he was hurt or in trouble? What if he was having psychotic episodes and he ended up hurting himself or someone else? All of these questions were thoroughly debated before the decision was made to do nothing at this point.

Saturdays were quiet for the most part. The day would start with a match of tennis in the morning usually followed by an early lunch. Today James had volunteered to help the town committee prepare for an annual craft fair, so Mona planned on reading all afternoon. The tennis match was heated but once again Mona had too much technique for James to overcome. The two now sat at the table eating sandwiches, only occasionally breaking the silence with a benign comment.

James could tell something was wrong by Mona's facial expression before she was able to let out a gasp. The blood drained from her face as she pointed toward the window. James turned slowly to follow the direction of her pointing finger which led out the window and across the street to two men sitting in a long black car. The driver was wearing sunglasses, just as Hank had described him.

194

"They are after him," was all Mona could get out.

"We have to get to him to tell him," James added.

"We'll never find him. There are too many woods. We could search for days and not find him. They must know that we are his friends if he has been on surveillance. I know they'll question us." Mona at this point had moved to the living area and peeked through the curtains.

"Exactly why Hank refused to tell us where he'd be..." James said, joining her.

They sat on the couch watching the car. They watched people of the community going about their daily activities. A few couples sat out on their patios and others carried groceries in from their cars. Gus walked by carrying his hedge clippers wearing a pair of gardening gloves, apparently returning from assisting someone with their landscaping.

"Look," James said. They're getting out of their car. "I think they are going to question Gus."

"He doesn't know anything. He doesn't even know Hank smokes pot."

"Can't he smell?" James asked, finding Mona's comment hard to believe. "I don't understand..."

Mona leaped off the couch. James tried to stop her but she smacked his hand away, so he followed her out into the yard and chased her across the lawn. She ran up to the man in the sunglasses and demanded to know what he was doing. The man ignored her and kept walking with Gus handcuffed and shackled toward the car. The other man opened the door and put his hand on top of Gus' head and pushed him down into the seat. Gus just kept repeating to Mona "Don't worry, don't worry. It's all O.K."

Mona and James watched the black car as it drove down the road and disappeared.

James forgot his charade that he had been playing out and tended to an extremely emotional Mona. She couldn't stop crying no matter how much James tried to soothe her fears about Gus. He did his best to assure her that this was some kind of horrible mistake and that Gus would be returned to the neighborhood soon. They made a few calls to people in the town who may know what was going on with the situation but found no information. In fact, it was James and Mona who carried the news of the apparent apprehension to many local people and by the time that James and Mona walked up town the next day, everyone was talking about the recent development with Gus.

The prevailing thought was simply that there had been some mistake made. The elderly sister was approached but had no real information and what she did say was hard to interpret because what little English she had mastered was covered with such a thick German accent. Mona and James stepped into the local five and dime, and over Mona's indignant protest, James bought a watch with a profile of the young Elvis and the later Elvis facing each other. The watch played "Love Me Tender" on the hour but stopped working completely only a few weeks after the purchase. James bought a blanket for Mona, one of the few items that she saw that appealed to her, because she was always cold. They ate lunch and then had ice cream and walked once more through the town.

As they walked toward the gazebo located in the center of town they noticed that a large crowd had assembled. A loud voice rang out from the railing of the gazebo and before they were even close enough to make out who it was from sight they knew from the sound of his voice who exactly it was. They didn't take off running but they both instinctively started to walk at a brisk pace. Neither of them spoke confirming what the other one already knew.

"I've never been an overly religious man as many of you can attest to," cried Hank, speaking out over the edge of the gazebo, looking into the middle of the crowd. "But I have spent three days in the wilderness and I have seen a sight that has transformed me. I am no longer who I was before I made my journey. In my solitude I came across a woman who had crashed her car. She was not hurt badly but she was shook to the very root of her bones. Not because of the crash but because what she had witnessed. When I emerged from the wood the sun was going down and it would soon be dark. I asked the lady if she was O.K. Her pants were ripped at the knee, which was badly scraped and bleeding. She said that she needed my help, not because of her injury but because of what she had seen. She wanted to make sure that she wasn't losing her mind. She asked me to follow her and I agreed. We started to make our way back the way that she had come. She took my arm and I supported her and then we walked back perhaps half an hour. We came to a great grain silo and she asked me to look at it and I did but I saw nothing. The moon was visible but only slightly as the clouds that passed by overhead obscured it every few seconds. She asked me if I could maybe drive her car from the ditch in which she had crashed. She was adamant that somehow I had to see the side of the silo so I put her car in reverse and then forward and repeated it until I had the car grunting, rocking back and forth, until it gained traction on the side of the road and finally loosed from the earth. I swung the car around. I put on the high beams and froze. I froze because what I saw before me I still can't believe. As clear as day, Jesus Christ with His arms spread out. He was calling for me. I know it sounds crazy and for those of you who know me, which are few but I see a couple in this crowd right now who know that I have been anything if not contemptuous of your religion. I have been rocked to my core. The lady and I walked out in front of the headlights and looked up and fell to our knees hands clasped. As I look out among you I see many of you who have wronged me. I was once a high school football star. Twenty years ago I would walk up town after a successful Friday night and men used to come out of the barbershop holding the newspaper with my picture and statistics to shake my hand. These same men, and some of them are right here today, just a few years later crossed the street to avoid me when I came back from the war. Now mind you, I fought like they did but only I wasn't at the right place at the right time for the right cause. I was a victim of my time. This is a story that is not only mine but is pervasive over small town America. But Mr. Smith, Mr. Simmons, Mr. McGerry....I see you there. You know exactly what I am talking about. But today is a day that you will carry your shame no more. I forgive you. Let me say it again. I forgive you."

Hank continued to enumerate the wrongs against him while some of the crowd booed and some of the crowd applauded with caution. There were different comments made among the people gathered there declaring or reaffirming that Hank was not quite right in the head. Rival church members plotted how they could induce what seemed to be a newly converted member of Christ to their church. Through most of the sermon, Mona and James remained quiet, only exchanging a few thoughts about the situation. Now that he was back unharmed, they only had one friend to worry about.

Hank finished his diatribe and the crowd dispersed and Hank walked down the Gazebo steps to see his friends. He recoiled briefly because of a deputy Sheriff who approached Mona and James. James reached his hand out to shake the hand of his cousin who was a few years older whom James had called when Gus was taken away. At that time his cousin, Nathaniel, had known nothing. Nathaniel was a bit distracted by Hank because of how nervous Hank was acting. After nodding to Mona, Nathaniel nodded to Hank. This is all Hank needed to put his paranoia aside and move closer to the conversation.

"Hey James, I have information about your friend that you were asking about, Mr. Schultz."

"O.K." James moved closer to Mona and took hold of her hand for the first time in weeks.

"Apparently, your friend may have some knowledge of a Nazi who may have been a prison guard or something. He was a guard at some camp and he has been charged with war crimes."

"That can't be possible," Mona said looking at James for reassurance.

"That's all I know," Nathaniel concluded with a general nod to all three before he moved past them.

"There must be some kind of mistake, right? I mean he probably knew a lot of people back in Germany who were in the army or a member of the Nazi party. That doesn't mean he did anything horrible," Mona said as tears started to stream down her cheeks. No one answered immediately as they tried to let this information sink in.

"Well," said Hank, "I always thought his good works were compensatory. I wish, for your sake, Mona, that I was more surprised but I'm not."

CHAPTER 18

Jason,

I hardly know where to start. You are not half the human being that your father was. It defies explanation that you came from a father who was one of the most remarkable men that I have ever known and a mother who is one of the most wonderful, compassionate woman on this earth. You tarnish their legacy. You disgrace your father's memory by your ignoble ignorance and your stupid third-rate-writing instructor cliché. "Show don't tell." Where did you pick that one up? A writing class taught by someone who had a couple of stories published in a review from a small college in South Dakota! Thank God Homer, Cervantes, Dostoevsky, Proust, Marquez, Roth and most of the other great writers did not change their work to heed such run-of-the-mill advice. What irks me most, Junior is that you probably don't even understand what that often misunderstood cliché' means. In fact, when I look at the markings of your pen, I know that you have absolutely no idea. I really think that you don't know what the hell you are doing so you probably write that on every manuscript so that you can cover for your ignorance and inability. You do, don't you? You're sitting there now knowing that you have been called out. Can't think of the last manuscript that you haven't with much false bravado written in large letters with red ink "show don't tell." I would think it dangerous for you to be in that position (no wonder nepotism is despised) if it were not for the fact that I am certain that any writer will look at your comments and dismiss them as sophomoric drivel.

I won't be making any of the changes that you "urge" me to make. In the old days, I would make the changes that your father suggested and then compare them to what I had and then decide whether or not I would make the change permanent, and I so often went with the suggestion of your father that in time I just made the changes that he suggested automatically, knowing that the work of art would now be more effectual, beautiful, and pertinent.

I'm back now and I shall no longer beat around the proverbial shrub. I've polished off two bottles of wine and I am damn well ready to tell you how it is. The only reason I have rode this train this far is because of who your parents were. Sound familiar? It should because it's the only reason you have this job. You disgust me. Put pressure on me? Correct me with your Ivy League clichéd bullshit! This is the last that you will hear from me. You will not get any more pages. I would rather use these pages to light a fire than to send them to you to let you butcher away. You want to know why this has been slower than I expected. Cancer. Terminal cancer. Most days I'm too nauseated and sick to even think about working. I may get a paragraph out a day here and a day there but it's a struggle. A struggle to make it through day to day let alone try to concentrate on anything productive and you give me some lame advice like "show don't tell." You have lost the opportunity to ever see any-thing I write again by your ignorant and degrading remarks. I don't mind constructive criticisms but I'm way too old for a schoolboy cliché. You don't have a clue do you?

Oh, yes, and as far as being consistent with Henry or Hank I like both. That is why I am leaving the inconsistency. Once I decide I just go back and make the changes. If I couldn't decide in the past I would just leave it as is and let your father decide and he would make the changes.

In memory of your dear father I am terminating this relationship. I know none of what I am working on will see publication but I really don't care. I have no doubt the end is near. I will attempt to finish. Give it to my cousin's daughter perhaps but I will make sure it never ends up in the hands of a third-rate hack like you. I should probably sober up before I send this but I won't, because if I did, I may not send it. And I want so badly for you to receive it at this moment.

Adieu,
E. Palamountian.

CHAPTER 19

Please ignore the letter I sent yesterday.
E. Palamountain
P.S. I'm experimenting with using plural forms for the narrator. While technically is shifts to first person(s) it retains a third person narrator feel. Trying to get my ahead around why that is so? Not sure if I'll keep it or not.

CHAPTER 20

Perry had been absorbed in numerous school projects and many of these projects made it necessary that he spend many hours in the library researching everything from Shakespeare to homo hublis to finding examples of Venn Diagrams. He hadn't seen Graham at all and, for the most part, he realized that this was probably the very reason why he had been so productive during the previous weeks, and with finals approaching, Graham's sparse appearances couldn't have been more timely. He had asked a few people around of his whereabouts and received vague information at best, and, unfortunately, we can add few facts other than he had found a new watering hole that held some sort of attraction for him. This attraction would, he would find out, be potentially dangerous for his well-being. In short, Graham had fallen in love, and though hard to tell precisely, this may be the first time Graham had fallen in love with someone other than a dead movie star.

So it was quite by chance that Perry ran into Graham in a small place called The Beer Barrel in north campus. Perry and Graham and most everyone else they knew rarely ever ventured up from south campus. For one, there was no bar where one could launder one's clothes and order pitchers of beer at the same time. Secondly, most of the live music, at least what they considered cutting-edge music, was performed at the south end of campus. Next among the reasons for the south end affinity was that the north end was cost prohibitive. There was no place where a group, fresh from selling their plasma, could all chip in a dollar and buy a bucket of beer, enough to last several hours. By the time the beer was three quarters empty, a person may have to tip the five-gallon bucket on its side to scoop a plastic cup full, and by that time, the beer was usually warm and stale but it was paid for.

Let us note parenthetically that Perry had learned his north end bias from Graham, who would rail against the increased prices, lack of bucket nights, lack of one-dollar Long Island iced tea specials, and, what galled Graham about the north end more than any of these reasons, it was where the fraternities and sororities gathered. He never articulated to Perry what exactly his problem with Greek life was, but he would sneer and grunt in disgust any time that the subject was brought up. Perry assumed, with very little support for such an idea, that Graham must have been either blackballed or beaten up by similar types in his younger years, or, perhaps, it was nothing more than class envy.

Graham was in high spirits, sitting at the end of the bar, listening to the jukebox, and having an in-depth conversation with the girl behind the bar. He was aloof when he first noticed Perry, more caught off guard, Perry would learn through conversation later, than indifferent. Perry had stopped in on an impulse with a few people with whom he was completing a group project. Perry sat with the group and discussed the project which consisted of an upcoming debate for Poly Sci. The students were instructed to debate the American involvement against the Nicaraguan rebels. The professor had instructed them to argue, vigorously, the opposite side of what they really believed. Perry was with the group then that was arguing for American intervention.

The group wrapped up their final point and began to grab their book bags when Graham approached Perry and shook his hand. Perry introduced a few of his fellow classmates, and upon Graham's invitation, decided to stay for another beer. Graham of course asked him about his new friends and if perhaps he was thinking of going Greek. Perry assured him that he was there only for school purposes and this brought a nod of approval from Graham. Graham proceeded to tell Perry exactly what he had been up to the last few weeks. For starters, Graham said, he had taken a new management position at the Italian restaurant where he had worked for the last year. More important, though, is that he had met her, and when he said "her" he pointed to the server behind the bar. He told Perry that she was "incredibly cool" and that she knew more about music than anyone that he had ever met. Looking around he lowered his voice to tell Perry that there was however one small hitch in the whole scenario.

"She's married!" Perry said with an incredulous smirk.

"Shush," Graham said looking around, not wanting the girl to overhear the conversation. "Yes, she's married. But so was Elizabeth Taylor when she met Burt Lancaster."

"Are you dating her? You know, having an affair with her?"

"Not yet, but believe me, it's not for lack of trying. Give me time, my boy, give me time."

"What about her marriage? Isn't it going well?"

"Quite the contrary. She's mad about her husband. In fact, I don't know if I have ever met someone who is any more happily married." Perry looked at Graham suspiciously. Graham didn't seem to be fazed until he noticed Perry's odd expression. "I wouldn't want it any other way. More of a quest you see. Would the Holy Grail have been worth searching for if was merely under the couch like some T.V. remote? And, check this out, not only is she crazy in love with her husband. She says that he is huge and that he can lift a car. The plot thickens my friend. The plot thickens indeed."

"Are you suicidal?" Perry said as Graham grabbed him by the arm and took him toward the bar.

"No, I am full of life. I have to have her," Graham said and then he said in a whisper, putting his hand up to Perry's ear, "at least once. I would like to have her for life but if that is not possible then I'd settle for just one night. One long, sweet night. I don't have a choice not to try at this point. I'm defenseless against fate, and since I am defenseless I may as well embrace it. *Amori Fati*, my young scholarly friend, *amori fati*, After all, one doesn't choose these situations these situations choose us."

"I don't buy it. I'm much more of a believer in free will."

"Ah, there's the rub. Free will isn't free at all…you pay and pay and pay for that will. Shh, enough rhetoric Horatio, the flower of my existence approaches."

"Aleisha, Perry, Perry, Aleisha." Graham grinned and with his hand pointed between the two repeatedly extending the introduction nonverbally.

"It's nice to meet you Perry," Aleisha said, extending her hand, "You're friend Graham here has told me about you. You know, you're friend Graham here is nuts."

"You don't have to tell me. I knew that five minutes after I met him." Graham took this as a compliment.

"Isn't she beautiful?" Graham said and although the question was addressed to Perry, Graham did not take his eyes off Aleisha.

"Will you stop already," Aleisha said as she threw a wadded dishrag at Graham.

"I try but I can't."

Although Perry had planned a night of studying followed by an early bedtime, as often happened when he was with Graham, he found himself hours later still sitting at the bar. The two had become intoxicated and they had even talked Aleisha into doing a few shots with them, something that she rarely ever did. Let us add also that once the liquor began to flow, whatever inhibitions that Graham retained, which were sparse at best, gradually began to loosen to the point until he regularly declared his love for Aleisha.

"Is it love or lust?" Aleisha quizzed him playfully, giving Perry a look of amusement.

"It's both. It's luvst," Graham said with a mild slur. "I am not a poet nor do I pretend to be but let me try to give you a sense of my luvst for you dear Madame." He prepared to tell his story and began to gesture more to make his point. Aleisha and Perry became his audience.

"Perhaps a few 'if I were' tales will show you just how ravenous this luvst is. If I were a king and I saw you bathing from afar, ah, the thought sends chills through my body, then I would send your soldier husband to the front line of a battle to get rid of him, and when he was gone I would claim you for myself.

"If I had a magician, I would use his powers when your husband was away and have him transform me into the physical likeness of your husband. And when I came in, you would welcome me into your bed.

"Let's see, if you were visiting me and denied yourself to me, then I would put a condition that I would leave you alone, and that would be that you could not drink water out of a designated glass, and I would put that glass between us as we slept. Unbeknownst to you, however, I would have instructed my cook to fix you the spiciest, saltiest dinner that he could create. Then, at night, I would lay and feign sleep, and wait for the thirst to overcome you so completely that you would be unable to resist the cool, clear water that was placed in the glass. You would be so incredibly thirsty that not to put your sweet lips to the glass of cool water would be to risk insanity. With one eye open I would catch you in the act, and according to the agreement I would enter your bed to claim what was owed to me."

At this point Graham took Aleisha's hand and kissed it.

"You are some flatterer," she said, with a slight blush spreading across her face.

"Can you believe this woman?" Graham said turning to Perry. Perry nodded feeling a bit uncomfortable to acknowledge that he agreed with the compliment.

The night turned into early morning and the drinking didn't slow down and Perry knew that the turn of events did not bode well for making his early class in the morning. After he listened to several songs that he had played on the jukebox, he excused himself and headed toward the bathroom. He steadied himself against the wall as he leaned over the urinal resting his head on the wall. He gazed at the graffiti on the walls trying to concentrate on the letters, expanding and receding, until he closed one eye, focusing on one letter at a time. Within the myriad of numbers and the names of rock bands, he focused on a small neatly written paragraph. He slowly read, his feet unstable, with a feeling the room was starting to close in around him. *And we are here as on a darkling plain,* he whispered, struggling to read the blurred words, *Swept with confused alarms of struggle and flight, Where ignorant armies clash by night.* Let us intervene just long enough to say that Perry had every intention of going back into the bathroom with a pencil and a bar napkin and writing down the poem, but when he came back out of the bathroom he saw Graham, asleep, his head on top of his arms, his arms folded on top of the bar. With this distraction he didn't make it back to copy down the poem and forgot about it for several weeks, and when he remembered it, he only remembered that there was a poem that he wanted to copy from the bathroom wall, but his memory was so impaired he couldn't remember anything about the poem. When he came across the poem over a year later in a class on the Victorians, he read through the poem for what he thought, at least, was the first time, with, for the most part, absolutely no recognition, until, that is, he came to the last three lines, and at that point, he froze until he read it again and then again and then a fourth time. *"Déjà vu"*, he said to himself. A fellow student saw the consternation on his face and asked him if everything was O.K. It took Perry a moment to collect himself but then he assured the girl that he was fine. Just a case of *Déjà vu* he told her. She told him that she experienced that occasionally and that it was weird. From that point on Perry looked at the poem often, trying to figure out why he had such an emotional connection with it. Graham was later to hypothesize that perhaps he was Matthew Arnold in a past life. Or, better yet, "perhaps you are the reincarnation of Arnold's murderer, which would explain the mystery of not only your mystical attraction to the poem but also Arnold's death. In fact," Graham went on, "if you were the murderer of Arnold, that would change what we know about history, because as to this point, nobody has the faintest clue that he was murdered, or, for that matter if he was at all."

"Do you live close to Graham?" Aleisha asked Perry as Perry tried to lift his drunken friend up from the chair as the lights came on.

"A few blocks."

"Just let me sweep and do a little clean up and I'll give you both a ride home." This came as a relief to Perry who had envisioned holding up his stumbling friend for several blocks. They laid Graham down in the back seat of the blue Chevelle as he muttered a few words to assure them that he was O.K. and more than capable to handle the situation himself. And then he proceeded to put his head against the back rest until it slid down the back to the bottom of the seat. "That can't be comfortable," Aleisha said, adjusting her rear view mirror, pausing to view Graham's crumbled body before moving the mirror so that she could view objects out of her back window.

"Ah, he's used to it." Perry replied, looking back to check on Graham. Aleisha turned on the radio after she pulled out onto the road. After listening to an insurance commercial she popped in a cassette tape and lit a cigarette, which she held a few inches out the window as a polite, though futile, gesture to respect Perry's non-smoking preference.

"What are we listening to?" Perry asked, unsure of what to think.

"Kitty Wells, you heard of her?"

"No. Do you know country music?"

"Well, I love it. It's an acquired taste for most, I guess, unless you're raised around it. I can tell you are not a big fan."

"It's alright. Not my favorite. We did see a guy singing a while back in that style who was very good though."

"Where?"

"At the Chicken Palace."

"Big guy?" Aliesha asked after she drew on the end of her cigarette.

"Huge. Absolutely huge."

"Uh-huh. Well, that's my husband."

"No way!"

"Yep, sure is."

"Holy shit. Does Graham know that?"

"Nope. He knows that I'm married and happily. Very happily. So, was Graham there when you saw him sing?"

"Yep."

"What did he think?"

"Oh my God, he loved it. It made his night." Aleisha nodded with a smile that couldn't contain the pride that she felt about her husband. "I think if he knew that that big guy was your husband then he may lay off."

"Oh, I figure they will meet soon enough. I always like to see the reaction of guys who hit on me when they meet Conway."

"I bet. He's a really good singer."

"I know. He used to be better. Much better. He used not to have the rasp. He was in an accident of sorts though. Many think that he is better now than he was before. I can't agree. I would never tell him that though."

"That's too bad," Perry said, taking a look back at Graham to make sure he was still breathing.

"Yeah, but he'll be fine. Who else was there?"

"At the Chicken Palace?"

"Yeah."

"Well, Ness was there."

"I've heard about Ness too. I haven't met him yet though. How did he like it?" she asked after a short pause, obviously fishing for more compliments.

"Oh, he loved it too. Those guys are into so many types of music, something new every day, it seems. What else does he do?" Perry continued.

"Right now, he's a bouncer."

"Where?"

"At the Coffee Tower."

"Coffee Tower, isn't that just a coffee shop, no booze?"

"Yep," Aliesha said as she flicked the remainder of her cigarette out the window and watched it spark and skip along the road through the rear view mirror.

"I've never been there but Graham hates it. Why would a coffee shop need a bouncer?"

"You know, I'm not really sure but I know that it is the highest paying bouncer job that I've ever heard of."

"Huh, strange," Perry replied trying to solve the mystery.

Perry continued to shake his head thinking about the trouble that Graham could be getting into.

"You know," started Aliesha, trying to fill the silence, "Graham is trying to talk me into driving to that silo. I guess your bunch don't know too many people with wheels."

"No, not really. He is gung-ho about making that trip."

"I might go. I've been talking to my husband about it. You guys chip in for some gas?"

"Oh, yeah, definitely," Perry answered while shaking his head in the affirmative.

"Take your next right and pull in the first drive. I'll take Graham in and let him crash at my place." Perry sat forward in his seat while he gave directions.

"Do me a favor," Aliesha said pulling another cigarette from her pack. "Don't tell Graham who my husband is. I really want to see his expression and I want to introduce them."

"No problem. I won't say a word," Perry said as he put Graham's arm around his shoulder, turning to walk toward his apartment door.

"Thanks, I appreciate that. Hey, do you know you're a man of few words?"

"I've been told that."

"Probably makes people think what's going on in that brain of yours that you keep to yourself."

"Thanks for the ride."

CHAPTER 21

"You gotta be friggin kiddin me!"

"Nope that's him."

"No way. I can't believe it. That's him. No way. She has to be pullin your leg. She's taking you for a ride man."

"I don't think so. I really don't. If you could have seen her I think you'd know what I mean."

"Son of a bitch," Graham said falling back into his chair. "She's married to that big ugly bastard."

"Yep."

"Son of a bitch." Between moments of silence when he would look up to the ceiling shaking his head he repeated, "son of a bitch."

"You've got no chance. First of all, she's big time in love with her husband," Perry said, doing his best to build a case for total abandonment, "and second, even if you do have a chance, which you don't, stay away because this guy will destroy you."

"He is big, isn't he?" Graham looked at Perry for reassurance.

"Huge."

"And ugly."

"Hideous."

"Ah, shit. See, this is what I hate about women. We could walk down the street today and find numerous examples of this exact same thing. If I show you a beautiful woman with a guy that looks like Lurch from the Addams family, I guarantee that 99 times out of a hundred he either plays guitar or can sing or something. Pisses me off."

"He can definitely sing."

"Yeah, and he's big." Graham repeated, though now he was nodding in the affirmative instead of shaking his head side to side.

"Huge." Awkward silence.

"I like it."

"Like what?"

"I'm starting to like it. He's talented and big but that just reinforces the fact that I have to have her at any price."

"Graham, you don't understand. She's crazy about her husband."

"Maybe so, maybe so. But women love attention and if you give them enough they become addicted to it. You know, love is a drug sort of thing."

"He'd mess you up."

"Ah, it would be a small price to pay. Every last fist to my face I'd accept gladly."

"You're crazy."

"Maybe. I'm going back tonight. I'm really starting to like this. Now, it's more than a challenge. It's a Homeric quest. I, Odysseus, he Polyphemus. He has the brawn but I have the wits. Wits win every time if the history of Western Literature is accurate. First thing is first. We must go back to The Chicken Palace. I have to see this guy again."

"Why? You could just go to The Coffee Tower."

"What da ya mean?" Protective, defensive.

"He's a bouncer there."

"The plot thickens," Graham said after he gave himself a short time to let this new information make sense to him. "C'mon, we're going there. I want some coffee anyway.

215

The two friends walked toward the coffee shop down Lane Avenue. They passed an assortment of bars, record shops, used book stores, and a variety of second-hand clothing shops which featured everything from retro apparel to inexpensive exotic jewelry to several dozen different fragrances of patchouli oil. The coffee shop, which was actually named The Coffee Tower, was sardonically referred to by Graham as The Ivory Tower. He mostly steered clear of the place, only occasionally stopping in when he needed a caffeine fix. Graham's visceral dislike of The Coffee Tower stemmed from a private room that was reserved for only certain people. Graham felt that he had every right to enter that room and resented its exclusion based on what he believed were basically illusory credentials. The two men stopped in front and listened to a guitar player sitting outside of The Coffee Tower. The guitarist was in the middle of a Neil Young medley when Graham sat down beside him and started to sing along. The guitarist, Luke, could be found around campus most of the time, playing his guitar, case opened, trying to eke out a living, which he could never quite do.

Though only a few years older than Graham, Luke looked like he was fifty. He had long hair and beard and his face was marked with deep lines and pockmarks. Luke had been around campus, off and on, for twenty-three years. He first arrived in the fall of '66 as a clean-shaven studious freshman from a conservative family, whose father and grandfather had been mayor of Bellefontaine. During orientation, the college president told the new students to look to the persons on both sides of themselves. He told them that on graduation day one of the three would no longer be there. There may not have been a worse time in history for Luke to be the one who didn't make it. Everyone who knew Luke in high school would have bet the house that he wouldn't have been the one, but Luke had always been controlled at home from his chores to his school work by strict parents who gave him little space to develop any type of independence. Luke was obedient, either out of the need for parental approval or from fear or both. At first autonomy felt strange to Luke, like he was visiting a country with a completely different cultural environment, where he had to readapt to all of the new rituals. Once he started to evolve in his new environment, he started to change at an exponential rate. His studies became secondary to the college nightlife. He spent Wednesday through Sunday going to bars and parties, jazz clubs, dances, and trying to keep up with his work by studying on Monday and Tuesday nights. Deep into the semester he would only make it to his morning classes once or twice a week. At the end of the semester he was put on probation, and by the next semester, he was out. By the following he was drafted into The United States Army and the party was over.

After Luke returned from Vietnam, he made an effort to return to campus and started to attend courses again but now he felt that everything was meaningless. He had no desire to attend classes with kids who, though only a few years younger than himself, knew nothing about life, nothing about how horrific people could be. So, he made his second exit from college, this time it was his own choice. He had learned how to play an acoustic guitar in Vietnam so he started playing it around town along with other odds and ends jobs, and this is when Graham met Luke--Graham was a freshmen.

"Here," Graham said to Perry, handing him a pocket full of change, "I'll take a cup of Kleindeutshe dark roast. Get what you want. I'm going to take a look around." Graham looked around like a private investigator, examining people and objects with a detached scrutiny. With all the subtlety that he could produce, he turned around and looked toward the room, and just as he had been told Conway Jones Jr. was posted outside of it, keeping guard. Conway was perched upon a stool with his arms folded, alert enough to be doing his job but he seemed lost in thought all the same. Conway looked up and met Graham's gaze but it was too late for Graham to look down or away so Graham nodded to the giant and the giant nodded back and then looked back down. Graham pretended to study the various art that hung along the wall-- art mostly created by gifted students. As Graham passed from one painting to another he focused all of his attention on the room and listened but could hear nothing. He finally found himself standing in front of Conway Jones Jr., and since Conway was sitting, they were almost eye-to-eye.

"You got credentials?" Conway asked.

"Not on me," Graham said, with as much confidence as he could muster.

"Sorry, I can't let you in."

"No, I know that you can't." Graham said as he tilted his head to see the men inside sitting around a table, he marked that Uriah the Historian sat at the head of the table, he seemed to be in an intense conversation. "Can I just put my ear up to the door?" Graham said in his most polite tone.

"I guess. Just for a second," Conway answered as he moved his massive body to the side.

Graham closed his eyes and put his ear between the two French doors, and though he wasn't sure he could make out every word he could hear Uriah's croaking, aged voice: *I am not a political scientist, so I hesitate even to surmise about any contemporary issue, but since you asked, I will certainly try to bring a historical perspective if you will forgive me in advance for the inherent deficiencies of the historians. We have heard this morning from exalted professors of sociology and political science, and while I won't dare venture outside of my own expertise into theirs, I will elaborate from an historical perspective. I am a believer that history does indeed repeat so if any of you would happen to see any parallels then so be it. I will caution any of you to see history as metaphor, because we historians only try to interpret the past; Once again, it is not* our job to use the past to interpret the present. Now, others can very well take our interpretation of the past and apply it to the present and for that matter even the future.

In the Congress of Vienna, led by Prince Metternich after the defeat of Napoleon, one can see the beginning of modernist reactionary politics. Metternich's conservative ideology was a reaction to the excesses of liberalism. Remember, liberalism is no longer liberalism once historical excess has been introduced. Once egalitarianism eclipsed the importance of liberalism in the French Revolution, the revolution had entered the realm of excess: The ghost of Rousseau had out-dueled the ghost of Voltaire and then released the Reign of Terror, with Robespierre and the radical Jacobins as its agent. So the reaction to that will be extreme and then open the door to a reaction that will place in power the original status quo, and usually that status quo will be immensely more empowered than it was originally. See it is the great historical paradox of revolution that goes to excess, and one can test it as one can test the boiling temperature of water at a given pressure, it is that stable. The revolution that goes to excess invariably leads to the exact opposite of its aims; it restores the status quo. Not only does the revolution restore the status quo, the power structure, in our example the crowned heads of Europe, but the restoration gives the regime more power, more stability, than it had before the revolution.

"So are you saying that this is the parallel to Thomas' puzzle about Reagan and the '60s?" A voice came from the other end of the table.

"I'm not saying that at all. You said that, not me. I'm a historian and it is not my job to say that," replied Uriah.

"Are you implying that?"

"A historian doesn't imply."

"Graham, Graham, here is your coffee," Perry said nudging his shoulder from behind.

"Thanks," Graham said to Perry as he nodded to Conway in appreciation. They sat at a table on the opposite side of the room. Through the window they could hear Luke playing his guitar and singing. They split the newspaper and began reading, but only after a few seconds Graham said, "I just can't believe it."

"What's that?" Perry replied.

"I can't believe such an angel is with that Frankenmonster."

"Well, it's true. I don't think there's anything that you're going to be able to do about it."

"Time will tell."

The noise coming from the adjacent room disrupted the conversation and the two listened intently. Uriah the Historian emerged and headed for the bathroom, slowly, shoulders hunched over, pushing his glasses up his nose with his forefinger. Graham shot a look at Conway, and seeing that Conway was looking inside the room, Graham headed for the bathroom himself. Perry looked on perplexed. Graham stopped outside of the bathroom and feigned attention to the surreal landscape until the old man emerged from the bathroom.

"Hello there Uriah," Graham said as the old man attempted to walk by him.

"Why hello there young fella," Uriah answered with vague recognition, motioning to Conway that there was no need for alarm.

"I don't know if you remember me but I'm Graham. I've talked with you several times at the Governor's Mansion. I'm a good friend of your son Ness."

"Why of course," Uriah replied. It was all coming back to him now. "How are you?"

"I'm just fine thank you. You know I always enjoy your lectures."

"Ah, thank you. What else can an ol' man do?"

"I'm quite the history buff myself."

"Are you? That's fine. Aren't you a professor if my memory serves?"

"No, I'm afraid I'm not," Graham said, a bit uncomfortably.

"That's a shame. I was about to invite you into our little room. Now, why did I think you were a professor?"

"Oh, that, embarrassing really. Some of the students call me that. Kind of as a term of endearment I guess. That's ironic huh, using professor as a term of endearment?" Graham gave Uriah a gentle tap on his fragile arm to accentuate the humor.

"He he he," Uriah giggled in a high-pitched tone, his forehead turning crimson from the strain of his laugh. "Say, are you published, maybe I could get you in as an honorary member."

"No, I'm not published. But check this out," Graham said cracking his knuckles, "Attila the Hun died in 453, the Hundred Years war, which actually lasted one hundred and sixteen years, ended in 1453 the same year Constantinople fell to the Turks, jump back one hundred years and one finds the Black Plague and the publication of *The Decameron*, jump back a year from 1453 and Leonardo Da Vinci was born in 1452 and died in 1519. O.K., hold on, I'm just getting warmed up. Speaking of Italian Renaissance artists, Michelangelo died in 1564, the same year as John Calvin, and oh what a year that was because not only was Shakespeare born that year but also Galileo.

"Of course 1492 is known for Columbus but it was also the year Ferdinand and Isabella unified Spain and not only drove out the Moors but also exiled any Jews who refused to convert and…and… let's see…Lorenzo Medici died, such a magnificent fellow.

"And yes, in 1776 we have *The Declaration of Independence* but there were also a few other monographs of some importance: Adam Smith's *The Wealth of Nations* and Edward Gibbons *The Rise and Fall of the Roman Empire*.

"*The Magna Carta* was in 1215 and Henry V won the battle in Agincourt in 1415. Don't you see, people take from now back to the constitution as an eternity but *The Magna Carta* and Agincourt are both in the distant past with no real separation? By teaching history

221

this way instead of chronologically or thematically it all starts to come into focus, even for the layperson. O.K, O.K, hold on to your hat because this could be my favorite.

"In 1648 The Thirty Years' War ended as did the Eighty Years' War, which not coincidentally had started fifty years before the thirty years war between the Spanish and the Dutch. Two hundred years later in 1848, perhaps one of the most pivotal years in history, revolution broke out across Europe, Marx published *Das Kapital*, James K. Polk declared war on Mexico, oh, my God what a year, Elizabeth Cady Stanton and Susan B. Anthony congregated at Seneca Falls New York and...."

"But those are just facts," the historian interrupted.

"Yes, but, it is a way to give a sense of the passage of time between historical events. It somehow connects it for me." Graham, out of breath, widened his eyes waiting for a response.

"Indeed it does. And I'm quite impressed but...well, I would like for you to join our society but without the right degree, I am unsure that there is anything that I can do. Are you at least published?"

"No, I'm not," replied Graham, losing some of his enthusiasm, yet again answering this question.

"That really is too bad," said Uriah with a mix of compassion and didacticism. "I like the method but there is no interpretation of events, no analysis. It was nice running into you. I really need to get back in there." The old man turned around to walk back into the room.

"Wait," Graham followed with contained desperation. "I have many ideas for articles and one in particular for a thesis. Graham grabbing his shoulder stopped the historian. Conway stood up but was waved off by Uriah. "It has to do with The United States," Graham spoke quickly because he knew that he had little time to work with and he realized that this might be his last chance to make

an impression on Uriah the Historian. "In the early years of the republic," Graham continued making intense eye contact, "more spe-
cifically between the years of 1825 and 1855, which were inciden-
tally the years that Nicholas the First ruled Russia, well, those thirty
years were what made modern America. See, it wasn't the Gilded
Age or Henry Ford's assembly line that created a modern America,
no the die was cast long before. In those thirty years it was the steam
ships, canals, railroads, that turned the tide on Jefferson's revolution of 1800 and once and for all killed his Rousseau-influenced
dream of some agrarian utopia and replaced it with..."

"I like it," Uriah said, interrupting Graham, "I think you may
have something there. But an idea for a great thesis is neither great
nor a thesis. You have to write it. Reenter the program, finish your
courses, and write it. Until then you will always be on the outside
looking in. I'm sorry but the truth is," Uriah said looking around
lowering his voice, "we all had to do it so you will have to do it
too. That's the proverbial bottom line." And with this Uriah gave
Graham a slight smile that contained a mixture of sympathy and
encouragement and disappeared back into the room.

Graham did his best to hide his agitation but Perry could see
that his friend was quite shaken, so he didn't pry into the conversation between Graham and Uriah. He decided to talk more about the
upcoming road trip. "Hey, Aliesha said that she may drive to the
silo to see that image. Maybe he won't come along." Perry pointed
to Conway only with his eyes.

"Fat chance." Perry took a sip of his coffee and indicated with
his facial expression that it had turned cold. "I'm cooling on the
idea."

"You're just having a bad day. You'll go." Perry knew Graham
would never sit out on such adventure.

"Probably."

"Hey, what projects have you been working on? Anything

223

new?"

"No, nothing that matters," Graham said, obviously feeling sorry for himself. "I have to go get this warmed up." One talent that Graham had that was beyond dispute was the capacity to cheer himself up, at least when he was sober. By the time he returned with his coffee, Perry could already tell a difference. "Actually, I have had an idea for quite some time but I might need your help. You game?"

"I guess," Perry said with a sense of dread. Perry had been working on saying "no" and he had a feeling that this was one proposition where he should run as fast and far away a possible. He didn't mind helping out but with his school load and his job at the student union he really didn't have time to commit to any projects but he didn't have the heart to be anything but supportive.

"O.K., it will involve writing for you." Graham was becoming more excited by the moment. "O.K., ready, here it goes: I have a friend who composes opera. He has a piece finished that he's shopping around with very little luck. As you know, over the years I've met many musicians; a lot of them owe me favors for one reason or another. Anyway, I was reading this article about this guy who makes instruments out of scraps, garbage really. Now, and this is where it gets good. Guess who did a stint at a scrap metal junk yard place on the south side a few years back? This guy right here", said Graham, using both thumbs pointing to himself. "So there are three pieces to this project well four really, the opera's libretti sucks and we need someone to write it and that's where you come in."

"Me?" Perry said, looking down.

"Yep."

"But why me?" I wouldn't know anything about that. How to even start."

"All the better!" You may stumble across something completely fresh. Think about it. An opera performed in a junkyard with instruments made out of scrap." Graham was gesturing wildly and Perry thought that he was going to start jumping up and down like a four-year old.

"Let's do it!" Perry said, swept up in the excitement.

"Great, I'll take you to see the junkyard. Let's get out of this place." Graham tilted his head back and drained the rest of his coffee.

"I really need to study though."

"It won't take long. You'll have all afternoon to study." It was obvious to Perry that Graham wasn't taking no for an answer. The two men headed for the door when Graham stopped and approached Conway and thanked him. He impulsively put his ear up against the French doors for a few final seconds: *The renegade Vice President went looking for his beloved daughter and sat in despair on the coast line of South Carolina, realizing that further searching was futile. He found some solace when one night looking out at the vast ocean, he heard her ghost, calling to him, soothing him in his time of torment, and some people to this day, say that if one is patient and listens carefully, one can still hear the voice of Theodocius Burr, shipwrecked, calling out from the black Atlantic.*

CHAPTER 22

Perry opened the door and Graham stood before him, back-pack and sleeping bag in tow. All the arrangements had been made for the trip. Conway and Aleisha would arrive after lunch and everyone would load up and hit the road. The trip was only a few hours so they planned to fill the tank (with everyone chipping in excluding the Jones' since they provided the car) and drive straight through. The papers had been reporting daily about "the image" so the route had been planned to mirror the trip that the Vietnam vet had taken when he ran into the fifty-five year old Catholic factory worker who had discovered the image of Christ on the side of the grain silo.

The small town only had about one thousand inhabitants but, since the news about the image spread, thousands every day were passing through to see the silo. The county sheriff's office requested help from neighboring counties to help police the area. Perry, who was the most reluctant pilgrim, had suggested that they cut the trip shorter by driving right to the image instead of going to the town and walking from there, which was reported to be about a five mile trip. There were two main objections to this plan: The first was that the traffic jams were so heavy within miles of the silo that the last few miles were taking up to ten hours to travel. Some sources had been cited as saying that the authorities very well may close the roads by the weekend, which made the choice of walking compulsory for all. This plan would never be put into effect because of the outcry from the sick and lame who were unable to make the long walk and who were making the pilgrimage in hopes of being healed.

The second objection came from Graham. He had read all of the newspaper accounts and he was struck by one Henry Hofstetter Jr. He not only wanted to meet this person who was roughly the same age as he was but he wanted to travel the same course. Mostly, this was because of various newspaper accounts. Those who simply drove to the silo, got out of their car and looked up tended to be either suspect, maybe seeing something but maybe not, or they tended to claim that they saw absolutely nothing but an oxidized blob with no discernible form. If the trouble was going to be taken to drive all the way up there, Graham told everyone, then we might as well do it right. The closed roads would aid him with any objections to his plan.

"Here," Graham said to Perry, handing him a sleeping bag. "I borrowed this from a coworker for you to use. Are you packed?"

"No not really." Perry sat back down on the couch, indicating that he was in no hurry.

"What's the problem here? We got to roll soon."

"I just have so much to do. I have another paper due and I have to prepare for midterms. I don't think I'm going to be able to make it."

"Here we go again," replied Graham as he rolled his eyes and let out a heavy sigh. "Listen, I can appreciate that you're worried about your education. I wish I would've been more worried about mine. I respect that. I really respect that. But this is going to be an educational trip, see? I really do believe that. And I owe it to you to talk you into going. Listen, you need a weekend out of this place. It will wear on you if you don't get a break once in a while. You gotta have some balance."

"Yeah, it's just that I have so much to do. I've fallen behind."

"O.K., listen, I need you to go. I'm not crazy being around Aliesha with that giant prick around all weekend. Pain in the ass having him around."

"He doesn't seem that bad to me."

"How would you know? The guy never says a word. He freaks me out a bit because I never can tell what the guy's thinking. I wish he would say something once in a while. The other night at the bowling alley, all he did was sit there and chain smoke. Man I wish I could see what she sees in him. Listen, you go and I'll make sure that you study your ass off until midterms are over. No bar trips, no mansion trips. No nothing, I mean no anything, until all of your midterms are over."

Perry packed his clothes in a large black bag. He found that he was probably taking too much for such a short trip but he didn't want to find himself in a situation, like rain, in which he would be unprepared. He came back out to the living room and sat his bag on the floor, and when he started to sit back down there was another knock on the door. He looked at the clock and wondered who could be at the door.

"That's probably Ness," Graham yelled from the bathroom.

"Ness is going?" Perry replied with surprise.

"Yep," Maybe Luke too."

Perry scanned the room and didn't see anything but a phone book which he assumed wouldn't count as an actual book. He went to answer the door when from the corner of his eye his saw his anthropology book and *The Mayor of Casterbridge*, both books he needed for midterm preparations. He grabbed the books off the couch and slid them far underneath the cushions, and took one final look around the room and opened the door to see Ness, his red eyes staring intently at Perry. Perry motioned for him to come in. Ness looked around the room, a gesture that Perry interpreted as a long look of suspicion. Perhaps he was reading too much into it. Perhaps he merely had a guilty conscious?

"Hey my good man," Graham said coming into the room, holding his hand out for Ness to grasp though knowing he wouldn't. Perry noticed that Graham always greeted Ness as if he hadn't seen him for years. "What's the news?"

"Man, I saw an incredible show last night downtown."

"Dude, why didn't you call?"

"Dude, you don't have a phone, and you didn't reply to the smoke signals I sent."

"That's it. I'm getting a phone as soon as I get back." Ness nodded sarcastically as if to indicate that he had heard this line before. "Seriously, I'm looking forward to coming back from this trip a changed man. You guys aren't going to recognize the new me." Ness nodded again the same way. "Well, I can see I'm amongst non-believers. You'll see."

"Who's driving, that big Indian dude?"

"Yeah, unfortunately," Graham said, with some exaggeration.

"Is Luke coming?"

"Who knows," Graham continued, "I invited him and he said he was into it so that means there's about a fifty-fifty chance."

"I hope so, he'll bring his guitar. I see grand possibilities here. Luke on guitar, that Indian dude singing, a camp fire…"

"In that case," interrupted Graham, "I hope he doesn't bring his guitar."

"Taking in the fact that I've never seen Luke without his guitar, which includes places like the laundromat and the grocery store, chances are pretty good that he'll bring it on a camping trip." Ness emphasized the last few words to indicate how absurd a proposition it was that Luke could somehow not bring his guitar.

"True enough. But let's remember that this is a little more than a camping trip. It's a pilgrimage."

"Well, to you it may be a pilgrimage. To the rest of us it's a camping trip, right?" Ness said, looking right at Perry. Perry turned his palms over to indicate that he was not going to take sides. He disliked the way in which Ness was always trying to put him on the spot by demanding he take sides. Graham had told Perry one night that it was just his way to help. Ness's complaint was that Perry was too passive and urging Perry to take sides was just one wrench in the toolbox to change that fact. "Anyway, they should be here any minute. It's a beautiful day. I think we should wait out-side." The two men moved toward the door while Perry shut off the lamps on his end tables.

"I'll be right there," Perry said. "I forgot something."

"What?" Ness shot back at Perry.

"Just something."

"Just something?" Ness repeated. "Anything we can help with?"
"No. I just want to bring another pair of socks. I forgot that we may be walking quite a ways." Perry said, looking down at the floor.

"Well, go get 'em. We'll wait for you," Ness said folding his arms, looking straight into Perry's eyes.

"Well, O.K." Perry walked down the hall and looked over his shoulder to see if he was being spied on. He walked into his room and closed his door. He should have put those books in his bag wrapped up in a shirt or pants before Ness arrived. How could he have been so careless? Maybe when they were all outside he would make another excuse and run back in, pull the books from beneath the couch...but going back in with his bag would be too suspicious. The words that Graham told him earlier replayed in his head. Yes, he would relax this weekend and worry about studying when he got back. He would take a book that he wanted to read. He surveyed his milk crates in his closet, which contained several books that he had bought used at a library sale. "Everything O.K. in there?" he heard Ness's voice from down the hall. "Yes, just looking for something clean." Perry grabbed *Dogs in the Cathedral* by David

Megenhardt and put it inside a pair of jeans and folded the pants over once and put them in the bottom of the bag.

"All set?" Ness asked Perry while he looked from his eyes to the bag and back to his eyes.

"Yeah, ready to go," Perry said, walking past Ness, avoiding any eye contact. "Wait one second, my mail." Perry grabbed his mail from the box right outside the door and carried it past Graham and Ness toward his desk. He flipped through the envelopes, which was an assortment of bills and junk mail until he came to an over-sized envelope that he knew instantly was from Reinbeck, Iowa. He looked at the envelope and debated whether or not to open it and see the question and if possibly the sender may have at last answered a question that Perry posed. He was in a dilemma because he really didn't want to open it now because he felt rushed but his curiosity to open the envelope was enough to make his hands shake. He began to tear the envelope open and without quite knowing why he shoved the envelope in the middle of the mail and put the stack in his top drawer to attend to later when he returned.

The three men sat outside on the steps making movements every time they heard a car coming down the road in the front or the alley in the back. A two-toned station wagon with paneled doors rolled along slowly down the alley and made a stop. None of the three gave much of a response because it was not the blue Chevelle that belonged to the Jones'. The station wagon didn't budge, and then the giant Indian got out and stood up, the top of the car only coming to his waist, and then soon after when Aleisha Jones rolled down her window and smiled and waived, they realized that their ride had arrived. They started toward the vehicle with all of their gear and Aleisha stood by the hatchback ready to assist them with loading. Conway stayed at the front, observing with his eyes hidden under a massive cowboy hat.

"What's with the new set of wheels?" asked Graham, posing

231

the question to Aleisha.

"Because," injected Conway with a rare comment. "Our family is increasin. We thought that this would be more fittin for our needs." Aleisha affirmed Conway's statement with a huge grin, holding her hands around her stomach.

"Well, isn't that something else," Graham responded thinking he was being clever with his intentional vagueness. Perry and Ness both hugged Aleisha and shook Conway's hand. Perry saw Conway smile for the first time. This guy is all right, Perry thought to himself. Travel plans were being discussed though Graham was conspicuously silent apparently lost in thought. "Got any names?" Graham said, looking back and forth between Conway and Aleisha.

"Conway likes Merle if it's a boy and Loretta if it's a girl. I like those names myself."

"All right," Graham couldn't hide his approval at Conway's taste in baby names.

"Well, we better get on the road," Conway said in his thick, raspy voice, already surpassing the amount of words that anybody except for Aleisha had heard him speak. He threw Graham the keys.

"What's this?" said Graham a bit surprised.

"I supply the car. You drive and supply the gas and drive. That was the deal." Aleisha knew that the arrangements were made while Graham was heavily intoxicated so she nodded to Graham assuring him that what Conway spoke was indeed the agreement.

"No problem," Graham said while moving toward the driver's seat. He moved into the seat and brought the seat belt in front of him. It had been a while since he had been behind a wheel of a car. He looked at everything from the hazard lights to the radio. He was pleased to see a cassette player. He figured there would be and he had a cassette of various recordings made for him by a friend who worked full time at a local record store; Graham's friend was a continual pipeline to the newest music, and Graham was excited to hear what was contained on the cassette.

"Anybody mind if I put in some music?" Graham said, with a tone that made the question sound rhetorical.

"A matter of fact I do," came Conway's voice from the backseat. "My car, my music."

Graham's inclination was to protest or at least appeal to the general sensibilities of the group, but when he adjusted the rearview mirror, and saw Conway's eyes peeking out from under his hat, he decided to leave the subject for now and put the car in drive and roll slowly down the alley, testing his ability to maneuver the wagon.

"Hold up," Ness said as he motioned across the parking lot. A bearded man with long hair carrying a guitar ran around the corner of the apartments, and the only reason why Graham didn't recognize Luke immediately, is because Luke, whom Graham had usually only seen sitting down on a sidewalk, ran so fast that his beard flew up in his face and his hair wrapped around his head. Graham came to a complete stop and Ness waived to Luke to come in the right direction. Aleisha opened her mouth and Conway knitted his massive eyebrows and they saw what looked like a flying hairball glide across the parking lot.

"Am I huh...huh, huh...too...huh, huh late?" asked Luke trying to catch his breath enough to get the words out.

"We could probably fit him, don't you think?" Graham asked, turning around to look at Aleisha and Conway.

"I don't see how," said Conway. Though Graham, Ness, and Perry sat upfront, Conway took up so much room in the back that he and Aleisha were fit just as tightly as the three men in the front and the back of the wagon was filled with luggage and camping materials.

"Luke," said Graham becoming very serious, "Do you remember what you told me about the last three hundred miles ride when

233

you went to Woodstock?"

"Oh, no," said Luke, who knew exactly what Graham was referring to. "There are two basic differences my main man. Firstly,
that was twenty years ago and I was a rustlin young buck with a
pink carnation and a pickup truck. Number two, and perhaps the
most important difference by far," Luke paused and grabbed his
beard and ran his hand down the length of his hair "Hendrix ain't
playing at this gig my broth."

"Let me talk to him for a second." Graham got out of the car
and walked Luke about twenty feet behind the car. "Now, Luke,
you don't want to miss this. This cat was a Vietnam vet- you're a
Vietnam vet. Don't you guys call each other brothers?"

"Yeah, but I don't see what that has to do with anything. I ain't
riding on the hood of that car."

"Wait wait wait wait wait just a minute. It will be just like reliving your youth. That was three hundred miles on top of some
day-glo magic bus through the chill of night with no food in your
stomach. This is less than a third of that trip during a beautiful afternoon. Look at it as a test to see if you still have that adventurous
spirit that you once had."

"Just go, Graham." Luke said shaking his head. "I got nothing
to prove. I'm too old to prove anything to anybody. Forget it, I'm
not going."

The station wagon roared down the road with an occasional
scolding coming from Conway from the backseat about the toll the
speed was taking on his new car.

"It's not new," Graham said without looking back.

"It's new to me," Conway replied with a sense of finality.

"Put in that tape," Conway said, putting his hand over Perry's
shoulder, indicating that the order was addressed to him. Conway
moved his head slightly back and forth to the music.

It wasn't god who made honky tonk angels

As you wrote in the words of your song
Too many times married men think they're still single
That had caused many good girls to go wrong.

When the song ended, Graham was in disbelief that the same song repeated again. "You got it taped on here again?"

"I got it taped on the whole damn side," Conway said with a huge grin, nodding his head. "And we're going to listen to the whole damn tape."

Ness and Perry looked at each other and Perry grinned and Ness let out a small chuckle, not so much because of how odd Conway's tape was but because they both could only guess what was going through Graham's mind.

So the song played over and over again but much to Graham's chagrin it grew on him. He started to really like the song and he found it comforting when he heard the familiar steel guitar come in, indicating the song was coming once more. In a moment of road hypnosis he found that he was singing the song to himself, lips moving, only when he came out of his trance did he look back and noticed that he was caught enjoying the song by Conway. The Karaoke King's eyes laid deeply buried beneath his hat as he looked on the conversion with mistrust. Graham recovered his stoic self and looked at the road uninterrupted except for Luke's beard that flew back and forth across the front of the window.

CHAPTER 23

There is no more gnashing of teeth over this project. One thousand pages in two years was a noble goal! Now, as I thumb through this manuscript of a few hundred pages, three and a half years after I wrote the first word, I see very little that resembles what I thought it would be. Notes, fragments, sketches, ideas. I have seeds of several novels, novellas, short stories, but the unifying theme is opaque at best. Personal revenge is as sweet for me as if I would have put a knife in his belly. He wanted more plot, so I gave him Gus as a possible Nazi! Why not? Sure it seems unexpected but it surprised me too. There's your "revelation" Jason. There's your "plot twist"! If it doesn't ring true don't blame me, blame Aristotle or Joyce, or some other standard bearer.

I've decided this will be my last diary entry, though I've been known to change my mind. I've destroyed most of what is left anyway. But don't, dear self, think that I am the least bit bitter anymore. I am not. Just when everyone seems to have left me, my sweet, sultry alliteration saved me, or at least what is left of me. I will give no details here but I feel a need to acknowledge you and your great gift, nothing less than a grand humanitarian gesture. No matter how you denied it, I know there was charity involved. I look into the mirror and see a stranger, ravaged by age and disease. She said she saw none of it and I believe her. Occasionally when I was younger, teaching a course, I would benefit from my little niche of infamy but I have been forgotten long ago. A used book sale in a basement! She read it and wrote to me and then came to me. I will be forever grateful to her--only partly because of the act, but more importantly for me, the memory. I have the impressions, and the empirical experience humanized this world again. Though I should write you a timeless ode, this is all I'll ever share. Thank you and adieu.

So very little of this book is my own. Reading through these pages I feel like a spy, a peeping Tom. I have intruded on people's privacy. Identity theft. I had no choice if I were to continue, I had nothing left. What a shame that all of the advice about writer's block, from listing exercises to automatic writing, no one ever mentions stealing. The type of stealing that I refer to shouldn't be confused with plagiarism. Plagiarism is an act so odious and amoral that I would cringe at the thought. Stealing someone's writing is more abhorrent than stealing someone's gold. But stealing someone's unwritten story, fiction or nonfiction (after all, how can we ever know for sure during the overhearing of a conversation, or a direct interview, what the truth really is, even if they believe it to be so. We can be no surer than Strindberg's captain in *The Father* of his own paternity, and if we ponder too long on such thoughts, like the captain, we will be destined for the straight jacket) it's open territory, free to be harvested by whatever method and with whatever seed that one sees fit. At least that's how I see it.

I will bring these characters together now or very soon, that detail has not worked itself out in my mind. I will "finish" but it won't be complete, not even close. I must do it while I have this burst of energy. I know from my own history that it will be brief and may not come again. What to do with Mona? I have at least vague ideas for the others but Mona is fighting with me, pulling me in different directions. I need to follow her but I can't seem to find her. When I'm wrong she lets me know it. She doesn't work. She doesn't sound right. She sounds too forced, too made. Well, I say,

I'm bringing you along by the hair of the head if that is what it will take! She spits in my face and refuses to cooperate. I need to get the ol' Zen books out, I guess. See if I can let her lead me, naturally.

Yes, yes, I know. I have walked the streets, the bars, the coffee houses. I've pulled my seat close to a near table and some young ladies grunt a pejorative before they moved across the room. The problem is there are no nineteen or twenty-year olds with worldly experience that have crossed my path. No young girls who haven't been sheltered by their parents. The women who had knowledge who would talk to me, the kind of knowledge that I imagine Mona would have were much older, thirty perhaps, but they had lost too much, shall I say "gusto". No that is not the right word. *Adventure?* No too pedestrian: *Boldness?* Yes, *boldness* may be the best I can do for right now. If I can somehow create her with the knowledge of a traveled thirty-year old and the boldness of a twenty-year old then I may have finally captured her. Ah, but I realize that I have limitations. I may not possess that type of skill.

Wasn't it Dr. Johnson who said something to the effect that one has to…Christ! I can't even formulate the thought. I can't even re-motely remember the quote but the gist of it was put the words on paper and worry about polishing it later…or…have all of the clay made before you worry about starting to sculpt it? I have to finish making the clay. I have to drive myself through foggy thoughts, and tension headaches, and nausea, and at the very least finish making the clay, and then I can worry about sculpting. What if I am all potential? What if I make the finest clay in the world but have less than perfect sculpting abilities? I have exhausted this line of think-ing. Am I starting to sink again? I have to at least bring some kind of conclusion to this. It is tormenting me like an open sore.

CHAPTER 24

The station wagon pulled off the side of the road behind a long line of automobiles. Everyone could see the town because of the tall grain elevator, and the group began exiting the vehicle; Luke dismounted the vehicle and stretched his back with an elastic expression that oscillated between pleasure and pain. The best estimate that anyone of them would venture is that they were at least three miles from town. A debate ensued about whether or not they should set up camp and make the walk or try to carry their gear closer to town. The gear would be heavy so a three-mile walk didn't seem the best of choices. Graham suggested that if there was a closer locale to set up camp, then they wouldn't have to walk back before they made the trip to the silo, but the thought of lugging the gear back to the car, if they were unable to find a suitable spot was too much of a deterrent, and since the signs in the farmers' fields stated only five dollars to camp, compared with what they assumed would be much more the closer they got to town, the decision was made to set up a camp and make the walk without the equipment. Luke said that he was too stiff to start walking and that he would relax and Ness opted to stay with him saying that they could catch up later.

The landscape was flat and the farm fields were only broken up by small patches of woods. Rolling, dense, gray clouds marched toward them threatening a storm; a gust of wind blew Conway's cowboy hat off and sent it toppling through a field. Aleisha ran after it and returned it to him. Though everyone had been following the account in the paper, nobody quite expected what he or she was now witnessing. Besides all of the campfires that were burning throughout the countryside, throngs of people were walking along the road and through the fields. Aleisha looked at one camp in particular with great curiosity. A woman dressed in a multi-colored robe and loop earrings motioned her over, almost hypnotically.

"Are those gypsies?" asked Aleisha.

"I believe so," Graham replied. "Why, you want to have your fortune told?"

"Yeah, I would. But not right now." She kept walking but she didn't take her eyes from the woman and the woman didn't stop motioning with her index finger trying to lure Aleisha to her. A man with long, black hair emerged from the tent carrying a baby and handed the child to his mother. The gypsy woman brought the child up to her breast without taking her eyes from Aleisha.

"That was kind of creepy. It's like she was trying to tell me something." Aleisha put her index finger through the loop on her husband's jeans for security.

"She woulda only taken your money." Conway said, uttering one of the few sentences that he would make on the trip. His silence fed his mystique. It is not that he didn't speak--he would have long talks with his wife. He would talk about what made him happy, what he hoped for the future, what he feared, but only to her. In a crowd or with company he would just listen. Aleisha was surprised that he talked to Graham as much as he had at the beginning of the trip. He could sing in front of people but those were other people's words or words he had written himself but words that were meant to be a part of music, not conversation.

There were several families of Mexicans--a few selling grilled food from the back of an old van. They stopped to eat and Graham pointed to a huge tortilla on the grill that was filled with meat, beans, and peppers, covered with various sauces. These tortillas were three sizes bigger than any that were made in the city.

"How much is one of those?" Perry asked pointing to the grill.

"One nickel," said a Mexican man who was about forty. He wore a cowboy hat and a denim shirt and had a friendly, comforting smile.

"One nickel! That would at least be a buck fifty." Graham said, the Mexican looking at him in disbelief.

"Do you speak English?" Perry asked, sure that there must be some mistake. A group of Mexicans were sitting on blankets, one strumming a guitar, watching the scene.

"*Si.*"

"Are you sure that is only a nickel?" Perry asked again.

"*Si.*"

"How much are the smaller ones then?" Perry said pointing to the other side of the grill.

"One dollar." The man said matter-of-factly.

"Now let me get this straight," Perry replied, "the little ones are a dollar but the big ones are only a nickel?"

"*Si.*"

"Well, O.K. I'll take a big one *por favor*," Perry said handing the man a nickel while taking the chance to use one of the few Spanish phrases that he knew.

Perry held the huge tortilla in his hands and bit into it an inch or so and started chewing. The effect started slowly. He opened and shut his mouth first slowly then very quickly as if he were trying to dislodge the food from his mouth and then he pursed his lips and blew through them twice in succession and continually breathed in and out as fast as he could. He looked at Graham and Graham stepped back, not knowing quite was happening. Graham could see that Perry's eyes were turning red and starting to water. Perry

241

took his hand and fanned air against his mouth as fast as he could. His hearing seemed to have ceased but he could see through his watering eyes that the Mexicans were all laughing at him, pointing toward his direction and slapping each other on the back.

"How much...how much for the coke?" Perry said pointing toward an ice filled open cooler.

"One can, five dollars!" The man announced. This was the punch line that the rest of the Mexicans knew was coming but it still sent them into spasms of laughter all the same as Perry dug through his pocket for a five-dollar bill as fast as he could and handed it to the man. He opened the can as fast as he could and gulped the cola down. Graham and Luke were bent over in laughter and even Conway couldn't help but smile. A boom of thunder followed too closely by a crack of lightning ended the laughter and the crowd instinctively ducked as if that would help them from being struck by lightning.

The group now walked through driving rain against a wind that made them lean forward to fight the emerging storm. As the rain fell harder and the sounds in the sky became more violent, each of them surveyed the landscape for an answer. They could ask various people who were in tents if they could come in but what were the chances that strangers would invite them? Also, if that happened they would have to be split up and none of them thought that was a good idea, at least for now. On each side there was nothing but open flat fields; Graham slowed down and walked on the other side of Conway, assuming that lightning would strike the tallest among them.

A man emerged from a lane that ran along side of a fence that split the large field.

"You fellas want to get out a da rain?" The man was about seventy-years old and the rain had parted his slick gray hair in the middle so that it covered about half of his abnormally large ears.

He had a 1973 three-speed Ford truck that was parked by a lean-to that he had constructed and covered with a tarp. Although he had no front teeth, and the teeth he had left were blackened, he didn't hesitate to give the group a large, hospitable smile. They hunched together beneath the lean-to. Aleisha was shivering so the man went to the back of his truck and opened a wooden box and brought her a gray, wool blanket.

"Thank you, Mr...?" Aleisha said, through her chattering teeth.

"Ernie Thompson."

"Thank you, Mr. Thompson."

"I ain't got no blankets for ye fellers but I got somethin' else thata warm your bones." Ernie went through the rain again and returned with a corked jug and handed it toward the men and there were no takers. Ernie uncorked the jug and took a large gulp from the jug and then shook his head with satisfaction as he brought his sleeve across his lips. "Sure?" He said again while holding out the jug.

"Ah, what the hell," said Graham, grabbing the jug to take a drink. "Wow! Hahh! My god, what is that!" Graham said as his face reddened and his eyes lit up.

"100% homemade moonshine. Been drinking it since I was nine," Ernie said, sustaining his smile, taking Graham's reaction as a complement to his distilling talents.

"Here," Graham said, handing it to Conway. Conway tilted the jug up and let the alcohol drain and then brought it down again. He blew through pursed lips and, while saying nothing, nodded in approval. He handed the jug to Aleisha who had to bring her hand from behind the blanket to take hold of it. She brought the jug to her nose to smell what her pregnancy was making her miss and then handed the jug to Perry who was still gun-shy from the burrito and in no mood to try some unknown firewater. Not one to withstand peer pressure, he succumbed to the goading of his friends and put the jug to his lips. To his surprise the alcohol seemed to cool his mouth, though it still made him close his eyes and grit his teeth.

"Go head. Passer round agin. I'm stocked up."

The rain had long since stopped but nobody was making a move to leave just yet. Perry stumbled out of the lean-to and went behind the tree to urinate. His head was spinning a bit, even though he had not drunk nearly as much as Graham and Conway, who seemed to be in an unspoken contest that Graham was destined to lose; no amount of liquor seemed to faze Conway.

"So you come up all this way?" Aleisha asked Ernie, "just to see this image on the side of the silo?"

"Oh no, darlin. I come up here to be healed."

"What's wrong?" asked Aleisha.

"I got cancer honey."

"That's too bad. I'm really sorry to hear that."

"What kind?" Graham asked.

"I got liver cancer." The group automatically looked at the jug that Conway happened to be holding. "It's not what you think. I don't believe it was the moonshine. I believe it was this." Ernie rolled up his shirtsleeves, one above the elbow and one above the bicep. Red scars dotted his entire arm. "See these scars. These are snakebites. It's the venom not the moonshine that's a got my liver." He pulled down his shirt to show that the bites were across his neck and chest. He lifted up his hair to show that he had even been bitten on the forehead. Believe it or not, I only drink a shot or two of that firewater a day. I know it may be a sin but it's always a way ta calm myself. Nowadays I'll mix a little sugar with it to get it down."

"How were you bitten so much?" Aleisha asked, not knowing what to say.

"I'm going to give you a very famous name among my people and chances are you never heard of 'em. Does the name George

Went Hensley mean anything to ya'll?" Ernie looked at all of the heads shaking no.

"Well George Went Hensley was known far and wide on the fact that he started findin' Jesus through the snake ya see. My folk was a part of the movement called the *The Church of God with Signs a Follow'n.*' My Daddy was one of the original followers of Mr. Hensley, along with fellers like Raymond Harris, Lewis Ford, and Tommy Harden. My Daddy, Mason Thompson, was a largely responsible for the spreadin of *The Church of God with Signs a Follow'n.* See, I grew up handl'n snakes prais'n the Lord. It was all I ever know'd.

"They outlawed it and Mr. Hensley brought one a' our lawyers who was a member of *The Church a God with Signs a Follow'n* and he fought the ban on first amendment rights straight otta *The Constitution* of these here United States. Well, we lost and what we called The Grand Persecution started. They locked our folk up but nothing save permanent incarceration was gon ta stop us from serv'n the Lord."

"Just how exactly," Graham intervened, "were the snakes going to get you closer to God?"

"It's just wasn't the snakes boy. The snakes was all that was banned. They are other signs. Speak'n in tongues..." at this point Ernie's eyes rolled up to the top of his head to the point that only the whites of his eyes were visible. He started to speak in a language that no one could recognize so at the surface it seemed like gibberish but the sounds were expelled with such a fluid cadence that the act seemed devoid of improvisation. He let sounds go loose and fast with the confidence of an auctioneer. "We call that speak'n in tongues. They never did outlaw that. All in all the signs included speak'n in tongues, cast'n out of demons, handl'n serpents, drink'n deadly things, and heal'n the sick. That all comes right from the good book. See and here's the kicker. Drink'n deadly things included the alcohol that ya'll is drink'n with me right now. They out-lawed that for a while too so the community not only had to deal with the persecution of snake handl'n they had to deal with the persecution of make'n and consum'n this here firewater."

"Whatever happened to Hensley?" asked Luke.

"Same thing happened to my Daddy. Killed from snakebite. Rattlers both of 'em. I took the rattler that killed my daddy and ripped its head off soon after my daddy breathed his last. I always regretted that. Wasn't the snake's fault. Those rattlers are deadly but not to me."

"They obviously got to your liver," Graham said in disbelief.

"No, I don't really think they did. These scars you see weren't from no rattlers either. I moved up into Southern Ohio to escape persecution with my mamma and sister not long after we buried Daddy. There weren't many rattlers so I handled copperheads. Rattlers would leave me two unnoticeable puncture wounds and I wouldn't even notice but them ol' copperheads is responsible for tattoo'n my body like it is. Their bites would make me sick and I would throw up with fever. That's why I finally gave it up. Didn't feel right anymore. I'm convinced it was the copperhead venom not the rattler venom that diseased my liver."

"Ernie, you're thinking that the silo is going to cure your liver cancer?"

"That's what I'm hope'n mam. That's why I made the trip."

"How long has it been since you stopped handling snakes?" continued Aleisha.

"Oh, I haven't stopped," said Ernie as he took a lid off a box that was placed in the corner of the lean-to, a movement that quickly emptied the space with the exception of Conway. "What's wrong with ya'll? This is just an ol' harmless river moccasin. It ain't poi-sonous."

"What the hell you doin with it!" Graham yelled, hiding behind a nearby tree.

"I ain't got no choice," said Ernie, barring his corroded teeth in amusement of how scared everyone was. "That's why they call me the snakeman. These fellers come right up to me. Even little garden snakes will slither right up on me if I'm takin a nap. Dis little angel ain't goin'a hurt nobody. Are you ma lady? Yes you are miss. Beautiful you ma lady?" Ernie was now talking to the snake very tenderly as he stroked the back of the snake's head before he returned it to the box.

"Why don't you let it go?" Aleisha asked with concern.

"Oh, I will. But I'm goin'a return that little lady to the river. She came to me for guardianship. Lost her way so I'll make sure she returns to her natural habitat for her own welfare. These creatures have gotten a bad rap, mostly from the good book but they do a lot of good."

"Are you that gentle with all of them?" Aleisha said, clearly touched.

"Yes'm."

Conway approached Ernie and laid his big hand on Ernie's shoulder, weighing down Ernie's wasted, cancerous frame. "Brother," Conway said, "I got some work to do on my believ'n as far as these kind'a things heal'n terminal diseases, but on one level that may be why I'm here too. But if you want to come with us to that silo I'll get down on my knees and pray with you for your cancer to be healed."

"Thank ya kindly stranger," Ernie said looking up at the giant. "If ya'll want to camp closer to town here I'll run ya out for your stuff."

"It beats walking," Graham said.

"I'll ride with you," Conway said, and then looked at Graham. Graham couldn't interpret this look but assumed it must be some kind of warning.

Ernie shifted straight down into second gear and when he was on the pavement he lifted his foot off the gas and pressed in on the clutch and shifted up into third gear. Conway steadied himself by holding onto the dashboard with one hand and the top of the truck with the other.

"Say," said Ernie, "you sure are a big feller."

"Yep."

"Do you like gospel music?" asked Ernie, turning on the radio.

"Yep."

"I thought you might, a feeling."

They passed all of the people that they had walked by once again. The Mexicans were still selling food and when Ernie and Conway rolled by the gypsies, the old woman spotted Conway as if she had a premonition that this moment would happen. She motioned for him to come to her. Conway tipped his hat and nodded and then pulled the mammoth hat back down over his eyes and stared ahead at the horizon.

Chapter 25

Mona heard tapping at the door but she ignored it, hoping either that whoever it was would go away or that James would be the one who answered. The tapping didn't stop and she could hear James snoring from the room down the hall. She threw a robe around her and stumbled down the dark hall and peered out through the slits in the door. Once she saw that it was Hank her frustration died down and she opened the door.

"Sorry," said Hank. "I knew you'd probably still be asleep." Mona looked out across the lawn. The first signs of daybreak were just starting to appear.

"Is everything alright?" said Mona quietly.

"Yes. I just wanted to tell you that I'm leaving early by myself."

"You mean to the silo?"

"Yes."

"But why?" Mona replied not trying to cover her disappointment.

"There are some stops I want to make along the way."

"That's O.K., I don't think anyone will mind. If you wait for the rest of us we'll make them with you. I don't think anyone is in a big hurry."

"No, this is something I want to do on my own."

"Alright. That makes me sad though."

"I'll wait for you once I get there O.K.? I'm taking a tent and a three day ration so I'll be there waiting for you."

"O.K. I wish you'd wait though."

"See you there. Go back to sleep." Hank started to walk off the patio until he heard Mona say something.

"I'm sorry, I couldn't hear you."

"You think he's guilty, don't you?" Monica repeated giving more volume to her morning voice.

"Yeah, I do, but I'm one to always think the worst of people."

"That's the most terrible thing I've ever heard. He seems like such a nice man, so gentle, so caring...I used to think about my father when I spoke to Gus and think only if he would've cared as much... " Mona said with tears welling up in her eyes.

Hank took two steps forward and stood in front of her with his arms spread out as if he were ready to be judged. "Do I seem like a nice guy, Mona?"

"Hank, you are one of the greatest people that I've ever met."

"Don't be surprised about the German then, I've committed acts beyond what you can imagine. Just taking orders, just like he was. We could have switched places, both young--blindly following authority and would have easily done the same thing as the other. I look at the black and white photos of these kids in Germany and don't see it as remotely possible but it's there all the same. I see it in the adults. Look at a picture of Goering or Himmler it's there. And to me, it was there in Gus. When Himmler or Goering looked at their grandchildren do you think they had the stern look that they have in their photos?" Hank watched her as she put her head down. "Life appears to change but it doesn't--its static. Change is an illusion that was born from our discoveries." Hank waited for a reply but none came. "I'll see you out there." He turned to walk away and stopped one last time. "Hopefully, Mona, your discoveries will be limited and small." She watched him as he crossed the lawn and then the road and then he disappeared into the woods.

He followed a trail in the woods for over two miles until it brought him to a ravine, and then he took out a long knife and cut his way through weeds and briar patches until he came upon an embankment that lead to an old set of railroad tracks that ran parallel to buildings and only crossed at the edge of the village. He stopped and leaned on the sign that welcomed people into the town. He tried kicking into the air to remove mud from his hiking boots. He found a narrow stick and scraped the mud that was packed between the cleats on the bottom of his boots.

He walked the tracks. He had walked a few miles when he came upon a trestle that he recognized. When he would explore the country side with a few friends of his from farms nearby, the boys would always put their ears down on the tracks, listening for any hint of a vibration so as not to get trapped on the trestle, knowing that even if they did not make it across the tracks, they would still probably survive the long fall into the river below. When he came back from Vietnam he would occasionally come out into the woods for two or three weeks at a time, and even though the trains still ran across the trestle, he wouldn't bother listening for any vibrations, he would simply not break stride and continue walking across the tracks, and he was never forced to jump into the river, and at that time, he wasn't sure he would have moved even if there was a train coming.

He ate his lunch sitting down halfway across the trestle, and as he chewed on bites of his sandwich he would drop small pebbles and watch the entirety of their long fall ending in a small ripple on the river below. Even after he had finished eating and had his backpack repacked, he sat there for almost an hour, thinking about many different things in his life, in fluid reverie. Not until the sun was directly overhead did he realize that he may be falling behind schedule.

He wasn't sure what he was seeing down the narrow tracks but he was sure that it was a person, and the closer he walked to the object, he realized that it was a child and a dog.

"What are you doing there?" Hank said, standing over the boy and his dog.

"My dog's sick," said the boy "I'm tryin to get him to the silo, to see if maybe he can be healed."

"Is that right," Hank replied, bending down to rub the dog's head.

"Yeah, and he won't go no farther and I tried to carry him but I got so tired."

"Here," said Hank, handing the boy his canteen. The boy drank the water fast, his lips pressing hard against the opening until he stopped and gasped for air. Hank felt the collie's heart and it was slow and the dog was fighting for breath. Hank wet his hand a few times and brought it against the dog's mouth.

"Your parents know your doin this?"

"No, I asked them but they said no. Said it wouldn't do no good."

"You're from town, aren't ya?"

"Yeah, I've seen you around too," said the boy.

"I'll tell you what," said Hank, "I'm going to the silo myself. I'll take your dog. There's no guarantee but your dog can't walk any longer and it looks like you're not going to be able to handle the walk either."

"Couldn't I walk with you?"

"I got a stop to make first. You look like you're on your last leg as it is. Plus, your parents are probably looking for you--worried sick."

"What if the silo doesn't help?"

"Then I'll make it as comfortable as possible for your dog."

"Can I be alone with her for a few minutes," The boy pleaded.

"Sure you can." Hank walked about twenty paces away and

gave the boy some privacy. He knew the boy was crying even though he had his arms around the dog and his face buried into the fur of her neck. It was only when Hank could tell for sure by the boys heaving shoulders that he went back to the boy.

"I lost a pet I loved once so I know what you're going through."

"You did? Was it a dog?"

"Nope, a rooster," Hank said cracking a grin when he saw the look of disbelief on the boy's face.

"Rooster--they ain't got much of a personality."

"Yeah, well, this one did--smart as a whip. Woke me up for school every morning right outside my window. Best alarm clock I ever had. He used to go fishing with me and he sat on my lap while I ate, pecking at the crumbs I gave'm."

"How'd he die, he sick?" the boy said to Hank, shielding his eyes from the afternoon sun.

"Nope, murdered. Killed by the government."

"What? What for? How'd that happen?"

"They were com'n after me, and he got in their way. I always believe he was try'n to distract them so as I could make my get-away. I told you he was smart, but by try'n to help me he paid for it with his life. They shot Bernard dead--just one more causality." The boy looked at Hank like they were really fellow travelers now.

"Take good care of her. Her name is Queenie."

"I will."

The boy gave his dog one more hug and said thank you and goodbye and then turned around and headed back toward the village and Hank could hear the boy sobbing from a distance. Hank picked up the dog and was surprised by how heavy she was, and he started doubting the feasibility of his offer.

He carried the dog for close to an hour before he took his first rest. When he laid the dog down, he noticed she was becoming more despondent and her breathing was becoming more labored. Hank said the dog's name and noticed that there was some reaction, nothing more than a whimper though. Hank shook his head realizing that the dog's existence amounted to nothing more than suffering, and he remembered another time when he carried a being who was suffering, and by trying to save that being's life, all he did was extend his suffering, and that being was a person, who was physically suffering much more than the dog to which he now attended. The man he carried groaned the name of his mother as if he were still a child and blood gurgled from his mouth and nostrils. If he had it to do over, Hank thought, he would have ended his suffering. With that thought Hank picked up the dog and headed away from the tracks down an embankment knee high with weeds and disappeared into a forest.

When he reappeared he was looking across a large field, newly planted with sprouts emerging from the mud. He looked across the flat land where the field was only broken by a farm a little less than a mile from where he stood. The longer he walked across the field the more his boots became weighted by the mud and drops of sweat dripped from his forehead onto the dog. His own breathing was now as hard as the dog's but came quicker whereas the dog's breaths came slow in convulsive gasps.

He walked upon an opening and surveyed the property. There were a few barns, a few more shacks, and an old run down house that was much smaller than he remembered it. The house was beside a circular drive leading to a gravel lane that cut between two vast fields. He walked around to the side of one of the barns and saw a horse. The horse was old and gray, unkempt, with clumps of burs tangled throughout its mane. The horse immediately responded to Hank, pacing back and forth waiting to be saddled or let out into the open yard. Hank laid down the dog and put his hand out and the horse came to him. Hank stroked the horse's neck for several minutes before he headed to the house. There were two vehicles in the drive, a pickup truck and a four door Bonneville.

"Yes," a strained voice answered through the screen door from the dimly lit room within.

"Hello," Hank called through the screen.

An old man appeared leaning on a walker.

"Yes," The old man said, half talking and half gasping. The old man had a bible in his hand and he clutched it to his chest.

"I need his gun. I have a dog here that is suffering. I want to end it."

The old man peered through the screen door so he could take in all that was in front of him. He looked at Hank and then glanced at the dog that laid stretched out in the yard. He turned the walker around and slowly receded back into the dim room. A few minutes later he appeared with a rifle slung across his shoulder. He leaned on the walker with one hand for stability so that he could put the rifle in his hands.

"Open up the door and get it," the man said as if he were giving an order that he shouldn't have to give.

Hank opened up the door to grab the rifle. He noticed the man's hands were arthritic and covered with gorged blue veins and liver spots. Without saying a word he checked to see if the rifle was loaded and started to turn. Before he was turned all the way around a bed caught his eye in the adjacent room. An old man lay in the bed and he was hooked up to many I.V.'s and had a mask that led to a hose that led to an oxygen tank. A woman that Hank did not recognize sat in a deathwatch next to the old man.

"Excuse me," Hank said, trying to make out what the old man said.

"I said he," looking over at the old man in the bed, "buried your rooster behind the tool shed if you want to bury your dog there too." The old man gasped for air and managed to finish with a hoarse, quivering voice "they didn't have to kill that rooster; the young one had an itchy finger. Your dad didn't mean for it to turn out that way. He just wanted you to serve your country like we did and our brother did who as you should never forget never came back from fighting the Nazis. I still believed that killed our poor mother," the man said now, talking to himself more than to Hank.

Without responding Hank went back out into the yard and picked the dog up and headed out toward the barn.

"You ever comin back?" The old man said as loud as he could.

"Yeah, I'll be back." Hank replied without turning around.

Hank spread the mound of dirt out across the grave with hands making big circular motions. The earth was still damp but it was drying fast. When Hank was digging the grave he feared that he may exhume Bernard's remains but it did not happen. He now stepped away to get a better look at the grave, and even though when grass did grow, there would be a mound, he still decided to mark the grave with rocks in case the boy ever wanted to see the final resting place of his dog.

Hank walked back up to the house and tapped again on the screen door.

"He's sleeping," his uncle said. "Do you want to come in?"

Hank came through the door and looked around and was surprised by how little had changed. The stovepipe sat in the middle of the kitchen and the plastered walls had faded into a lifeless green. The house used to smell like whatever season it was but now it just smelled musty from being closed up for so long. Hank drank a glass of water and his uncle took him into a dark room that used to be a living room but now was turned into a room arranged for a dying man. Henry Hofstetter Sr. lay taking deep breaths that reminded Hank of the dog that he just buried.

"He doesn't have much time left, but he's prepared to meet his maker. He and I have had many a deep conversation over the last few weeks during the short periods where he's awake. Talked about you a lot. Lot of regrets," the uncle said while examining Hank's reaction to his words. "He probably won't make it through the night," the uncle continued, "This is your last chance to forgive him."

"I feel like it's he who should be forgiving me," Hank replied.

"Perhaps, but it's too late for that now."

The uncle and the nurse left the room and waited on the porch. Hank emerged a few minutes later and announced that he would be on his way. The uncle and the nurse went back inside to continue their deathwatch, and Hank looked around the farm. This would be his now and to his surprise, he could see himself living out his days here too, returning to the place of his childhood to grow old. He could be self-sufficient, and he would rarely have to travel into one of the surrounding towns, and if someone wanted to visit him, Mona and James perhaps, they could come and spend as much time as they wanted. That barn though, he thought, I'm going to burn it to the ground. He watched the barn as he walked by it and replayed the whole scene in his head, including the murder of his pet rooster.

"Excuse me," Hank was startled, turning around to see who spoke to him but he saw nobody. "Who said that?" he said, continuing to look around but saw nothing but the old horse.

"I asked if you were coming back for good this time," the horse said looking directly at Hank with a look that could easily be interpreted as profound sadness. Hank was still but walked closer to the horse. "The old man is dying and the world is a bit concerned about its future."

Hank looked directly at the horse: "Yes, I'm coming back for good this time. I've been away for too long. This is where I've always belonged. Were you just reading my mind?"

"Lord no, if I could only do such things. I can't read the minds

of people but that doesn't mean that I don't know what is constantly on their minds. Would you like to know?" The horse continued
to stand still without blinking.

"Yes, I would."

"The reason I know is it's the same thing with me and it was the
same thing with the old rooster Bernard. And don't assume that I
have some mystical wisdom because I know these things. I don't.
In fact I know very little. I just wanted to know if you'd be back and
when. I've grown old waiting."

"I'll be back late tomorrow night at the latest," Hank replied,
looking deep into the horse's eyes.

"I see, and did you know the old man will be dead by then?"

"I knew it was a strong possibility."

"It is more than a possibility I assure you. Is that why you're
coming back? Because the farm will be yours?"

"I suppose so."

"I see," said the horse as if in judgment.

"I have to go. I have people to meet."

"Yes." The horse watched Hank as he turned and headed back
toward the woods. The horse began to sing as he started his song
Hank's pace increased until he was crossing the field in a slow jog.
The song of the horse filled his ears as he ran:

> Wine is already sparkling in the golden goblet
> But do not drink yet; first I will sing you a song
> The song of care shall sound laughing in your soul.
> When care draws near, the gardens of the soul lie waste
> Joy and singing fade away and die
> Dark is life; dark is death.

CHAPTER 26

Expanded by one, the group entered the village. They walked in a parallel line like a gang of outlaws entering a ghost town during the old west. Ernie had told Conway that he was not greeted by the locals cordially when he had entered the village for supplies the day before. Conway assured him that he had no reason to worry, as he put his massive hand on Ernie's shoulder to signal assurance. The town would have been busy on this weekend even without the image because of a craft market that was scheduled, luring hundreds of people to the village, but the image had swelled the town by several thousands. Entrepreneurs were lined up along the streets but instead of the usual craft market items, booths were sat up that were selling various paraphernalia pertaining to the image. One booth had coffee cups with a picture of the silo with the words "The Image" written below it. Luke and Ness both bought "I Saw the Image" shirts and put them on. A clear picture of Jesus was super-imposed over the silo so the face covered most of the picture. Ness announced that when he got home he had every intention of crossing out the word *saw* and writing the word *survived* over the crossed-out word. Graham commented how the scene was just as the papers had described it.

There were posters and pins and hats and patches too. The stars and stripes hung from poles and windows in a voluminous display of patriotism.

"You would think this is the 4th of July," Aleisha said.

"Every day is the 4th of July in these corners of the world," Graham replied.

The group stared at what was probably the biggest flag that any of them had ever seen. It was draped in front of a township building that was otherwise covered with moss.

Even with the cast of characters who had made their way into town since the discovery of the image on the silo, the group still was noticed. Conway, of course, always garnered attention but even Luke with his long hair and beard, and Ness with his penetrating red eyes would normally be a topic of conversation and this was no exception. While the village certainly was taking advantage of the economic opportunities, the members of the community who were not profiting were incensed at the invasion. The majority were not entrepreneurs and shopkeepers but residents who had lived there their whole lives and in many circumstances belonged to families who had lived in the village for many generations.

Two women sat on their porch shaking their heads in disgust at the travesty, making inaudible comments about all the freaky people. The women, who were around forty, still wore the beehive hairdos that they had donned in High School in the '60s. Even the girl with the blue streaks in her hair was still a topic of conversation. The ladies had a whole summer to get used to daily changes of hair color from blue to orange to red to platinum but they still couldn't warm themselves to such outrageous conduct. The girl was standing over a table at one of the flea markets trying on a large silver ring formed in the shape of a skull.

Mona liked the way the ring reflected the sunlight. She held it up away from her body and turned her hand back and forth and watched the ring with deep concentration. She looked at it with admiration and though she had the appearance of appraising the ring, still being in a decision phase, she had mentally bought the ring the moment she laid eyes on it. The ring automatically became an extension of her and she was sure that she would be unable to remove it even if she tried. She would be forced to buy it. She kept staring at it as she paid the woman behind the table and continued looking down at it hypnotically, as someone newly betrothed would her engagement ring.

Mona continued to look through the merchandise going to one table after the next. James would be working until the evening and shopping at the market was a good a way to pass the time as anything else.

"Excuse me, can I see that ring?" Graham said without any other introduction.

"Sure," Mona said, holding her hand up with great pride.

"That is really cool. A little *momento mori*. Nothing like that to keep perspective. Where did you get it?"

"A table back there," answered Mona, looking over her shoulder, "but it was the only one like it."

"You are not from here, are you?" Graham said looking Mona over. He was right in assuming that a girl dressed in black with her hair spiked with blue streaks was more than likely not a local girl.

"No, I'm not."

"Just passing through?"

"You could say that."

"Who's your friend?" Mona asked, looking at Perry a few feet away petting a dog.

"Who him? Oh, he's just a hitch-hiker that we picked up driving a few miles past the penitentiary. Between you and me," Graham continued lowering his voice and putting his hand on Mona's shoulder, "We've been trying to lose him since we got here. Weird guy. He kept saying weird things about praising Satan and stuff. I think he probably killed his family or something."

"Hey Graham, I'm going to grab a coke do you want anything?"

Perry said walking up to him.

"Listen, guy, I don't know what your game is and who you really are but take your pentagram and your Alice Crowley fan club propaganda and leave me alone. Anyway, can't you see I'm otherwise engaged? Engaged in conversation with this beautiful young girl," Graham accented his last phrase through his teeth as if Perry should take a hint.

"Oh yeah, no problem. I'll see ya around." Perry began to walk away.

"Wait," said Mona, grabbing Perry by the arm. "You don't look like a convict. You don't look dangerous at all."

"I'm not a convict," Perry said slowly, sure that somehow he was not catching on.

"See," interjected Graham. "Anything you ever read about psychopaths they're excellent liars. Extremely convincing. Now, scram before I yell for the sheriff."

"So how long have you known this guy?" said Mona, making eye contact with Perry and ignoring Graham.

"Too long, as you may gather."

"O.K., guys. Where are you from?"

Perry, Graham, and Mona sat on a bench and talked for nearly an hour. They covered everything from why they had come to the village to how they all agreed that they disliked hair bands. Mona was introduced to the rest of the group and now sat under a tent eating barbeque with the rest. Ernie took a flask from his pocket and passed it around. The sip immediately made Mona's face turn warm. Conway expressed his concern to Ernie about what the effect on his liver may be. Ernie reassured him, once again, that it wasn't the moonshine but the snake venom. Aleisha said she needed to find a bathroom and Mona offered to take her to James's trailer.

"Would you like a wine cooler?" Mona asked Aleisha after she was through using the bathroom.

"Got a beer instead? Conway wouldn't like it but having a beer once in a while isn't going to hurt anything. It's not like I drank any of the snakeman's moonshine. "

Mona handed Aleisha a lite beer and opened the wine cooler for herself. Aleisha asked a few questions about the village, some of which Mona couldn't answer. Mona asked various questions about the group and Aleisha told Mona what she knew of Luke, Graham, Perry, Ness, and Ernie. She spent the most time telling Mona about herself and Conway. This story inspired Mona to take Aleisha's hand and squeeze it. She told Aleisha that she still couldn't comprehend what human beings were capable of.

"And you said Graham is in love with you?" Mona said, implying disbelief that anyone would declare their love for a wife of a giant.

"Well, he thinks he is. It's infatuation most likely. Men have always thought that they may have a shot with me because they can't comprehend that I could be in love with Conway. They don't understand but I do and that's all that matters."

"Isn't he afraid of your husband?"

"I'm sure he is but he acts like he isn't. I talk to Conway and it doesn't bother him none as long as he doesn't cross any lines or disrespect me and he won't--he's harmless. Conway was messing with him a bit, mentally, before we took off. He made him drive and listen to one song over and over. It was pretty funny."

"Tell me about Perry?"

"I noticed you two looking at each other--women's intuition. You live with a guy here though don't you?'

"Yes but it's only temporary. He's just a friend. I plan on moving down to where you are in just a few weeks."

"Well, isn't that convenient. Perry's a nice kid. So quiet. Smart but he needs to make sure he doesn't spend too much time with that group. I'd hate to think he would be hanging around campus ten or even twenty years from now working part-time jobs. Listen, when you come down make sure you stop at The Beer Barrel and see me--I bartend there. Meanwhile, talk to Perry. Very nice young man, like I said a bit quiet, reserved, but he can come out of his shell from time to time."

The two girls walked back up the sidewalk toward the center of town. It wasn't hard to find the group though the town was even more crowded with people before, Conway still stood well above the crowd.

Graham had entered a discussion with an amateur filmmaker who had come from the local college to shoot footage for a possible documentary. Luke was playing his guitar and Ness was stretched out beside him shaking his head to a Neil Young song.

"I've been waitin for ya," Conway said to Aleisha. Ernie here has done over taxed himself and I'm going to take him back to rest awhile. I'm going along to make sure everything goes smooth. He wasn't treated too nicely his first trip in here."

"And who's going to protect your little ol' wife?" Aliesha said, reaching her hand up against his cheek.

"Oh I don't have ta worry bout her," Conway said, winking at Mona. "She's meaner than an alley cat. She can take care of herself for an hour or so." Conway kissed Aliesha.

"Conway, I'm having some people over tonight for a few beers and barbeque. You are welcome to come," said Mona.

"That'll do just fine. You gonna be up to that Ernie?" Conway asked.

"I imagine I will but even if I'm not I've done fine for over a half a century and nearly a score so I don't reckon it'll be any different tonight."

"Thank ya ma'm," Conway said to Mona while removing his hat. Conway and Ernie walked off together leaving only Aleisha, Mona, and Perry. It didn't take Aleisha long to realize that she was the third wheel and soon excused herself under pretense of wanting to look closer at some Indian jewelry at a table she had eyed earlier, on the way into town.

Mona showed Perry where he could buy a soda. Perry stood in front of the pop machine wondering if he was seeing the price correctly. Mona assured him that the price was accurate and that everything cost less in the village. They walked along making small talk and looking at various items and commenting on the people who had flooded into the town. Mona suggested that they sit down on one of the benches that were placed along the sidewalks.

"I love to people watch," said Mona, making direct eye contact with Perry, holding her stare until Perry diverted his gaze to the ground. Mona asked Perry numerous questions and the more he answered the more excited she became about finally entering college. She had made her point and was more than ready to jump into a new life. "I'll be down there in just a few weeks. I really don't know anyone except I know there were quite a few classmates that went to state but frankly I don't care to see them, so I'll probably find my way around the place myself. I've been there for a visit but it seems so big."

"It's big, that's one of the things that I love about it: music, museums, film, it's all there. That's why I'm on the five or six year plan."

"It looks like your friend is on the twenty-year plan."

"I think Graham is on the lifetime plan."

"Does he have a degree?" Mona said, trying to pick a piece of gum off her shoe.

"You know, it's hard to tell with him. I'm not even sure that Graham is his real name. Or what he says is true of false."

"He seems entertaining. Is that why you hang around with him?"

"Partly, he's interesting at times. I feel sorry for him too."

"Why?"

"Because he gets so down some times--he'll become interested in something and he'll be completely fired up about it, and that passion is contagious, but then you will see him the next day and you can tell by his expression that his mood has changed. He's quieter and apparently full of despair like everything is bad. Then you may run into him a couple of days later and the sun is out again. In fact, not only is the sun out it's the middle of summer."

"Come with me," Mona said, taking Perry by the hand without even waiting for his approval. She took him down an alley between two of the taller buildings in town. She took him where another alley intersected and turned left and followed the buildings as they became shorter. She released his hand and told him to follow. She climbed up on a truck bed and walked, then raised herself up to the top of the truck. She put both hands on top of the lower level roof and asked Perry to give her a boost and then she swung one foot on top of the roof and with Perry's help lifted herself up on the roof. Perry was able to lift himself up behind her. They climbed from one rooftop to the next each rooftop bringing them higher above the village. Mona walked right up to the edge and looked over while Perry stayed behind. She motioned him toward her and he cautiously made small steps and peeked over the edge. He had lost his sense of space and had no idea how far they had climbed until he looked over and his natural reaction was simply to move back about five feet away from the edge.

"Are we scared of heights?" Mona asked Perry with an amused tone.

"*We* are actually scared of putting ourselves in danger," replied Perry.

"O.K., we will play it safe. This is how you want to do it." Mona lay down on her stomach and edged herself just so she could see over the edge. After a little coaxing from Mona, Perry joined her. They could see across the whole village from this point. They watched everything from a preacher surrounded by a group of people as he prophesized the apocalyptic meaning of the image. They couldn't make out all of the preacher's words but when he raised his voice at the end of a paragraph and pointed his finger into the air and yelled "repent, repent" his words would echo off the brick wall across the alley.

"Hey, I want to have you and all of your friends over for a little get together tonight--nothing too late because most of us are planning on setting off early." Mona again stared straight into Perry's eyes waiting for a reply to her invitation.

"I'm sure we can stop by for a while."

"Yeah, the guy I've been staying with is having some people from work over too."

Perry looked at her in surprise and then looked away trying his best to mask his mild astonishment.

"Don't get me wrong. We're just friends, acquaintances really. He just gave me a place to hide out for a while. I don't want you to have the wrong idea," she said putting her hand on his elbow.

"Since it's his place he's going to be cool with all of us showing up?"

"Yes, he is cool with whatever I tell him to be cool with."

"What is his name?"

"James."

"Does he like you more than a friend?"

"Of course he does."

"Sounds like a tricky situation. I thought…never mind. I'm not sure what I thought."

"I've been weaning him off me though. It's working with mixed results." She waited for Perry to make a comment or ask a question but since he didn't she kept on talking as if he did. "Well, I've been upfront with him all along. He knows that I'm leaving in a few weeks to enroll and that I wanted to take a year off. Originally I was going to travel Europe or something exotic but I didn't have the funds. I met James at a party so now I've been here--couldn't be more different than Europe. James denies it but I'm pretty sure he has something for his boss. She annoys me. I never met her but she still annoys me."

"How so?" Perry said breaking up the monologue.

"Well, she always has James listening to these motivational cassettes and it has kind of brainwashed him. One thing James always was is nice and now I can't even have a conversation with him without listening to a string of clichés about, I don't know, you have to make your own luck or some such nonsense or 'confidence is the key.' It bugs me because it doesn't strike me as real confidence but false cockiness. He attributes Tina and her tapes to his success. I mean he's doing really well. He sells vacuum cleaners and he's been number two in the company recently. I think he's going to have enough money to buy a house soon. But it's not because of the tapes or Tina it is because of me. He was a total loser before he met me. He's tall and well built and girls like him but there's nobody home upstairs. I prefer intellectuals." Mona paused.

"The kind who wear glasses." Perry blushed slightly and pushed his glasses up his nose. Mona noticed the nervous gesture.

After clearing his throat, Perry was eager to change the subject but while he thought he was going to talk about the image he said: "Do you happen to like intellectuals that are perhaps shorter than most and carry a few extra pounds?"

"My favorite." Perry leaned over but Mona pulled back. "But I also like intellectuals who move slowly."

"Jeez what's wrong?" Perry said looking at Mona's expression, thinking that somehow he misunderstood completely what had been happening between them.

"Remember when I said I was hiding out?" Mona pointed down

and to the left and continued without waiting for an answer. "That is the reason. See that man who the television crew is interviewing?"

"Yeah, I see him."

"That's my father!" Without saying another word Mona grabbed Perry's hand and led him back down the rooftops to the lowest level. She crouched down on all fours behind a brick chimney and put her finger to her lips letting Perry know that she wanted him to be quiet. She put her head around the chimney and strained to listen to the interview being conducted on the sidewalk below.

"Well, Professor, what do you think about the image?"

"I think the real story here is actually the Nazi. Alleged Nazi, I mean."

"There may be tens of thousands of people who walked by the image of Christ. There may be ten people here investigating the Nazi story."

"True but numbers don't validate reality. The Nazi story may have proof. We will never have proof about the image. I have been studying these phenomena for over twenty-five years, and I never thought I would have the luxury to study one this close to my own home. I've traveled half way around the world and here it happens about twenty miles from my own house."

"Why so skeptical, Professor?"

"Many reasons. For example, no one knows what Jesus looked like. There are no pictures, no remaining descriptions. We do know that cultures, especially European cultures, have tended to draw his likeness to their own. Early images resemble Alexander the Great for example. There are numerous paradigms throughout history, including the German Northern Renaissance painter Albrecht Dürer. Jesus started looking like his self-portrait until the Nineteenth Century for the most part. And trust me, Leonardo's Jesus does not look like he could have lived in first-century Palestine."

"Yes, Professor, but what do you say to someone like nineteen year old Melissa Hartfield. Melissa come here for a second. Melissa, I see you have a shirt on with a drawing of the image. What do you think about this phenomenon?"

"Well, I just know it's a sign of the second coming."

"How do you know that? We've probably interviewed over thirty young people who say the same thing," said the reporter, placing the microphone back in front of the young girl.

"I feel it. Something's changed within me and in this town. Plus my minister has told us to repent."

"Very well. Thank you, Melissa. What do you think about sentiments like that?" The reporter said placing the microphone back in front of the professor.

"Well, firstly, I think that having an image of an image is postmodern. Beyond that, I really can't comment on that. I've learned over the years that it will do no good so I stopped debating that frame of mind years ago--so, no comment. Again the Nazi seems to me to…

"What's up with the Nazi?" Perry whispered to Mona.

"He's so damn smug."

"Who, the Nazi?" Perry said, knowing full well that she meant her father.

"The alleged Nazi's name was Gus. I mean is Gus. And it's not true. From what I hear he isn't even being accused of anything they just want him to identify someone else that they suspect. Perry, all you would have to do is meet this gentleman once and you'd know that it's not true."

Perry could see she was becoming emotional about the subject so he did not say anything in reply. He just put his hand on her shoulder.

She watched the crowd disperse once the interview was over and the cameras walked away. She watched her father walk away too.

"Hey, I'm going home now. I want to lie down and get ready for tonight. Aleisha knows how to get there O.K?" She reached over and kissed his cheek so quickly that she was climbing down the roof before he had time to think it all through.

CHAPTER 27

An overcast sky dimmed the moonlight. There were many people sitting outside in the trailer park. Some were barbequing a late dinner, others waiting to see if the clouds would dissipate so they could gaze at the stars. There were two groups in front of James's trailer. His group stood around an awning where a keg was centrally located. James and most of the sales force of the company stood around Tina Winner while she talked shop. She held their attention like a guru. Out in the yard Mona had set up lawn chairs and buckets and had laid a blanket on the ground. Perry sat on a chair next to Luke who continued to strum his guitar. Mona sat on a turned over bucket and Conway sat on a blanket with Aleisha and Ernie sitting on either side of him.

James was very uncomfortable with the strangers. He was usually cordial but he remained cool during the quick introductions. Mona was not much of a hostess to the other group either. She had never met Tina Winner. While refusing to become intimidated, Mona found that she was unsettled by her presence. Now, though, she didn't look nearly as imposing as she had imagined. Gone were the high heels and business suit and she was now dressed in a light flannel shirt, jeans, and hiking boots, which, much to Mona's chagrin, probably meant that she intended to tag along with the group on their journey to the image.

The good news, though, was that the others were dressed more casually: boat shoes, polo shirt, pressed tan pants, gold watches, necklace, and a few bracelets. Mona wasn't sure that she knew any of these men but she was certain she knew their kind. They were the type that would badger her when she would change her hair color several times a week. Blue one day, red the next, then purple. They were also the type that would hit on her when and if they ever had a chance to get her alone. Mona looked at her new friends; she would take the giant and the snake-bitten man for company ecstatically over the other options that were available to her. The whole scene made her replay the day in the near future when she would leave this town.

Her thoughts, interrupted, found a new place of concentration when Graham and Ness walked up with two other men she had not met.

"Hey, see, I found the place," Graham said, looking at Aleisha.

"That's because you haven't had too much to drink yet."

"True, guilty as charged. Hey is that keg for us?"

"Go ahead," Mona said nodding her head toward the patio.

Graham had on a tie-dye shirt and ripped jeans. He grabbed a plastic cup and started to fill it with beer when one of the young men from Winner's group approached him.

"Hey, you going to throw in a few bucks for that?"

Graham stopped as if he didn't understand the question. "Hey, I was invited here. And besides I'm broke."

"Well, chief, if you're broke maybe you shouldn't mooch. Put the beer down." The young man was short and stocky and his face turned bright red and his pink scalp flourished under his short, black hair.

"Ah, c'mon dude be cool. I'm in no mood for a hassle."

"That's some shirt you got there. The '60s are over in case someone hasn't told you."

By this time the crowd had gathered around them and James

273

had come between the young man and Graham. The guy was telling James that he should not let the stranger drink for free when they had all thrown in for it.

"Forget it," Graham said putting the beer down. The young man looked satisfied yet still had a look of anger.

"Mind if I have one of these?" Conway said stepping in and taking a cup, ducking in under the awning. He looked straight at the young man. "I don't have any money either but I'm real thirsty. You're not saying anything so I'm assuming it's O.K."

The young man looked down and whispered something that was inaudible.

"Sorry but I didn't catch that," Conway said looking down at the young man.

"Yes, I said, go ahead."

"Well, I thank you for your hospitality. By the way, is it alright if a few of my friends here wet their whistle? It's been a long day."

"I guess."

"Any you other fellers have a problem with it?" Conway said looking at the rest of the group. "Ma'm" he said putting his hand to his hat looking at Tina Winner. Everyone said something to the effect of "help yourself" or shook their head no.

Conway picked up the glass and handed it to Graham and then went back and sat next to Ernie without getting anything for himself. He saw that Ernie was shivering so he unbuttoned his outer shirt, took it off, and draped it over Ernie like a blanket.

"When you get a chance, see if that guy would like a job in collections," Tina whispered to the humbled young man.

"This town is unbelievable. Have any of you seen anything like this before. I mean, who would have thought that some oxidized image could have caused such a stir," Graham said, eyeing how much beer he had left in his cup.

"It's not just any image. It's the image of Christ," said Ernie.

"Do you really believe that, Ernie?" Graham asked, not in his usual tone but in a tone that was sensitive not to challenge a dying man.

"Well, I surely didn't come all this way for my health," replied Ernie "well, actually, I did come all this way for my health but ya'll know what I mean."

"What's wrong?" asked the filmmaker whom Graham had met earlier in the day.

"My liver's in a bad way." The filmmaker said nothing but drew back his lips and shook his head to convey sympathy.

"We heard some guy being interviewed today," Perry said, "who said it was impossible to know if that was the image of Christ or not, and it didn't matter what the image looked like, even if someone thought that it was the spitting image."

"How can anyone know that for sure?" Ness was skeptical of skepticism.

"The guy's point," Mona interjected, "is that nobody knows what Jesus of Nazareth looked like. Representations of him have changed from time to time and from culture to culture. So, the woman who discovered that image has preconceived cultural notions of what Jesus looked like, as do the thousands of pilgrims who have made this journey."

"We're going to that silo tomorrow Ernie and you're going to get better. Don't pay any attention to all this talk." Conway said, putting his massive hand on the sick man's head.

"Oh, it don't mean nothin to me. I know what I know." Conway gave him a small smile.

"I don't think that argument has much to do with the price of eggs in Toledo," said the filmmaker.

"What exactly does that mean?" Mona said, surprised at her own defensiveness.

"It simply means that the good professor has a point. I'm familiar with him because I have already interviewed him for this documentary and I know his argument. His point would be right on if people were claiming to have seen the historical Jesus on the side of a silo, or barn, or tree or whatever but I think that misses the point. During my research, I've read more than a few articles concerning this. When Leonardo or anyone else depicted Jesus they were not concerned about likeness. Listen, Leonardo had an idea that the world was much older than the 4,000 years believed at the time by just taking a walk in the mountains and looking at the rocks, he certainly knew that the historical Jesus did not look like his Christ. Christ is subjective, Jesus: objective.

"I wish I had the books with me to show you the paintings but people depicted Christ in different manners through different ages. Two modernists' depictions that are striking to me are by the French painter Rouault and the German painter Emil Nolde. The paintings are expressionistic and very different from one another. In Rouault, Christ is soft and compassionate, with large eyes, which gives him omnipotence, but it is a futile omnipotence. I like to imagine that Christ is looking over Europe in 1938 and seeing the coming catastrophe but is powerless to stop it. Nolde's Christ in *The Last Supper* is one of the masterpieces of German Expressionism. Christ has an angular, ambiguous face, fire- red hair and small beard. To me, while Rouault's Christ is full of empathy, Nolde's Christ, while feeling the fatalism and the futility of Rouault's Christ, has no empathy. He is beyond empathy. He no longer has the capacity for such emotions. Rouault's Christ is somehow showing the modern world as a knife in the gut. But as different as these two depictions are from one another and the rest of the depictions throughout the ages, they are both depictions of Christ, and though I won't see it to tomorrow, that oxidized figure on that silo may be also. To say that it definitely is not is as wrong-headed as saying that it definitely is. The possibility has to be left open. There should always be room for mystery."

"I sure would like to see them pictures."

"We'll find'm. In the library or the bookstore," Conway said looking down at Ernie.

"What the hell?" Luke said stopping the omnipresent strum of his guitar. "See that lady?"

Gus's sister stood bent over a walker. Her white hair matted over her wrinkled, pale face. If she had been an apparition even the most dogmatic skeptic would not have been converted. She was a big woman and her body shook, which rattled the walker. Mona called for James and the two of them walked over to her. They talked with her for several minutes until James came over and went inside the trailer reemerging with milk and a few other items. The two of them came back after several minutes, each joining the same group as before. Tina Winner and the rest of the sales staff were getting louder as the keg was drained. Any other night the police would have been called by now but with the thousands of strangers in the town, a few drunken people were the least of the police's problems.

"Is she O.K.?" asked Aleisha.

"I think so. We thought about calling an ambulance but she begged us not to. I think she may be dehydrated but we're not sure. We had her drink some milk. I think she will be alright tonight but I'm calling Human Services tomorrow." Mona was starting to wish that she could be by herself. She didn't have time to think about it because her thoughts were interrupted by wailing.

"Do you know what that is? You seem to know the most among us?" Graham said looking across the circle at the filmmaker.

"No, idea. I've been studying a lot for this film but I don't know everything. Could be some cult with some ritual I guess." The cries in the night increased in frequency and duration and it cast anxiousness over the whole group. James and his friends listened for a while but soon resumed their party. One of them, in an attempt at humor, howled loudly between his cupped hands, mimicking the sounds of despair that rang through the night.

"That's starting to freak me out. Sometimes it sounds like wolves howling." Aliesha said with a slight shiver. "Maybe we should head back to camp?"

"I reckon. You ready ta go Ernie?" Conway said.

"Yessir. I'm mighty tired."

The sounds of sirens mixed in with the howls in a crescendo of confusion. A dozen flashlights became visible in a jagged line moving back and forth across the street stopping and starting again. At this point the two groups converged and though no one had any idea there was little doubt that something was out of order. House lights were being turned on up and down the street and the lights became brighter. There was some general discussion about what the possible problems could be. Had the crowd or certain groups in the crowd started some type of trouble? Theories began.

Three elongated shadows appeared beneath the streetlight in front of the trailer court followed by three deputy sheriffs. The first thought that went through Mona's mind concerned James's friends and what she considered to be their "loud, obnoxious behavior." She also had a brief thought that it was a good thing Hank left early because there was no smell of pot in the air.

The three deputies shined their lights across the yard and then in the face of the people at the party, making them shield their eyes, all except Conway who had his eyes hid under his cowboy hat. The young deputy nodded to Mona. She diverted her eyes to the ground.

"Listen, we are letting everyone in town know that if they have come to see this image out here on this silo they can move on." The elder deputy patted the air as to silence the general malcontent that his remarks caused. He had repeated this several times this night so he knew the routine.

"The mayor has been barraged with complaints. This town has been a good host but there is no longer a reason for you to stay. The image is no longer there. Somebody what's the word? Desecrated it." The gasp in the crowd toned down the deputy's voice. "I know many of you have come a long way and this means a lot to you. Somebody covered it with paint. They've ruined it. There are night-lights being set up as we speak. Painters are repainting the whole thing. Now, we can't make you leave but there is no reason for you to stay. If you are set up outside of town that is fine. I suggest you either go tonight or camp and leave first thing in the morning. I have no authority to make you but we are asking in a civil manner. We would really appreciate your cooperation. The grocery stores are bare and there is nothing for you here. The citizens of this village need a return to normalcy."

The two older deputies walked on and the younger one walked up to Mona.

"Why?" Mona asked in a whisper.

"This gentleman travels to his fishing place the same way every day and I guess the traffic made him snap. We have him in custody."

"That's senseless."

"Can I stop by later. Can you get away?"

"No, I'm leaving soon and I'm beat. You can stop by before I take off."

By the time Mona turned around Tina was driving her four wheel truck down the lane and the rest of her sales force was gone too. There was a circle made around Ernie who was sitting on the ground. Mona couldn't tell if he was crying or not.

"I came all this way," he kept mumbling to himself. Conway knelt down and put his arm around him.

"You said that you were heading somewhere else before you

heard about this. Where was that?" Conway asked.

"Mexico."

"We can drive him and we'd be there in a few days." Conway said looking at Aleisha for approval. She nodded to him to show her support.

"I can't expect you to do that." Ernie said, his voice shaking.

"An army couldn't keep me from it," Conway said, looking directly at Ernie.

"O.K.," Conway announced, "this train is leaving tonight. Thank you for your hospitality, ma'm." Conway said, tipping his hat to Mona.

"You're welcome. I'll see you again. Soon."

"Call me when you come down, O.K?" Perry said to Mona extending his hand.

"You will be the first call I make."

Conway took the initiative to walk off into the night and Perry started to follow.

"No, wait," Graham said grabbing Perry by the arm. "You have to wait. This messes up everything. I need your help to make this film."

"There is no film. The image is gone."

"No," said Graham, starting to gesture wildly. "The one we were going to make after that. We can make it tomorrow now. Listen, there is this city of tires outside of town. I saw it with my own eyes this evening. It's as tall as a building and goes on as far as you can see. Michael here is going to film it. Luke and Ness are going to help me and I want you too. I want you to put on a mask see. Signal through the fire Artaud kind of stuff and have everyone take turns stepping forward on top of the tire pile. Then I want to do voiceovers consisting of Hamlet's monologues."

"How we going to get back? Our ride is leaving." Perry looked out to make sure Conway wasn't too far gone to catch up with yet.

"I don't know, Perry, we'll figure a way. This is too good to miss."

"I can't miss class on Monday."

"This is the real class," Ness said, adding more pressure.

"No, I can't. I can't just blow off school." Graham and Ness looked at each other in disbelief.

"Ah, leave the kid alone." Luke said sitting against the side of the trailer.

Perry ran into the lane and disappeared.

"We'll just have to find someone else. Let's get back to camp." Graham thanked Mona for the invitation and told her that he looked forward to seeing her again soon. Before he disappeared into the night with the rest of his party he promised to show her around campus the right away.

James and Mona stood alone in the yard, dark and quiet now. The yard was full of empty plastic cups.

"Let's go in," said Mona.

"I'm just going to clean this up."

"It can wait until morning before we go."

"Go where? You go ahead in. I can't leave the yard like this. There is nowhere to go now."

"We have to go. Hank is out there somewhere."

"He goes out there all the time."

"Yes, but he is expecting us and I'm going, with or without you."

Chapter 28

James opened the door and looked for the first signs of day. He was still groggy, sipping coffee, but he felt good because his body was restored by deep, untroubled sleep. He was packed with his backpack full of food, drink, a jacket, sleeping bag, flashlight, and a spare set of socks. He opened the door where Mona lay still and he strained to hear in the dark, and for a moment he thought she was gone until his eyes adjusted and he saw her form bundled up laid deep inside a quilt. He whispered first and then called for her again, raising his voice until she stirred.

They walked out into the yard. A mist hung over the earth and in the mist they looked at each other acknowledging that it was time and they walked across the lane. Their boots sunk into the ground, which was wet from the dew of the morning. The sun was now partly visible and provided spectrumed color through the moisture of the air. They entered a trail at the edge of the woods and walked a narrow dirt path between large sycamores that covered the forest making the day grow dark again. They resumed without speech as they crossed a creek stepping on moss-covered rocks holding their arms perpendicular to their bodies, casting spindly shadows against the water, balancing their bodies against the stones' surface and the pressure of the flow from the current. They stepped out of the creek and walked sideways up a steep bank keeping at times one hand against the ground and occasionally crawling on all fours until they reached a ridge that led to a lane that lay between two fence rows. They walked through fields until mud hung heavy on their boots and each step was taken with labor forcing their hearts to drive beads of sweat out onto the surface of their skin.

The sun approached the center of the sky and they stopped and drank water from their canteens and dug the mud out of their boots again. They walked through an overgrown path and James kicked his leg up bringing his knee to his chest and laid his boot down heavy on the weeds that blocked their way. They came to a clearing where a little graveyard was built upon a small hill. The graves were old; some were worn so much the writing had disappeared into the stone. Weeds grew over the markers and had to be pushed back to see the carved names. Mona stopped and read the names of people who were long since forgotten, swallowed by history. Names like Javis Feltus, Orance Rogers, and Ansida Pennington. Mona pondered would the carving "Mona Nash" on some future stone monument have any significance 150 years from her last breath?

Looking at all the names in the cemetery, she wondered what they loved, what they disliked, what made them smile, which flower they favored? It's not that long ago, she said to herself. My great-grandfather could have been alive when they still had blood coursing through their veins-- his life beginning while theirs was ending? But, what was his name? Edward I believe. Not so long ago he was alive. This century even I think. What was his middle name? I don't believe I've ever known that. What was his favorite food? What brought him joy? Just a few generations and I have no idea.

They walked away from the graveyard and Mona felt compelled to look back until the markers appeared smaller and then became invisible. She couldn't get the idea out of her head that the great-great grandchildren of Javis Feltus or Orance Rogers were more than likely oblivious that their family was even buried there. Or maybe

Javis or Orance had no children and that forgotten cemetery was the conclusion of everything that they had been. What is the point of their graves if nobody knows they even existed? Mona forced herself to move on and she started to think about her impending move and all of the people that she had met the day before. She imagined what it would be like seeing them again and soon she forgot about the graves.

They reached the trestle and looked apprehensively across the river. James had crossed over the trestle many times in his childhood and as far as he was concerned as long as he didn't look down there was no reason to fear anything. He leveled his ear against the track and closed his eyes and tried to feel for the slightest vibration. He stood up and grabbed Mona's hand and walked from one step to the next staring straight ahead. Mona looked over the trestle to the river below and stopped. She picked up a pebble and let it drop watching its long journey into the still waters. They crossed over the river and reaching the far side of the trestle sat along the side of the tracks. The afternoon was waning and there was still no sign of Hank.

They ate their supper and discussed the possibility that they may not find Hank before nightfall and if they didn't they were prepared to camp and continue the search for at least another day. Perhaps they would still visit the silo even though the image had been destroyed. They sat up and stretched and decided they would walk the tracks for a few miles more before they made any more decisions. They walked along the gravel; and occasionally James would balance on a track casting more shadows on the embankment.

They rounded the bend and stopped because they saw movement far down the tracks. They walked closer and soon there was no doubt that a person was walking toward them. Soon enough it was evident to Mona and James that it was not Hank but though neither of them said anything, they both had an inclination of whom the approaching person was.

"James, do you know who I am thinking that is?"

"Yes, I do, and I'm thinking the same thing. But it can't be."

"Oh, James, it is. I'm sure it is."

Mona and James started a slow jog toward the figure and the person put her arms out and when they were within fifty feet there was no longer any doubt in the mind of James or Mona. Their jog developed into a full blown sprint and James reached her first and then Mona soon after and they threw their arms around the woman and though Mona was short of breath she couldn't help but laugh and continue to call the woman's name.

"Fanny, Fanny," Mona cried, "I can't believe it's you. Oh, Fanny, thank God."

James who could at times be quite reserved held nothing back and he took Fanny's hands in his and looked into her eyes. "This makes it all worth it. The whole trip. I don't care if that image is gone, Fanny." James threw his arms around Fanny and then released her and then Mona in a moment of elation put her arms around James. They looked at each other in disbelief and Mona kept shaking her head and just kept repeating Fanny's name. The two pilgrims finally started to believe that they had made contact with the one person whom they never expected to see on this journey.

They sat for an hour asking each other questions and becoming reacquainted. They sat in a circle holding hands with Fanny as she talked with them and answered so many questions that they had asked each other many times before.

"Any news of Hank, Fanny? We're worried sick about him."

Fanny told them that they had no need to worry. She had indeed seen Hank but not at the silo. She gave them directions to go and to count seven fields that were separated by either a lane or a tree line. She told them to walk down the embankment to where the steel fence ended and a split-rail fence began. And they did and the sun was setting now and they came to the split-rail fence and looked over the field. And just as Fanny said there would be, a palomino horse was grazing in the field. They walked up by the horse without getting too close. The horse came up to them and turned around. Mona felt compelled to follow the horse and James followed Mona. It was getting darker and the horse went up on its hind legs and came down again and then broke into a slow trot.

Mona and James could hear voices growing louder as they followed the old gray palomino, and the smell of smoke began to overwhelm them. When they had traveled half way across the field they could now see small flames running up the side of a building and the larger the flames grew the more furious the sounds from the fire grew too. The horse was running and they also ran toward the building, thinking that perhaps someone could be in danger. It was dark now and the light from the fire became their guide because the horse had momentarily receded out of sight. They came upon the inferno and stepped out of the field unto a grass yard. The horse had arrived there before them and stood at the edge between the field and the yard. Mona, James, and the horse looked on as people, naked and hypnotic circled the burning barn shouting words and chanting phrases that none of them could decipher. Men, women, and children ran around the barn, their skin reddened by the heat of the massive fire. A man with a long beard led the group and the people responded to his presence by mimicking his movements as he ran around the barn occasionally falling to his knees and holding his palms face up in some ecstatic trance. Directly behind him came three women and two small children who knelt and then came up on their feet again and resumed their frantic circling of the barn. Behind them ran Hank, bent over, reaching toward the ground and then reaching for the sky, opening and closing his eyes for several seconds at a time. Mona and James watched Hank until the south wall of the barn began to crumble into the center, the fire hissing with violence and then the remainder of the wall crashed unto the earth with such a force that a flame shot up into the black sky. Mona and James eyed the propelled flame as it climbed and burned and then dimmed before falling back to earth as ash turning to dust revealing the first star of the night.

About the Author

ROB JACKSON received a B.A. from Ohio State and a M.A. from John Carroll University. He was an editor for Cleveland's literary journal, *Muse* and presently is a senior editor for *Great Lakes Review*. He lives somewhere in Ohio.

CPSIA information can be obtained
at www.ICGtesting.com
Printed in the USA
FFOW01n1456050215
10849FF

9 780990 543510